The *Reckoning* of Barnard Joseph Snodgrass

BOOK ONE

The Making of a Hero

B. L. SANDERS

ISBN
Paperback: 978-1-967668-48-9
Hardcover: 978-1-967668-49-6

Disclaimer

The Reckoning of Barnard Joseph Snodgrass is mainly historical fiction. The story is fiction, set in historical events. The non-historical people are fiction. Since there are 8.2 billion people living on Earth, and a kazillion more who came before us, the chances are astronomically possible that you will recognize characteristics in one or two of the FICTIONAL characters that you possess. TOTALLY COINCIDENTAL. But if you are flattered by those characteristics—great! You are enriching humanity. ON THE OTHER HAND, if you are not flattered, then you might consider changing your behavior. You most likely will feel better about yourself. And you most definitely will improve humanity.

Acknowledgements

First, if *The Reckoning of Barnard Joseph Snodgrass* becomes a success, then I thank whatever caused me to have the three-consecutive-night dream that gave birth to this story. On the other hand, if it does not become a success, then I curse whatever caused me to have that three-consecutive-night dream that turned into a twenty-five-year nightmare.

Second, THANK YOU to all those real people who lived the historical events depicted in *The Reckoning*. If it was not for you, this story would only be fiction.

Third, THANK YOU to those friends who read a few of the chapters and bluntly critiqued my work. It made the story better.

Fourth, THANK YOU to the medical experts who reviewed the appropriate passages and made it more realistic.

Fifth, THANK YOU to all those people who input information onto the Internet. It made my research much easier.

Sixth, THANK YOU to all those at McGilligan Publishing who edited and formatted the book, improved on my cover art concepts, and guided me through the world of book publishing. They made *The Reckoning of Barnard Joseph Snodgrass* publishable.

Finally, THANK YOU to the readers of *The Reckoning of Barnard Joseph Snodgrass*. If it was not for you, I would have wasted twenty-five years of my life and would be looking at a set of very expensive books.

From the bottom of my heart, sincerely,
B. L. Sanders

About the Author

Born in 1950 in Wichita, Kansas, **B. L. Sanders** was the first of two children raised by a stay-at-home mother and a father who worked as an expeditor at Boeing. From an early age, Ben was taught the importance of studying hard, earning good grades, and staying in the good graces of his teachers—lessons often reinforced by his mother, sometimes with a yardstick and the warning, "Wait 'til Daddy gets home." Though his father never resorted to spanking, he had what he called a "very strong middle finger," which he used to deliver a firm thump to the side of Ben's head—believing it was closer to the brain than a spanking.

Thanks to that upbringing, Ben became the teacher's pet in nearly every classroom.

He went on to earn a B.A. in Elementary Education, as well as both a B.S. and M.S. in Total Quality Management. At Boeing, he monitored and presented the status of both military and commercial programs to upper management. Later, he served as a Quality Improvement Consultant, supporting seventy different groups.

Ben has been married and divorced twice—an experience he believes needs no further elaboration.

To the Reader

The Reckoning of Barnard Joseph Snodgrass is about a man who is accounting for what he did in his life. It is a trilogy. You are a juror in *The Reckoning of Barnard Joseph Snodgrass*. At the end of Book 3, you will be asked three questions to answer. First, where will Barnard Joseph Snodgrass spend eternity: Heaven or Hell? Second, which female character is Barnard Joseph Snodgrass' guardian angel? Third, what kind of angel is she—an angel from Heaven, or a fallen angel from Hell?

At the end of Book 3, you will be asked to cast your decisions on these three questions at a website. Then, when you submit your decisions, you will find the verdict of *The Reckoning of Barnard Joseph Snodgrass*.

Contents

1

Between Before and After

FRIDAY, 31 December 1999

George Bailey's smile fills the large television screen as the bell on the Christmas tree jingles. "Attaboy, Clarence!" he exalts as *It's a Wonderful Life* concludes, "Auld Lang Syne" resonating from the surround sound speakers hidden in the walls of the house. Instantly, the lime green LCD clock on the video recorder changes to 11:58 PM.

Sprawled on a recliner in the opposite corner of the room is a man sporting a short gray beard, his long body partially wrapped inside a thick brown bathrobe, its hood covering his head, making him look like the exhausted Jedi Knight, Obi-Wan Kenobi, relaxing in a galaxy far, far away. Dangling from his left foot is a tattered leather slipper teetering on the brink of joining its partner on the stained gray carpet. Next to the slipper, a stemmed flute lies in a purplish pool. On the nearby end table is an almost empty bottle of Merlot with a much-used gun-cleaning kit open beside it, its contents lying haphazardly within as if having been used and flung back inside. Scattered on the tabletop and carpet lay eleven .45-caliber shells, their copper heads and brass casings gleaming from the light of the television.

The man stares at the big screen television. It is a blank stare—a stare of indifference even though the clear picture and sound equals that of any theater with THX.

"Follow the light," directs a female voice from the blackness inside his head. The voice is soothing to the man's soul—kind, compassionate,

friendly, yet authoritative—a voice the man could listen to forever.

Deliberate but awkward, his steps follow the dash of brilliant white light he approaches but never reaches in the otherwise total blackness. He hears nothing, not even the pounding of his hypertensive heart. The incessant buzzing from Tinnitus in his ears is silent. His footsteps make no sound, nor does the crackling of his arthritic knee. The blackness is deafening.

"Sit, Barnard," the voice calmly orders.

"How do ya know my name?" He stares at the light now illuminating something resembling a chair—maybe metallic—undoubtedly futuristic. It seems only a hint of a chair, a shadow, an outline—an aberration. It does not appear to be there, but then again, it does, like a hologram or something certainly out of The Twilight Zone.

"I know everything about you, Barnard Joseph Snodgrass. Age: forty-nine years, seven months, twenty-four days. Weight: 240 pounds, so you're obese and have been most of your life. Do you want me to list your ailments and medications?"

"Who are you?" Barnard's voice does not reflect the anxiety that normally runs through his veins when puzzled.

His right arm twitches and the barrel of the revolver resting in his lap moves against the channel selector of the remote control. In one-second bursts, Xena yells and freezes in midair; balloons rain down from another party; a giant alien stands before the U.N. pledging to serve Man; Ron demonstrates the Veg-O-Matic, and a pink cloud moves across the central states.

The LCD clock changes to 11:58:25, and another few seconds join their siblings in history while a festive Times Square pours into the man's family room, a room without family on this joyous night.

The brilliant beam flashes, blinding him.

"I said—sit."

Instantly, the bright white light engulfs him, and he finds himself reclined exactly as if in his recliner. His body fits perfectly. It is like sitting on a cushion of motionless air: not cold to his flesh or hot, not hard or soft. It is as if his surroundings have finally conformed entirely to him.

*Suddenly, he discovers his hairless nakedness. **"Hey!"** He tries to stand, but nothing moves. **"What the hell?"** Only his mind frantically struggles to free himself from the invisible but real bonds. Finally, exhausted, his chest heaves one last time, then collapses.*

A glimpse of the mouthwatering ad for his favorite pizza cannot whet his appetite. No fleeting peek at the bikini-clad bombshell Marine JAG colonel can command his manhood to stand at attention as she has so many episodes before. Nor can the howling wind whipping sheets of sleet against the nearby window send a chill down his spine. And the first few notes of the doorbell's chime, "Jingle Bells," or the phone ringing and the voice on the answering machine cannot attract his attention.

*He glares into the bright splash of light that is now before him. **"What the hell's goin' on?"***

*Instantly, the light vanishes. Blackness. His body glows a fluorescent blue; his fingers and toes tingle as if asleep. **ZAP**. His digits curl into painful knots. He shrieks, flesh quivering, hands and feet jerking in spasms, arms and legs twitching excruciatingly. At last, a final groan gurgles in his throat, and his naked body lies silent. The blue slowly fades to black.*

The leggy brunette swaggers out of the interrogation room. Fox Mulder leans to the right to prolong his view of the stunning woman in the chain and silver micro miniskirt. "I don't know about you, Scully," he says to his slightly amused partner, "but I'm feeling the great need to blast the crap out of something." The X-Files episode, "First Person Shooter," continues, the remote now resting on the floor, the revolver lying upside down between the man's bloodied thighs.

The television jubilation shifts to a Dallas ballroom as a younger host takes over for the ageless Mr. New Year's Eve. "Okay, Central Time Zone, this is for you. Three. TWO. **ONE!**" The VCR acknowledges the new era: SAT 01/01/00 12:00:00 AM. "**HAPPY NEW YEAR!**"

Brilliant bursts of fireworks spray the television screen. Dazzling flares of light dance in the glass fireplace guard, in the golf wall hangings, and in two pictures of a young girl proudly displayed on the end tables. Even the man's eyes reflect the sparks of color but do not flinch as the old millennium gives way to the first moments of a new thousand years and the hope for a better future.

The small, bright white light reappears.

Barnard grimaces, still recovering from the shock. "Please tell me what's goin' on."

"That's better, Barnard. This is your Reckoning."

"My reckoning? What's that?"

"Everyone eventually has one. It's the time between Before and After—when a soul accounts for what he or she has done."

"Soul? Is this Judgment Day?"

"No. Judgment Day is after The Reckoning."

"I don't understand."

"I know. Look at the Reckoning as you would preparing your annual tax return. It's the time you revisit how you spent the major events of your life to determine if and what you owe. View Judgment Day as an audit from a not-so-friendly IRS."

"So, I'm dead, and this is Purgatory?"

"Not necessarily."

*"**What?**" The unsatisfactory answer brings a hint of irritation to his voice.*

Blackness. Fluorescent blue. Pain. Spasms. Convulsions. One last gasp before the bright white light flashes in front of him.

*"**W-what the hell's goin' on? Who are you, anyway? Am I dead or not?**"*

Blackness...

*"Oh **shit!**" He braces for another shock. It is the worst. Then, the light reappears—not so bright, much easier on the eyes, and larger. With bulging eyes and gaping jaw, he stares into the light at a pair of the most dazzling legs he has ever seen, glistening as if gently rubbed with the finest oils, tanned to golden bronze, and perfectly muscled like those of a prima ballerina.*

"Ho-lee smoke." His sigh is heavy. Longingly, he gazes upon every sultry inch of the lovely limbs, from immaculately pedicured toenails painted an exotic bluish-green to deliciously bare hips. "I've seen those legs before."

"In your dreams," the voice replies.

And around my neck, he thinks.

"You've always been a connoisseur of the—oral arts."

"What?" The remark catches him off guard.

"To answer your questions: this is your Reckoning; I'm your guardian angel, and not yet."

"Guardian angel?"

"Yes. Who did you think I was—your fairy godmother?"

His eyes follow the sleek curves of her legs, from the slenderness of her ankles and the erotic beauty of her feet—bare and encased in silver, strappy, stiletto sandals—to the sexy bulge of her shapely calf and teardrop muscle always accentuated when legs are crossed. "I should say not." His mouth drools, not the only body part to drool. A burning sensation flows through his body. However, he is not glowing. He looks down and grins, eyes gleaming. "Who needs the Senator's little blue buddy, now?"

"Mmmmmm. You certainly don't." Her voice is lustful. "You've always been a legman."

"Highways to paradise."

"Uh-oh. I hate to put a damper on our flirting, but we need to get going."

"Where to?"

"Your Reckoning. We have a lot to cover."

Instantly, blackness again befalls Barnard Joseph Snodgrass.

"Hey! Where'd ya go? You're not gonna leave me here, are ya?"

In a brilliant white halo, the angel reappears, a flowing gown of chaste white silk draping her heavenly—naked—body, translucent for adoring eyes to behold her splendor. "Of course, I won't leave you, Silly. It's your Reckoning."

He looks past the diamond face chain mask to the almond-shaped eyes staring at him. "I knew it was you."

"Of course you did. Now take my hand."

He stands with her hand in his. "Uh. How 'bout—." His empty hand covers his aroused crotch.

"Oh no, no, no. You mustn't hide anything."

"I'm naked! And I've got…"

"Ooo, I know." The angel's face beams. "The Reckoning requires the bare-naked truth. It'll behoove you to be—well—impressive."

"Impressive's one thing, but havin' a naked boner for My Maker to see is quite another."

"Not to worry. Your maker has seen every boner you've ever had. Besides, who do you think gave you the ability?"

Barnard cannot move his eyes from her. However, he knows he does not have a choice, not with an angel looking the way she looks. "Hey, uh, if you're my angel, then where're your wings?"

"Did you hear any bells ringing?"

"Well, no. So, it's true—every time ya hear a bell ring, an angel gets his wings?"

"No, Silly. That's only in a movie. Let's go. We have a life to revisit."

"Where to?"

"Your boyhood home."

"Why there?"

*"Friday, February 12th, 1954." As she escorts him into the bright light, she says, "And what's with this—**his** wings?"*

2

A Hero is Born

FRIDAY, 12 February 1954

7:00 a.m. A stocky boy in Superman pajamas runs from the bathroom to the living room, opens the double doors of the 1952 Admiral 21" console, turns on the television, then rotates the channel dial to 12 (CBS). Reading the black hands and fancy numbers on the porcelain dial under the twelve-inch-tall glass dome of the 1909 German disc-pendulum-anniversary clock sitting on top of the TV, he yells, "**Kenny! It's seven o'clock! Cap'n Kangaroo's comin' on!**"

A small, slender boy wearing Batman pajamas runs into the living room and flops down beside the bigger boy. Sitting cross-legged in front of the television, they stare at the fuzzy screen as the cathode-ray tube slowly hums to life.

A moment later, a woman in a plaid pedal pusher, long-sleeve blouse, white cotton socks, and well-worn black pumps walks up to them. "Barney, Kenny, you boys brush your teeth?"

"Yes, Mommy!"

"Open up." She inspects the teeth of her two-year-old and soon-to-be five-year-old sons. "Good job." She wipes a little toothpaste smudge from Kenny's cheek and pats the tops of their heads before walking into the bathroom to clean the foamy toothpaste spots from the sink.

"**Yea!**" the boys yell as the Captain opens numerous doors on the entry door and peeks or waves at them. Each time, they enthusiastically wave back, yelling, "**Hi!**"

7:15. A car horn beeps, and the man sitting in his rocker lays the newspaper on the coffee table, stands, and rustles his fingers through the tykes' hair. "Boys, you help your mother today. Dottie, I'll clear the drive tonight." He dons a worn and stained khaki Mackinaw coat, its shoulders bearing the faded outlines of long-removed patches. He opens the front door. The bitter cold rushes through the screen door, chasing away the warmth in the living room. Quickly, he closes the door as he steps out into the winter morning darkness. The boys run to the picture window and rub small circles in the frosted pane, their breath fogging the glass as they watch their father trudge down the snow-packed driveway to the waiting car. The boys wave as their father closes the car door, then resume watching Captain Kangaroo.

8:00. With the television off, the boys play with their toy soldiers while their mother prepares to bake a cake for Valentine's Day.

8:20. The boys rush into the kitchen, their eyes gleaming with anticipation, and hover like vultures, watching for the opportune time to pounce. Then, Barney implores, "Mommy, can we lick the bowl? Pleeeease?"

"Since you said the magic word—yes, you may." Carrying the mixing bowl to the kitchen table, she sets it between them as they climb on their chairs. Before she can hand them spoons, like bulldozers, their little fingers sweep the reddish batter from the side of the bowl. She puts the two nine-inch round pans in the 325-degree oven and closes the door, then begins mixing the frosting.

8:55. Dottie takes the cake out of the oven but leaves the door open to help heat the room. The boys hurry into the kitchen to dive into the white frosting, but their mother announces the worst news they could hear, "Not yet. The cake must cool first. Then I'll put the frosting on; **then** you can lick the bowl. Go play. I'll call you." They leave the room with exaggerated sighs and slumped shoulders.

9:00. The boys see their mother go into the bathroom and close the door. Quickly but stealthily, they creep into the kitchen and pull out the bottom cabinet drawer. Kenny, the lighter of the two, steps on the drawer and climbs up on the countertop, removes the lid to the cookie jar, hands Barney two chocolate chip cookies their mother had baked the day before, and then climbs off the counter. Just as quickly and quietly, they return to the living room, huddle behind their father's recliner, and devour their loot, giggling softly at their small thievery.

9:02. Dottie exits the bathroom and, on the way to the kitchen, glances into the vacant living room. "Hmmm." Turning about-face, she walks to their bedroom to find her offspring nowhere. Quietly, she returns to the living room and peers behind their customary hiding place. "What are you little dickens doing?"

"Nut'un," Kenny says with a mouthful of evidence.

Dottie bends down and takes a closer look. "So, what are cookie crumbs doing on your lips?"

The boys chuckle, their cookie-covered teeth exposing their caper.

Standing with hands on hips, she glares at the four large eyes staring back at her, then smiles. "I thought you two were awfully quiet. Wouldn't a glass of milk go good with those cookies?"

The boys swallow, and grinning with delight, leap to their feet, and run into the kitchen. A moment later, all three are sitting at the kitchen table, each eating a milk-dipped chewy chocolate chip cookie.

9:20. Dottie quizzes her boys on the alphabet and counting to one hundred. Then, she lays face down the fifty-four cards of a standard playing card deck and leaves the boys to play *Concentration* while she goes into the master bedroom to resume her sewing project. After the first game, Kenny has thirty-eight cards, Barney sixteen. "**I win!**" With his arms raised in victory, a triumphant Kenny runs to their mother to announce his win. She gives him a kiss and sends him back to defend his title.

9:30. Beaming with pride, Kenny makes another victory lap, and Barney, in a frustrated tantrum, throws the cards all over the dining room. When Kenny gets back for the third round, he screams Barney's infraction.

The continual *zzzzz* of the sewing machine stops, and the wide-eyed boys anxiously watch the hallway. A moment later, their worst nightmare walks into the dining room and sees the evidence all over the floor, dresser, and table. "Barnard Joseph Snodgrass, that's poor sportsmanship. Shame on you. Daddy would be **very** unhappy with you. Now, you pick up every card. And how many were you playing with?"

"Fifty-four," Kenny blurts out.

Dottie glares at her youngest, who is smiling proudly. "Did I ask you, Kenny?"

Kenny's grin fades. Looking down in shame, he shakes his head.

"Barney—make sure there's fifty-four cards when you're finished." Dottie returns to her sewing. A few minutes later, she peeks into the dining room to see her boys playing the game. She walks up to them. "Did you find all the cards?" Barney nods, and Kenny shakes his head. "How many cards did you find?" Barney shrugs. Dottie repeats her question, and Kenny says, "Fifty-one." She shakes her finger at him. "**Barney**, how many cards are missing?" He shrugs. Kenny cups his hands around his mouth and whispers, "Three."

"You both find the **three** cards." She watches them hunt. "If you haven't looked, check the kitchen."

Kenny runs into the kitchen. "**I found one!**" He continues looking, then yells, "**I found anudder one!**"

"Hey! You're not supposed to look," Barney says. "**Mommy!**"

"He's helping you. That's a good brother. Brothers should help each other. One more, and you can play." She watches them for a moment, then says, "I wonder if I should call Gramma."

"**Yeah!**" They run to the phone.

Barney climbs on the chair beneath the phone. "Can I dial?" As he reaches for the phone, his eyes bulge as he spots the prize wedged between the wall and the phone. "**I found it!**"

"Hey! Don't bend it. Be gentle like if you were holding a little kitten."

"Can we read *The Three Little Kittens*?" Kenny asks as Dottie watches Barney count the cards.

"For naptime. Now, you play one more game." She shuffles the cards and hands half to each boy. "You put them on the table. And don't peek."

Barney shakes his head. "I don't wanna play."

"Why? I thought you liked *Concentration*."

"Cuz Kenny wins all the time."

She looks at the victor, who is smiling from ear to ear. "Well, you play more, you'll get better and finally beat your little brother."

"Nuh-uh," Kenny says. "I remember where **every** card is."

"I know you do, Sweetie. You beat all of us. That's why playing against you is real good practice."

Again, Kenny shows a proud, toothy smile.

"Still don't wanna play?"

Barney shakes his head.

"Okay. How about color books?"

9:47. The boys are kneeling on the living room floor, adding color to the images in their favorite color books, *Sergeant Preston* for Barney, and *Steve Canyon* for Kenny.

Dottie goes into the kitchen and starts frosting the two-tier cake. When finished, she says, "Boys, who wants to lick…?" She laughs as they rush into the kitchen and hop up on their chairs as their mother sets the frosting-lined bowl and spatula between them. "Dig in."

"Thanks, Mommy."

She kisses the tops of their heads. "Thank you for saying thank you."

10:10. Kenny snuggles up to his mother, and she stops sewing. "What?"

"Can we read this?" He holds a Little Golden Book.

"This one again?" Dottie caresses him. "Haven't you memorized it already?" He shrugs, and she sighs. "Okay. Let's go in the living room."

A moment later, Kenny is sitting on his mother's lap immersed in Lewis Carroll's *Alice in Wonderland Meets the White Rabbit*. Then, after the second time through, Dottie sets that book aside and holds Anna Sewell's *Black Beauty* in front of him.

"Barney! Black Beauty!" Kenny yells.

Barney runs into the living room and jumps onto the sofa. He kneels beside his mother as she opens the book to the bookmarked page. Then she begins reading where she had stopped the day before.

10:30. After another chapter is behind them, the boys resume coloring, every few minutes running to their mother to show her their masterpieces while she adds a few more stitches to her sewing project. Then, just before eleven, she says, "Boys, how would you like to make Daddy a Valentine's card?"

11:00. While Dottie watches *The Tennessee Ernie Ford Show* on NBC, her boys sit at the dining room table coloring original Valentine gems on folded construction paper. Then, during a commercial, she inspects their artwork and praises them. "You need to sign your names so Daddy will know who made these beautiful pictures." She helps her boys print "To Daddy from" and their names on their respective artwork. Finally, the boys stand the folded cards against the table's centerpiece, and she returns to her show.

11:30. As Dottie watches two fifteen-minute soap operas on CBS, *Search for Tomorrow* and *The Guiding Light,* her boys crawl from their bedroom to the dining room and back, Barney pushing his 1/36 scale metal blue 1948 Ford F-1 pickup truck with Kenny's blue-and-white police car giving chase, its red dome flashing and siren blaring.

"Kenny, bring me your car, Honey." He does, and she slides the lever on the underside of the car, shutting off the light and siren. "Just until my show's over. Then you can turn it on."

Kenny resumes the pursuit, and Dottie returns to watching her programs in relative quiet.

12:00 p.m. Dottie and the boys gobble up homemade chicken noodle soup. Then, Barney hugs his mother. "Can we have some cake?"

"No. That's for Valentine's Day. But I made **cupcakes**." Their mother gives each a red velvet cupcake with cream cheese frosting and topped with a conversation heart. "Can you read what's on your heart?"

"Sweet Heart!" an excited Kenny says while Barney says, "Cutie Pie!" They lay big smackers on their mother's cheeks before exclaiming, "Thank you!"

12:20. With the covers pulled up to their chins; the boys snuggle in their beds as their mother reads a few more pages in *Black Beauty.* Then she kisses their foreheads and leaves them in dreamland.

12:30. Bundled up in her boots, coat, hat, and gloves, Dottie steps onto the porch and starts scooping the snow off the porch, the steps to the driveway, and finally a path to the street.

1:30. To chase the chill from her bones, Dottie sips a cup of hot coffee while curled under the thick woolen Afghan her mother-in-law knitted a couple of years before and watches *Art Linkletter's House Party* on CBS.

2:00. She quietly dusts the furniture while the boys sleep.

2:20. Suddenly, The Lone Ranger and Hopalong Cassidy burst into the living room, their six-shooters exploding from their mouths, **"Bang! Bang! Bang!"**

"Gittem up, Belle Starr, or we'll blast ya!" the masked man orders.

At once, the woman drops her dust rag and reaches for the ceiling. "Ya got me, sheriff," she says dramatically, her eyes wide with playful fear. She looks at the two little gunslingers pointing four silver cap pistols at her. "Why don't you and Hoppy see if you can catch my gang of—**cookie** robbers?" Their eyes widen. "They're around here somewhere. I'm sure there's a reward for their capture—especially if you recover the—**cookies**." She points to their bedroom and they hop along on the trail of the imaginary desperados. Meanwhile, Dottie sneaks into the kitchen and puts on the table two cookies on a saucer along with two glasses of hot chocolate.

A moment later, Barney says, "Keep yur hands up, hombres!" before her boys walk into the kitchen, their guns still drawn. "We got 'em! **COOKIES!**" They holster their guns, hop on their chairs, and gobble their law enforcement reward.

For the next hour, "Gittem up! **Bang! Bang! Bang!** Got him!" fills the house.

4:30. The boys are watching *Howdy Doody* on NBC.

4:50. The crunch of tires on the snow-packed street tears the boys away from their show. They run to the picture window and quickly wipe away the condensation. Then, with noses to the cold glass, they yell, **"DADDY!"** They watch their father walk up the cleared path at the side of the driveway. As soon as he enters the house, they wrap their arms around his cold legs. He closes the door. "Take this to the kitchen." He hands Kenny his lunch pail. "Sure, smells good."

"Chicken noodle soup," is the answer from the kitchen. "It'll be ready in about half an hour."

"That'll give me time to clear the rest of the drive. And boys, thanks for clearing the snow off the porch and driveway. I really appreciate it."

"**We didn't do it!**" Barney exclaims.

"Hey. You don't have to yell. If you didn't? Then who in the world did? You Kenny?"

He shakes his head as "And you're welcome, James," comes from the kitchen.

He grins. "Thanks, Dottie. I do appreciate it." He steps outside, grabs the snow shovel, and begins clearing the rest of the snow from the driveway as his boys wipe a circle on the frosted picture window and watch. Then Barney runs to the kitchen and pulls on his mother's sleeve. "Can we go out and help Daddy?"

"No, Honey. It's way too cold. Besides, Daddy'll have to come inside in pretty soon."

Head bowed and shoulders slumped, Barney trudges back to the window. "Naw. We can't go outside. Daddy's comin' in pretty soon," he mutters with a pout.

Kenny whispers in Barney's ear, "We ask Daddy. He'll let us go outside."

A couple of minutes later, Dottie walks up to them. "So, what are you drawing?"

"Daddy." Kenny points to the stick man. "See? He's shovelin' snow."

"I see. And that looks just like Daddy." She looks out the window. "Wave at him." The three wave at the man leaning on the snow shovel as he takes a breather, bursts of steam shooting from his mouth with every huff and puff. He waves to them. "Why don't you finish your pictures so you can show Daddy when he comes in?"

5:30. The boys are scribbling classics in their coloring books as Dottie opens the front door. "Jim, it's five-thirty. Come inside and warm up."

"I'm almost done."

5:40. Jim stomps the snow off his boots before entering the living room. As soon as he closes the door, the mouthwatering aroma of homemade chicken noodle soup and freshly baked dinner rolls sashay into his nostrils, watering his taste buds.

"Daddy, can we go outside? Pleasssssse?"

"No, Barn. It's too cold. Besides, it's dark, and Daddy has to thaw out." Jim removes his coat and hangs it up, then sits down on his recliner.

At once, the boys climb on his lap and give him a kiss on his red cheeks. "Wow! Your cheek's **cold**."

Jim laughs as he grabs his boys and pulls them close to him, pressing their faces against his. "Keep Daddy warm," he says, chuckling. They scream. He laughs, then kisses their cheeks. "But tomorrow, we'll go out and build a fort or an igloo. Whadaya say?"

"Yeah!"

After Dottie calls Jim and the boys to the kitchen, he spots two large cards on the dining room table. "Hey! What's this?"

"Valentine cards." Barney jumps on one chair and retrieves the two large cards.

"But Valentine's Day is Sunday. You want me to open them now?"

"Yeah."

Jim looks at the unrecognizable pictures. "They're beautiful. Thank you!" He gives each a big kiss on the cheek. "We're gonna put these on the fridge."

The family sits down to supper, capped off with Red Velvet cupcakes.

6:00. The boys watch *Kukla, Fran, and Ollie* on ABC as Jim sits in his chair reading the evening newspaper, *The Wichita Beacon*. "Ike's sending advisers to South Vietnam. Where the heck's South Vietnam?"

6:15. Jim watches the *John Daly and the News* on ABC. The host reports, "After authorizing $385 million over the $400 million already budgeted for military aid to Vietnam, President Eisenhower warns against the U.S. intervening in Vietnam."

"**What?**" Jim exclaims. "Then why the—did he send advisers?"

"What, Daddy?" Barney asks.

Jim shakes his head. "Oh, nothin', Barn. Go back to playin'."

6:30. Kenny and Barney, who is hugging his stuffed German Shepard, watch *The Adventures of Rin Tin Tin* on ABC.

7:00. With the television off, the family begins playing *Chutes and Ladders*. Since the spinner-arrow is broken, they must roll a die.

7:25. The phone rings. Barney pushes Kenny down to beat him to the phone. "Hello? **Hi Granma!** We're playin' *Chutes and Ladders*. Daddy won the first game. Okay. **Mommy!** Granma wants to talk to ya."

Dottie walks into the dining room, takes the phone, sits on the chair beneath the phone, and begins talking.

"I have to make a pitstop." Jim points a stern finger at his youngest. "**Kenny, do NOT touch anything.** Barn, you watch your li'l brother. Make sure he doesn't put anything in his mouth. I'll be back in a minute." Jim walks into the bathroom.

7:26. Barney watches his little brother like a hawk watching dinner shiver in the grass. For a moment, the room is silent except for the occasional furnace burner igniting. Then, as if struck by a sudden thought, Barney jumps up. "I'm gonna get my Rinty book. Do-not-put-anything-in-your mouth. Promise?"

Kenny nods.

"Promise."

"I promise."

"You know what Daddy and Granpa say 'bout promises."

"Never break a promise."

"Okay." Barney sprints to the bedroom, retrieves Frank Kearns' book, and returns in record time. He looks at the board. "Did you move anythin'?" He scans the board, suspicion growing in his gaze. Then he looks at Kenny, who is holding his neck, his face getting redder by the second. Then his eyes roll back in his head, and his limp body collapses to the floor. At once, Barney launches a bloodcurdling "**DAADDDYYYYYY!**"

The sound pierces the house, freezing Dottie mid-sentence. She drops the phone as Jim bursts from the bathroom, his eyes wide with concern. They see their youngest lying motionless on the floor. A wide-eyed Dottie stops dead in her tracks, her hands over her mouth. After the split second of shock passes, Jim hurries to his youngest and picks up the small, lifeless body. His hands tremble as he checks Kenny's throat, his mind retreating to an Italian battlefield. "**Dottie, call an ambulance!**" She hangs up, then dials zero as Jim examines Kenny's throat and finds the culprit. He turns him over and firmly whacks him between the shoulder blades. Nothing comes out. A harder whack. Nothing. The third time is the charm, and out shoots the six-sided die, clattering onto the floor. Kenny gasps, coughs, jerks, and quivers—then wails. Jim wraps his arms around him and gently rubs the back, slightly bigger than his hand. Kenny bawls, tears shooting from his eyes, mucus running out his nostrils. Dottie rushes into the living room. "He going to be okay?" Jim nods, then points at the die lying on the floor. "Well, maybe this'll cure him of puttin' things in his mouth **that ain't food.**" Jim wipes Kenny's face before picking up the die. "You think I should thump ya for puttin' this in your mouth?"

Kenny shakes his head and wraps his arms around his father's neck. "Daddy, I love you."

"I love you, too, Squirt. But you didn't answer the question."

Kenny hugs him even tighter and says, "I promise I won't put nuttin' in my mouth ever and never again."

"You know what Gramps said about promises."

Kenny, still catching his breath, answers, "You never, **never, NEVER** break a promise."

"That's right."

"Daddy," Barney says. "Kenny broke his promise to me."

"He did? What promise was that?" Barney tells him, and Jim glares at Barney. "You left him alone to get a book?" Barney swallows hard as his shoulders slump. "Huh? Answer me." Barney starts to cry as the faint whine of a siren breaks the tension. "Your little brother could've choked to death."

About thirty seconds later, the loud siren fades to silence, but the red light continues sweeping across the curtains and the two small windows on the front door. Dottie hurries to the door as the ambulance stops at the foot of the drive. The two technicians hurry up the driveway. She opens the door and lets them inside, then tells them what happened. One technician checks Kenny's heart, lungs, and eyes. "Everything seems okay. You might watch him the rest of the night and let your family doctor know what happened. He may want to see him."

"Okay. Thank you." Jim shakes hands with both techs, as does Dottie, then closes the door behind them.

Five minutes until eight, as she rocks Kenny, Dottie says, "Barney, please put the game away."

Jim goes to the basement.

A few minutes later, Jim returns and sits in his recliner. "Barnard Joseph Snodgrass, front and center!" With slumped shoulders and chin pressed against his chest, the wide-eyed boy reluctantly obeys. Jim looks at him. "I should thump ya for not watchin' your li'l brother. But you did yell for help as soon as you saw Kenny chokin'. So, you helped save his life. Therefore, for displayin' quick thinkin' durin' a life 'n' death situation, I award you the fourth highest military medal, The Bronze Star." On Barney's shirt, Jim pins the red ribbon with a vertical blue stripe down the center, flanked by thin vertical white stripes.

Barney lifts the five-sided star. "It's heavy."

Gently but firmly, Jim holds his son's arms as he stares into the big brown eyes. "It is. It'll always remind you of your duty to protect Kenny." He gives his son a kiss on the cheek—and a pat on the butt.

Barney hurries to his mother and shows her the medal.

Then Jim looks at his youngest, who is watching the award ceremony with great interest. Gesturing with his forefinger, he beckons Kenny to approach. The little boy jumps off his mother's lap and runs up to his father. Jim glares at him. "I should thump ya for puttin' that die in your mouth." Kenny's enthusiasm vanishes as his head bows, but Jim lifts his chin with a nudge of his finger. "You're almost three years old. You're a big boy now. You know better than to put things in your mouth that aren't food. Right?" Kenny nods timidly. "But, instead of a thumpin', I award **you**, Kenneth Joseph Snodgrass, The Purple Heart, for almost dyin'—and scarin' the livin' bejeebers outta Mommy and me. **Don't do that again, Buster.**" On

Kenny's shirt, Jim pins the purple ribbon with a white stripe running down the edges. Then, he looks directly into his son's eyes. "You're not a baby anymore. Only babies put things in their mouths that they shouldn't. Don't **ever** put stuff in your mouth that isn't food because next time, you won't get a medal—you'll get a **hard** thumpin'. Understand?" Kenny nods, and Jim gives him a kiss on the cheek and a pat on the butt. Kenny runs back to his mother and shows her the medal.

"Boys, I didn't hear you thank Daddy for the medals."

"**Thank you, Daddy, for the medal!**" the boys say, almost in unison.

"You're welcome. But next time, it's a thumpin'."

Twenty after eight, Dottie says, "Let's get you guys ready for bed." She herds them into the bathroom, where they brush their teeth and wash their face and hands after using the toilet. Then, they put on their pajamas and return to the living room. Kenny climbs on his father's lap, and Barney snuggles against his right side. Jim looks at the medals now hanging on their pajama shirts, and for a split second, his mind returns to the action that earned him those awards. But only for a split second.

Barney hands him Edgar Rice Burroughs' *Tarzan, Lord of the Jungle*. "Daddy, will ya read this 'til Mommy gets out of the bathroom?"

"Sure. Ya know this is one of my favorite books?"

Both boys nod.

Fifteen before nine, Dottie walks out of the bathroom wearing a quilted bathrobe over flannel pajamas, her hair rolled up in curlers, feet in furry pink slippers.

"Okay, boys, time to hit the sack," Jim says.

"Mommy, will ya read *Black Beauty* to us? Pleeease?"

"Until Daddy gets out of the bathroom."

They scamper into their bedroom, where their mother tucks them into their chilly bed.

Nine o'clock, Jim steps out of the bathroom to find the boys' bedroom door mostly closed and Dottie sitting on the sofa crocheting her doily. "One hellava day."

Dottie looks up at him, tears filling her eyes. "When I saw Kenny…" She shakes her head. "If you hadn't been here…"

"But I was." Jim sits beside his wife. "Maybe this'll teach the li'l squirt not to put things in his mouth."

"What if it doesn't and you're not here?"

For a moment, Jim stares across the room, then says, "Monday, call the doctor's office and tell 'em what happened and ask 'em where we can learn first aid."

"For a second, I thought we would have a new arrival. But you gave him a second lease on life."

Barnard shakes his head in disgust. "It would never have happened if I had obeyed my dad."

"Years later, you beat yourself up over the incident, not ever giving yourself credit for not panicking and thus saving Kenneth's life. And you know what he did in his life—all because of how you responded to a life-and-death crisis."

"Just call me George Bailey," Barnard says, kind of kidding.

"Let's not get a big head," the angel replies, not kidding. And speaking of life-and-death crisis…"

The rumble of the electric motor lifting the two-car garage door, a key rattling inside the kitchen doorknob, the kitchen door slamming against the cabinet, and quick footsteps tapping on the tile floor indicate help is approaching. But is it approaching fast enough—and soon enough?

11:58:15.

"I think we better get going."

"Where to?"

"You ready to party like a five-year-old?" The angel lightheartedly grabs his hand and pulls him into the light.

3

The Bestest Birthday Ever

SATURDAY, 7 May 1955

"**Gammaw!**" Kenny runs to greet the gray-haired woman stepping into the living room. He wraps his arms around her left thigh before reaching up and grabbing her little finger. "Come see my pitcher."

"I will, Chérie, as soon as I put this food in the kitchen."

"Hi, Granma!" Barney hurries to her, giving her a loving hug. "Guess what today is."

She looks at the wallpapered ceiling, shakes her head, then looks down at him. "Oh! I remember. It's your daddy's birthday."

His eyes bulge, and his head cocks back as he stares up at her. "Granmaaaa!" He slams his hands on his hips. "It's **my** birthday, too!" He holds up his right hand, five fingers parted. "I'm five years old. Did you forget?"

Just then, a balding man steps into the house carrying three gift-wrapped boxes, and Barney's face explodes in an ear-to-ear smile. "**Granpa didn't forget!**" He runs over to the Snodgrass patriarch and gives him a big hug.

"Happy birthday, Barn. Put this on the coffee table." He hands him a three-foot-long gift-wrapped box.

"**Wow!**" Barney's eyes bulge as he takes the present from his grandfather and sees his name on the card. "What is it, Granpa?"

"If I told ya, wouldn't that spoil the surprise?"

"No!"

25

His grandfather chuckles as he sets the other two gifts on the mahogany coffee table sitting in front of the floral-upholstered sofa.

"Well, can you keep a secret?"

A wide-eyed Barney nods eagerly.

Grandpa rustles the boy's hair. "So can I, Kiddo."

"Granpaaaa," Barney whines as Kenny looks at the gifts on the table, then starts to pick up the long one. "This is heavy."

"Good. It's mine." Barney grabs it.

Jim steps out of his bedroom. "Hi, Pops." They hug as his father says, "Happy birthday, Jimbo."

"Daddy, can I open a present?"

"You know better than to ask. You'll find out what you get after we eat."

"Boys, whadaya say we go in the backyard and play some catch?" Grandpa suggests.

"Yeah!" As they run to their bedroom, Grandpa steps into the kitchen. "Hi, Dottie."

"Hi, Joe." They hug and kiss on the cheek. "Love your bowtie."

"Thank you. Brigitte gave it to me for Valentine's Day."

"I kinda guessed with the red hearts. Look what my three boys gave me." She proudly holds out her left arm, displaying a gold bracelet with three stones: one round emerald and one round sapphire flanking one slightly larger rectangular emerald.

"Beautiful."

A moment later, the boys rush into the kitchen with a baseball, their gloves, and wearing their New York Yankees caps.

In the backyard, Grandpa kneels on one knee and says, "Boys, come here." They walk to him, and he taps the medals they wear on their shirts. "Kenny, are you keeping nasty things outta your mouth?"

He nods emphatically.

"Barney, you always lookin' out for your li'l brother?"

He also nods, though not as assuredly.

"That's good. I'm proud of ya. Now, Kenny, you remember how to catch the ball?"

"Gampaw! I remember everything." He holds the large mitt open in front of him, and his grandfather tosses the ball into the glove, which is only about five feet away. He catches it with both hands, then looks around as he winds up.

"No. You look at the target when you wind up. Now, do it right."

Kenny looks at his grandfather's bare left hand, winds up, takes aim, and throws the ball —drilling it into the grass. "Li'l low, but right on line. Keep your eye on the target." Grandpa lobs the ball overhanded to Barney, who is standing about ten feet away. He snags it in the web of his father's glove. "Good catch, Barn." Holding his left hand in front of his face, he says, "Keep looking at the target and throw the ball right here." He taps the palm of his left hand.

Barney stares at the bare hand, winds up, and throws the ball to his grandfather, who catches it with both hands directly in front of his face.

"**That's the way!** Good control."

They continue playing catch until Jim joins them a few throws later.

"Pops, whadaya think of West Germany becomin' a sovereign country?" Jim catches the ball from his little one.

"Just as long as we don't let the SOBs start another war." Grandpa watches Barney snag another softly thrown ball from his father. "Good catch, Barn."

"I think they've learned their lesson. And it's only right since the Allies recognize their sovereignty, and they joined NATO two days ago."

"Wouldn't surprise me if the Russkies made the East Germans join the Warsaw Pack in a couple months."

They continue playing catch until, from the open kitchen window, Dottie announces, "Lunch is ready."

Immediately, the boys toss their gloves in the air and sprint towards the side of the house, only to skid to a halt with, "**Hey!** What do we do with our mitts?" With shoulders slumped, they turn around, pick up their gloves, and then sprint into the house as Jim and his dad shake their heads.

"C'mon, Pops." Jim tosses the ball to his father.

"They're just like you," he says, putting his right arm across Jim's shoulder.

"Ya think?"

"Oh yeah. I had to tell you and your brothers to pick up your toys, or they'd still be under that old oak tree."

Jim chuckles. "How did that poem go?"

His father smiles. "Under the old oak tree, between her legs, I could see a little brown spot with some hair on top. It looked like a June Bug to me."

They laugh, and then Jim says, "Guess they're a few years away from learnin' that one."

"You can include it with The Birds and The Bees."

They go inside, wash their hands, and take their places at the ends of the dining room table.

Dottie looks at her oldest. "Barney, would you please say Grace?"

With heads bowed and fingers interlaced, Barney says, "Grace," and everyone chuckles except his mother, who glares at her firstborn.

"Oh, Dottie, give the birthday boy a break," Jim says. "Besides, ya gotta admit, that was pretty funny."

"Did you put him up to that?" Staring at him, she detects a cat-ate-the-canary grin on the corner of her husband's lips. "**You rascal. You did!**"

Everyone bursts out laughing. Then Barney starts over. "Thank You, God, for our food today. Thank You, God, in every way. Amen."

"That's much better." Dottie picks up the bowl of mashed potatoes, dumps a spoonful on her boys' plates, then her own, and passes it to her mother-in-law. The meatloaf is next, followed by brown gravy, then canned carrots from their garden, Grandma's Brussel sprouts with real bacon crumbles, and finally, her homemade dinner rolls. But every time someone looked at Barney they would grin or chuckle, then everyone would burst out laughing.

"Well, I read somewhere that laughter adds a few years to your life," Jim says.

"Then we should live at least ten years longer." Grandpa chuckles again. Then he pats Barney on the head. "That was a good one, Barn. I bet God's even laughin'."

"I sure hope so," Dottie says sternly, and again, everyone bursts out laughing, even Dottie.

Finally, with the main meal finished, the women clear the dirty dishes from the table before Dottie sets the birthday cake on the table between the honorees. With everyone watching, she lights the five two-inch-tall red candles before the blue "35" candle standing in the middle of the cake. "Okay, make a wish and blow your candles out. No!" She quickly covers Kenny's mouth before he can dampen the cake. "You have to wait until your birthday in September."

Everyone laughs before Jim and Barney close their eyes. Barney wishes to himself, *I wish I could play baseball with Willie and Mickey,* then opens his eyes and extinguishes the six flames with a lungful of moist hot air.

"Hey, Buster!" Jim stares at Barney. "You blew out my candle."

Barney shrugs. "Your wish was too long."

The adults howl, then Dottie says, "He must've been wishing I would hurry up and cut the cake." The mirth continues.

Before she can pick up the cake, Barney plucks a candle off the cake and sticks the frosting-covered end in his mouth, a moment later pulling it out clean. "Mmmm!" His eyes are wide with delight.

"Can I have one, Barney? Please."

"Well, since you said the magic word." Barney hands his brother a candle. Then, they both lick the frosting off the remaining candles.

"It's a beauty, Dottie. Thank you."

"It's the same every birthday." With Grandma following, Dottie takes the cake into the kitchen and sets it down on the turquoise Formica tabletop. A minute later, they bring everyone a saucer with a slice of cake and a scoop of vanilla ice cream.

"Our favorite Barn. Red Velvet Cake with Cream Cheese Frosting and vanilla ice cream." Jim closes his eyes as he savors a mouthful of the cake and ice cream combo.

"You're not tired of it?" Dottie asks.

"Heck no!" Jim cuts into the thick wedge. "I'll never get tired of this. How 'bout you, Barn?"

He shakes his head, his mouth full of cake and ice cream and some on the corner of his mouth.

A couple of minutes later, Jim takes the last bite of his cake, puts his fork on the saucer—almost free of crumbs, leans back in his chair and pats his moderately sized potbelly. "That was **deeee**-licious. I am pleasantly miserable."

The boys mimic their father, and the adults laugh.

When everyone has finished their dessert, they retire to the living room, where Jim drafts Kenny into handing out birthday presents.

Kenny hands his father the first present.

"Whadaya think this is?"

Kenny shrugs.

"Shake it."

He does but hears nothing.

Jim whispers in his ear, and Kenny says, "A shirt or PJs."

"Help me take the paper off." Jim and Kenny attack the festive paper.

"When do I get my presents?"

"Barney, you know we watch each person open a gift," Dottie says. "Your turn's next."

Kenny lifts the top of the box and exclaims, "A shirt! I was right!" He jumps up and runs around the room with his arms raised.

"Thanks, Mom, Pop. I can always use more dress shirts and ties."

Dottie catches Kenny on his second victory lap. "Give Barney a present."

He picks up one and gives it to his brother. "This is mine. Guess what it is."

Barney shakes it, and everyone hears clanking. "I think it might be—uh—a car or—."

"They're Matchbox cars!" Kenny yells. "You'll like 'em. They're—."

"Hey! Don't say another word," his father warns. "Remember, Lose lips…"

"Sink ships," a dejected Kenny says. "Daddy, I remember everything."

"Then remember this: If you tell what's in a gift, then you spoil the surprise."

Kenny and the rest watch Barney open his gift. "Wow!" He lifts out a green Road Roller with red rollers, a green Muir-Hill Dumper with a red dump tray, a red Massey Harris Tractor, and an orange Euclid Dump Truck with a gray dump tray. "Wow! Thanks, Kenny."

"You welcome, Barney." Kenny gives him another present.

Barney uncovers a rectangular box with Strato Bank printed **on it. He** pulls out the light blue metal mechanical bank, his third one from Duro Manufacturing of Detroit, Michigan. **"Thanks, Granma!"** He jumps up and wraps his arms around her.

She chuckles. "You're welcome, mon chéri. You fill your other banks?"

"Not yet. But they're gettin' pretty heavy. Ya wanna see?"

"After you and your daddy open all your presents."

"Here." Grandpa hands Barney a dime. "See if you're a good shot."

Barney takes the coin and pulls back the small red plane on top of the rocketship until he hears a click, then places the coin in front of the plane. He pushes the button at the tail of the plane, and instantly, the plane launches the coin through the slot on the planet. It rattles inside until it comes to rest at the bottom of the sphere.

"Now, Barn, you're ten cents richer."

Jim opens another gift and pulls out a pair of black dress pants. "Dottie, how did you ever know?"

Chuckling, she shrugs. "Lucky guess? And believe it or not, they're in your size."

"This is from me and Barney." Kenny hands his father a small box.

Jim opens it and pulls out a bottle of Old Spice. He stares at his boys. "You think I'm stinky?"

"Sometimes—when you work," Kenny replies, and everyone bursts out laughing.

Jim grabs his boys and pulls them to him before giving each a kiss on their cheeks. "Thanks, boys. It's my favorite aftershave."

Then Kenny hands Barney the long, gift-wrapped box, and Jim says, "Barn, guess what it is."

He looks at it, then, with wide, excited eyes, says, "**A baseball bat!**" He looks at his grandfather for confirmation but gets none. "Uhhh, a fishin' pole?" His grandpa shakes his head, so he tears off the wrapping paper and opens the plain cardboard box. At once, his jaw drops, and his eyes almost pop out of their sockets, for in the box is a three-foot-long wooden rifle and a box of roll caps. "**Granpa!**" He charges into his grandfather. "**Thank you!** I love it." With his arms tight around his grandfather's neck, he starts to cry.

His grandfather pats him on the back. "Barn. Don't cry."

"But—I'm—really—really—happy."

Everyone laughs. Then Grandpa says, "Well then, it's okay to cry if they're happy tears."

"Barn, Grandpa made it." Jim picks up the gun to admire the fine workmanship. "Pops, ya outdone yourself with this."

"Thanks, Jimbo. It was a lot of fun making. Barn, you know what rifle this is?"

"Davy Crockett's Old Betsy!"

"Pops, you oughta make some more—all kinds of guns—and sell 'em at the fair. I think you'd make some good money."

"I'm in the process of making a few—but none like this one. This is one-of-a-kind."

Jim's eyes widen. "If you need any help—sanding, varnishing—whatever."

"Okay. Hey Barn, come here. Let's load this and see if you can fire it."

Barney runs into his bedroom. A moment later, he returns wearing his coonskin cap and intently watches how his grandfather lowers the metal lever, which brings down the housing where he inserts the roll of caps. Then he brings the end of the caps through the frizzen. "Each time you bring the hammer back, the caps advance one place. And the only time you pull down on the lever is to reload another roll of caps. Okay?"

"Yeah! Can I shoot it? Can I?"

Grandpa hands Barney the rifle. He quickly puts the butt against his right shoulder, cocks the hammer, and pulls the trigger.

POP! The cap explodes. Everyone jumps and laughs.

"I love this, Granpa! Thank you!" Barney cocks the hammer again and pulls the trigger.

POP!

"Great," Dottie says. "It's going to sound and smell like firecrackers all year round."

"Well, I guess that's it. Thank you all for the gifts."

Barney stares at him.

"What? Aren't ya happy with Matchbox vehicles, a bank, and Old Betsy?"

Barney's eyes well up as his head bows and nods ever so slightly.

"Oh! Wait a minute. Dottie, did we forget a present?"

"Hmm. Let me think." She stares at Barney's wide, anticipatory eyes. "Well—maybe."

"I wonder where we left it."

"Let's go out on the porch."

Barney is the first one outside.

Then the garage door opens, and everyone sees Jim standing with a new twenty-inch opal red F-32 Schwinn American Flyer bicycle with white-wall tires—and training wheels.

Barney jumps off the porch. However, instead of rushing up to the bicycle, he rushes up to his father, wraps his arms around his waist, buries his face in his father's belly, and sheds more tears.

Jim kneels and hugs his son. "What? You don't like it?"

Sobbing, Barney replies, "I love it. This is the **bestest** birthday I ever had."

Jim points to the end of the block. "Nick and Nikki are ridin' their bikes. Give it a spin." Jim walks the bicycle to the street, and Barney gets on. Then, Jim gives a gentle push as Barney steps down on the top pedal, and off he goes—a little wobbly, a little slow, this way and that—but without any help.

Kenny and the adults watch the newest member of the neighborhood bicycle club join his best friend and sister as they ride from one end of the block to the other. By the time Barney returns, Jim is standing in the middle of the street, holding his Revere 8 mm Model 88 Movie Camera to his right eye as he records his oldest son's first bicycle ride.

"Yep." Barnard wipes away a tear. "That was the bestest birthday I ever had."

"You only had five at that point," the angel replies. "And you didn't remember the first three."

*"You're right. What I mean is—**that**—was the **very** best birthday I **ever** had."*

"Well, you didn't get your wish."

"I was five. Can't really expect to play ball with The Say Kid and The Mick when you're five. But then, sometimes wishin' is better than gettin'."

"You're kidding."

"Is that a question?"

"No. I know you're kidding because no way is wishing for a bike better than getting the bike. Or wishing to play baseball with your heroes is better than meeting them. Or…"

"Okay, okay. You're right."

*"Of course, I'm right. I'm always right. Now, if you've finished celebrating the very **bestest** birthday you ever had," the angel says sarcastically, "let's go to your grandparent's farm."*

"All right! I always loved goin' there—except…"

The frosty air chases the man inside the house. He turns into the living room and stops, seeing the limp body. "**JOE!**"

12:58:35.

They step into the darkness.

4

When the Night Explodes

WEDNESDAY, 25 May 1955

6:40 a.m. As the sun peeks over the eastern horizon to a cloudless blue sky, a whiny Collie scratches at the kitchen screen door.

"Patience, Roscoe." Grandma wipes her hands on the old apron she sewed years ago as her almost three-year-old grandson scampers toward his four-legged pal. "Kenny." The reining Snodgrass matriarch collars the speedster before he can cross the span of the kitchen's linoleum floor, discolored from decades of activity. "Mon Chéri, give him this."

"Oui, Grand-mère." Kenny grabs the sausage link as his grandmother replies, "Excellent Français, Mon Chéri." She kisses him on the top of his head. "Merci, Grand-mère."

Barney pushes open the door, and the dog rushes the boy with the food, but instead of bowling him over, he sits panting with tongue out, tail wagging, his left paw eye-level with the tyke: Roscoe's way of begging.

As Grandma clears more breakfast dishes from the table, she praises, "Good boy, Roscoe. Kenny, give to him."

The lad holds out his hand, and with one wet swipe, the dog snatches the link, not a tooth touching the boy, who lets out a loud squeal and giggles before wiping his wet hand on his shirt. Then, he gives his furry friend a big hug as the dog devours the treat.

"Boys, time to brush teeth." Grandpa cannot keep up with the two as they sprint into the bathroom, where Barney spreads toothpaste on his brother's brush, then his.

"Ooo, Granpa," Barney says, wrinkling his nose as his grandfather plucks his dentures out of the water. "Why don't ya have teeth in your mouth?"

"Well. Don't brush your teeth every day—ya get to brush your teeth like ya polish your shoes."

Kenny chuckles. "Gampaw, you sound funny with no teeth."

"I have teeth! See?" He holds his uppers in front of Kenny's face, and the boy bursts out laughing, spraying foamy toothpaste on the false choppers, Grandpa's hand, the sink, and down his chin.

Barney stares at his grandfather to see what he will do, then quickly spits his toothpaste into the toilet before launching a loud laugh, as does his grandfather.

"Granpa, why don't ya eat breakfast?" Barney asks after rinsing his mouth out.

"My breakfast is havin' two cups of coffee while I read the paper."

After assuring everyone rinses out their mouths and after biting down to test the fit of his cleaned dentures, Grandpa asks, "Who wants to see the sun wake up?"

"**I do!**" The boys race through the house to the kitchen, grab Grandma's dress, and pull. "C'mon Gammaw! We gonna wake up the sun." Pulling her from the dishwashing chore, the boys escort her to the front door where Grandpa is standing. He holds the door open as the four go outside and sit on the porch swing. Looking eastward, they watch the dark royal blue sky slowly grow lighter and lighter. Then, a reddish haze spreads across the lower horizon before turning amber, then gold, then a light lemon.

"Sun's opening his eye!" An excited Kenny jumps off the swing and runs to the railing as the lemonish horizon vanishes, and a light blue dominates the sky.

"Oh, what a glorieux sunrise," Grandma says. "It will be a beautiful day."

Grandpa gently pushes Barney off his lap. "Now that the sun's awake, who wants to feed the chickens?"

"**Me!**" The boys race around the house and across the backyard to the fenced enclosure, Roscoe nipping playfully at their heels.

"Watch how I do it." Farmer Barney dips his hand in the bag of feed and slings the grains on the ground.

"I know how!" Kenny grabs a handful of feed, tosses it on the ground, and laughs as the chicks and chickens peck away at their meal. "We did it yesterday."

A few seconds later, Grandpa arrives at the coup. "Holy cow!"

"**Where?**" The wide-eyed boys scan the premises.

Grandpa shakes his head. "No cow, not even a holy one." He stares at the feed slung from one end of the coop to the other—and into the nearby yard. "Just an expression. Good job, boys. I think that's enough food for 'em," adding under his breath, "'til next year. C'mon. Let's collect the eggs while they're eatin'."

The boys carefully gather the eggs from the four dozen roosts and carefully place them in baskets. When the last basket is full, they carry them into the kitchen and hand their cache to Grandma.

"Merci Cheri." She pats each boy on top of the head.

Then, they eagerly follow their grandpa to the garden, where he shows the boys which carrots to pull from the ground. "You remember how to harvest carrots from yesterday?"

"**I do!**" Kenny yells before Barney says the same.

"Show me." Grandpa watches each boy grab a stalk close to the ground and wiggle it a bit before gently pulling up.

"Perfect. You boys'll be farmers in no time. Go ahead and pull the rest just like that."

As the boys harvest baby carrots, Grandpa cuts the heads off some broccoli and places them in a basket. Then, taking their bounty to the well, they wash off the dirt and eat a carrot or two before taking the rest to Grandma.

8:15. With their work finished, the boys play in the ten-by-ten-foot sandbox with their trucks, tanks, and toy soldiers while Grandpa works on the tractor's engine.

8:55. The boys play tag, running around the thirty-five-foot-circumference trunk of the largest and oldest oak tree in Cowley County.

9:00. A frustrated Kenny stomps towards the tractor. "Gampaw. Barney's cheatin'."

"How's he cheatin'?"

"I can't catch him." Kenny pouts, wrapping his arms around his grandfather's thigh.

Grandpa chuckles. "You're playin' Tag, right?"

Kenny nods.

He kneels and whispers in the little ear, "You start to run around the tree one way, then go the other way real quick, and you'll catch Barney. Try that."

Kenny's eyes burst wide as he runs towards the tree where a laughing Barney is waiting.

Grandpa leans over the engine but watches to see if Kenny can implement the new tactic.

He runs to his right after his giggling brother, who keeps a few paces ahead. Then, the chaser turns and runs in the opposite direction. A second later, with loud screams, the brothers crash into each other. From on his back, a jubilant Kenny yells, "**YOU'RE IT!**" and looks at his laughing cheering section who is clapping greasy hands together.

Barney chases Kenny around the tree once before he catches him. Then they quit. Barney whispers in Kenny's ear. A moment later, they walk towards the tractor.

Huffing and puffing, Barney leans against the front tire. "Grampa, will ya swing us? Please?"

"Are ya tired of chasin' each other?"

They nod.

"Okay. For a li'l while." He wipes his hands on the grimy cloth while the boys run to the black patched tractor inner tube hanging by a rope tied to one of the seven thick branches jutting from the massive trunk. Kenny waits for grandfatherly assistance. A moment later, Grandpa lifts Kenny onto the inner tube. "Hang on." Assuring the boys are grasping the natural sisal rope in front of them, he pulls back and releases, sending the smiling lads yelping. When they come back, Grandpa gently pushes them again.

"Higher, Gampaw!"

Grandpa complies with Kenny's order, earning loud laughter from his grandsons.

9:05. Grandma walks up to her husband. "Mon Chéri, will you get butter for the mashed potatoes and green beans?"

"Of course." He wraps one arm around her waist as they watch the boys swing double, Roscoe running back and forth as if trying to catch his friends. "Remember how we swung our children?"

"Oui," she replies, her eyes becoming glassy.

"I know." He gives her a tender kiss on the forehead. They watch the giggling boys swing and spin. "We'll see 'em Decoration Day."

9:19. With everyone's bladders empty, Grandpa loads the boys into the black seven-year-old Ford pickup for their one-mile trek towards the small rural town of Udall, Kansas, population about five hundred.

"Boys, you know when I bought this truck?" They shake their heads. "I bought it the first day I could buy a new truck to celebrate VE Day. You know what VE…?"

"Victory in Europe!" the boys yell.

"That's right. You know why I celebrated that day?"

"Cuz Daddy came home from fightin' the Nazis," Barney quickly says.

"Well, even though the war ended in 1945, Daddy didn't come home right then. He had to stay and make sure the Germans would stay whooped."

"And they're still whooped!" Barney exclaims.

"Yes, they are. But as soon as he came home, I bought this truck. Grandma cried when she saw him."

"Why?" Kenny asks.

"Because she was really, **really** happy."

"Like Barney on his birthday?"

"Yes."

"If she was happy and Barney was happy—why did they cry?"

"Well, when a person cries, they can have happy tears or sad tears. And…"

"She had happy tears—like Barney," Kenny finishes the sentence.

"Yes. **Very** happy tears." He slows at the railroad crossing and looks both ways before entering the town. "You know your daddy had three brothers who were killed in the war?" The boys nod. "She cried then. Me too. Those tears were very, very sad tears." They nod again.

"Gampaw, how do you know if they're happy tears or sad tears?"

"Your heart tells ya. If you want to laugh, then they're happy tears. If you don't want to laugh, then they're sad tears."

"Gampaw, you know this is Daddy's Purple Heart." Kenny pats the pin attached to his shirt.

"I do. You told me when we celebrated your daddy's and Barney's birthdays." He stares at his grandson. "You still puttin' things in your mouth you shouldn't?"

Kenny shakes his head emphatically. "I promise Daddy I wouldn't, and you never break a promise 'cus if ya do that makes ya a liar, and the Bible says ya better not lie 'cus Santa Claus'll know and he won't give ya a present on Jesus' birthday."

"That's right." Grandpa looks out the door window and grins. "That's good. Only babies put things in their mouths, and you're not a baby anymore. Are you?"

"No! I'm three years old and eight months old." Kenny holds up his thumb, middle, and forefinger.

Barney points to the medal he wears on his shirt. "Daddy gave me his Bronze Star for savin' Kenny."

"I know. You told me. That was very heroic, Barn. I'm proud of ya. You need to look out for your li'l brother."

"I do." He hugs Kenny.

"Kenny, you know who's on The Purple Heart?"

"George Washington, the first president of the United States of America."

"Do you know **why** he's on The Purple Heart?"

"Yeah. Daddy told me. In 1782, General George Washington created the medal, so his head is on it."

"Exactly right."

As the old truck sputters along the rutty dirt road, a dust cloud swelling behind, KWBB Radio, Wichita, Kansas, starts playing "The Ballad of Davy Crockett." At once, the boys burst into song along with Fess Parker, the star of one of their favorite television shows,

"Born on a mountain top in Tennessee, Greenest state in the land of the free…"

As the boys' concert ends, Grandpa parks the truck in front of the general store, then escorts his grandsons to the soda fountain where they share the best drink ever conjured up: a Cherry Coke Float with precisely three squirts of cherry juice and two scoops of vanilla ice cream topped with whipped cream and a Maraschino cherry.

"Granpa, who gets the cherry?" Barney asks as Kenny gets on his knees, ready to pounce on the bright red reward.

"We'll play Rock Paper Scissors. Two outta three wins."

Two matches later, "Mmmm." The stem sticks out of Barney's smiling lips as he sucks the whipped cream off his prize.

"Gampaw, I like this the best." Kenny slices some light brown foam from the side of the ice cream."

"I know. That's delicious." Grandpa swipes his spoon on the edge of the whipped cream and then in his mouth. "You know what that is?"

"Yeah. Frozen Coke."

As they eat, Grandpa and the owner chat about the outlook for the upcoming wheat harvest and if the Kansas City Athletics can beat the Tigers later that evening.

"Gampaw, Detroit is in fourth place, and Kansas City is in seventh place."

"You know the standings?" the owner asks.

Kenny nods as his grandfather says, "He reads the newspaper—all of it—every day."

"How old are you?"

Kenny tells him with the aid of a thumb and two fingers.

"And he remembers **everything**."

"Must be nice." The owner wipes off an area of the counter that is not in need of cleaning. "Who beat my favorite team, the Pittsburgh Pirates, yesterday?"

"Nobody. Pittsburgh whooped the Brooklyn Dodgers fifteen to one. Bob Friend was the winnin' pitcher. Johnny Podres was the loser." Kenny gives the owner a big, toothy smile. "That was a trick question. Daddy does that, but I win all the time. You wanna know 'nother game?"

The owner chuckles. "No. I believe you. You're a very smart little guy."

"Thank you. Gampaw, will ya buy us baseball cards? We worked a lot this mornin'."

"Yes, you did. Isn't this drink enough payment?"

"No!" the boys exclaim, and the owner laughs.

"Well, I guess so—if ya finish **all** of the Float."

The boys suck down the rest of the drink right to the bottom. Then Grandpa spends a dime for two packs of six Topps baseball cards and a slab of bubblegum in each pack. "You save the gum for after lunch."

They collect the groceries, hop in the truck, and head back home.

"Thanks, Grampa, for the Cherry Coke Float and the baseball cards," Barney says.

"Yeah, Gampaw. Thank you." Kenny wraps his arms around his grandfather's neck before giving him a big kiss on his weathered cheek.

"You're welcome, Boys. And thank you for sayin' 'thank you.' That's very nice."

"Daddy told us always say 'thank you' when someone gives us somethin'," Barney says.

"And we promise Daddy we would," Kenny adds.

"And never break a promise," they say together.

10:30. They arrive back at the farm. The boys leap out of the truck and sprint into the kitchen. "Gammaw, Gammaw," Kenny yells. "We had Cherry Coke Float, and it was **deeeee-licious!**"

"And Grampa bought us baseball cards," Barney adds. "C'mon, Kenny. Let's see what players we got."

Both boys head into the living room where they sit on the floor, open their wax packs, set aside the pink Bazooka Bubblegum pads, pick up the top cards—the ones lightly coated with the mouthwatering confectioners' sugar, and inhale.

As her husband lays the groceries on the table, Grandma, standing akimbo, glares at her husband. "Cherry Coke Floats?" A few choice French words follow.

He shrugs. "With three squirts of cherry juice."

With a disapproving huff, she returns to making ham sandwiches and gives him a final comment, "We eat at noon, Mon chérie. Be hungry. Be **very** hungry."

He gives her a kiss on the cheek. A dimple dents the opposite one.

Noon. As Grandma sets the kitchen table, she wonders what the boys are up to since she has not heard a peep out of them for some time. So, she steps into the dining room and sees their small bodies sprawled out on the oval area rug she had woven out of many old clothes. Shaking her head, she smiles and tiptoes through the kitchen, picks up two lunches, and goes outside to the picnic table her husband had built when their children were about Barney's age.

"We eatin' out here?"

"Oui. The boys are sleeping in the living room."

He chuckles. "I think chasin' the chicks did 'em in."

"Or maybe their bellies are full of Cherry Coke Float."

"With three squirts of cherry juice."

4:36. Grandma is peeling potatoes as KWBB Radio, a service of the Wichita Beacon evening newspaper, broadcasts, "Scattered severe thunderstorms with the possibility of tornadoes are expected from 4:30 to 10:00 p.m. tonight in the area of Dodge City to Amarillo, Texas to Wichita Falls, Texas to Ardmore, Oklahoma to Wichita, Kansas to Dodge City. Wichita is on the extreme northeast edge of this area and is less vulnerable to these storms than the area southwest of here." Then, the station returns to playing country music.

4:40. The station rebroadcasts the severe weather warning.

4:58. Grandpa plops down at the kitchen table. "Finally got the tractor carburetor clean." He wipes the grease and grime from his hands. "Tomorrow, I'll take the boys for a ride."

"Radio announce severe storm warning." Grandma peers out the window as Hank Snow concludes his hit song, "Yellow Roses."

Then, the radio announcer repeats the warning.

"See? That is three or four times he says it."

"Don't surprise me. There's quite a bank of dark clouds buildin' up in the southwest. But we got nothin' to worry about. We're on the farthest point of the storm area. And Dodge is about a hundred eighty miles away." He shakes his head dismissively. "Plenty of time for the storm to die out."

"What if it does not?" Grandma cuts the last potato into fourths and places the pieces in the large saucepan.

"Then we go to the shelter. We've used it before—back in October. Remember? That storm didn't do any damage."

She fills the pan with water until the potatoes are submerged an inch, then sets the pan on one of the stove's burners. "Oui. But we have the boys, and we must be more careful."

Grandpa stands and walks up to his wife and wraps his arms around her waist. "We'll be careful," he whispers in her ear before giving her wrinkled cheek a tender kiss. "I'm sorry I fed the boys floats so close to lunch." He gives her another kiss. "We'll be careful. Promise."

5:00. Grandpa waits for the boys to finish watching another of their favorite shows, *The Mickey Mouse Club* on ABC, then asks, "Who wants to check out the storm shelter?"

"**I do!**" The boys leap to their feet.

"Turn the TV off. And someone get the flashlight."

Barney quickly twists the television's volume knob until it clicks as Kenny retrieves the olive-green U.S. Army angle head TL-122 flashlight from the stand beside the front door. Then they run outside, Roscoe right behind them.

Grandpa opens the wooden doors, and Barney shines the flashlight into the dark hole. "**Oh!** Grampa. Spiderwebs."

"Better get rid of 'em before Grandma sees 'em. She hates spiders."

"Me too."

"Get the broom from the garage." Grandpa watches the boys race to the garage, then he hears Kenny scream and run out of the garage, Barney giving chase with a well-used corn-fiber broom between his legs.

Grandpa laughs. "You'd make a good Halloween witch." He takes the broom and wipes all the cobwebs off the walls and ceiling of the six-by-six-by-six-foot cinderblock-walled shelter. "There. Now, let's have a look." Kenny sits on the cinderblock bench as Grandpa looks around the room. "Boys, if the storm is really bad tonight, we'll come down here." He turns on the Coleman lantern and the GE portable radio. "Good. Both work." He turns them off.

"Is it gonna be bad, Grampa?"

"I don't know, Barn. But it's always better to be ready for a bad storm."

Kenny digs in the sand floor. "Can we play down here?"

"No. This is not a place to play. That lantern is only for emergencies. And Kenny, the floor is sand because if we're down here for a long time, that hole you're diggin' will be our toidy."

"**Yuck!**" Kenny drops the shovel and hurries up the stairs, Barney right behind him. Grandpa chuckles as he follows them—much slower.

"Gampaw, ya know some spiders won't hurt ya." Kenny proceeds to name each one and what they look like. Then, he names and describes the poisonous spiders.

"How do you know all that?"

"Daddy and Mommy help me read the En-cy-clo-pe-di-a Brit-tan-i-ca."

"Very good! Those are two very long words."

Kenny nods. "Mommy and Daddy tell me to divide long words in parts."

"There are lots of interesting things in the encyclopedia. Barn, you read it?"

He shrugs. "Mommy makes me read Black Beauty. But I don't like to read. It's boring."

"Oh no! Readin's excitin'. You can read about Superman and Batman in comic books. You can read about other countries without goin' there—kinda like takin' a vacation in your own home. You can read about the presidents, other historical figures, and characters like Tarzan. And you like Mommy and Daddy and Grandma and me readin' to ya at bedtime. Right?" They nod. "One day your li'l kiddos'll want ya to read to 'em. Ya **don't** wanna say—well, I can't read."

"Can we play catch?" Barney asks, hoping to change the subject.

"Sure. Get your gloves and ball. I'll meet ya in the backyard."

The boys race to the house as Grandpa closes the cellar doors.

A minute later, Barney and Kenny stand a few feet away from their grandfather. Roscoe sits between the boys and Grandpa, tail wagging, eager to participate. Kenny throws the ball to Grandpa. Roscoe's head jerks as he watches the ball into Grandpa's hands. Grandpa tosses the ball back to Barney, and Roscoe's head jerks as he watches the ball fall into Barney's glove. And so it goes, back and forth, ball and head. Then it happens. The one thing a dog longs for—a dropped ball. Before Barney can lean over, Roscoe lunges for the rubber sphere, swipes it on the first bounce and off he scampers.

"Uh-oh," Grandpa says. "If ya wanna play some more, you better play with Roscoe." He chuckles, watching the boys run after the Collie as the dog plays a one-sided game of Keep Away. He glances up at the ominously gray and rolling clouds. He whistles before calling, "Roscoe, come here, boy." The boys race the pooch to their grandfather but come in a distant second. "We better go inside before we get wet."

The boys let out disapproving groans before Barney says, "It ain't rainin', Grampa."

"I know. But it's gonna. Just look at those clouds. C'mon. Besides, Grandma'll have supper on the table, and I don't know 'bout you, but **I'm hungry**."

Almost on cue, Grandma steps outside and sets Roscoe's bowls on the porch. "Supper is ready." Roscoe drops the ball and runs to his food.

5:15. "Mmmm," Grandpa and the boys eye the heaping bowl of mashed potatoes, a cube of butter melting on top; another bowl with steaming hot green beans freshly picked from the garden, four long strips of fried bacon lying on top; the creamiest country-style gravy;

and a basket of lightly browned dinner rolls. Grandma places the crispy main attraction in the middle of the table, now creating one vacancy in the coop.

"Boys, will you say grace, please?" Grandma requests. "And I don't mean just—grace."

They all laugh before bowing their heads, and with hands folded under their chins, the boys make grace short and sweet, just as their father taught them. "Thank You, God, for food today. Thank You, God, in every way. Amen."

After supper, Grandma and Grandpa are washing and drying dishes as the boys attempt to play Keep Away from Roscoe. However, the pooch is quicker than the boys and often snags the rubber ball, then plays Catch Me If You Can with the giggling boys giving chase.

6:30. As they watch television, the local weatherman says, "I apologize for interrupting *Walt Disney's Disneyland*. The Weather Bureau has issued a Tornado Watch for south-central Kansas and north-central Oklahoma until nine o'clock tonight. Severe storms …"

Blinding lightning flashes across the sky and nerve-jolting thunder rocks the earth while wind-whipped rain lashes the house. Grandpa and Grandma quickly close the windows.

7:30. With the TV program ending, Grandma says, "Boys— bedtime. Get your PJs." With halfhearted moans, the boys stand, and Grandma ushers them to the bedroom, where they get their pajamas. A moment later, they are in the bathroom, Grandma giving each a sponge bath. After brushing their teeth, they put on their pajamas and go into the living room. Kenny, with his Steiff Orsi Teddy bear, climbs on Grandpa's lap and lays his head on his chest while Barney curls up on the sofa, hugging his stuffed German shepherd pup, Rinty (Rin Tin Tin).

"Looks like they're played out," Grandpa says.

"I know." Grandma lays an Afghan on Barney. "Aren't they cute? They should sleep good tonight."

"If Mother Nature lets 'em."

8:00. The cuckoo clock chirps, and a loud rumble of thunder opens the eyes of a startled Barney. "Granma, can we sleep with ya? Pllleeeassse."

"Are you afraid of a little thunder?" Grandpa asks as the radio announcer tells the fans to stand for The National Anthem.

Kenny crawls off his grandfather's lap. "C'mon, Grampa." Grandpa stands, and he and his grandsons face the radio with their hands over their hearts as a band plays a song honoring the home of the brave. Then, in the end, they return to their previous positions— Grandpa slowly rocking Kenny on his lap and Barney cuddled next to him as they listen to the ballgame and the interrupting weather updates until the eyelids of the little ones grow too heavy to stay open.

Halfheartedly, he shakes his head and shrugs, then asks, "Grampa, who's playin'?"

"Tigers and Athletics. It's the bottom of the first. No score."

"Will ya tell us a story or read a book?"

"Tell us how ya met Gammaw," Kenny says.

"Not that old story again," she says. "We told you a million times."

"Uh-uh!" Kenny says emphatically. "You told us six times."

"Well then, you should know it by heart."

"I do. But you tell it really, really good."

Grandma and Grandpa look at each other. Then, with a sigh, Grandma relents.

"Yeaa!" the boys yelp victoriously just before an explosion of thunder rocks the house, sending the boys into the arms of their grandparents. Then Kenny, kneeling on his grandfather's lap, stares into his eyes and asks, "Gampaw, please let us sleep with ya. Pleeeease."

Grandma and Grandpa look at each other. Then Grandpa grins and Kenny immediately wraps his arms around Grandpa's neck and gives him a hard kiss on the cheek. "Thank you, Gampaw. I love you."

He chuckles. "I love you, too, ya li'l stinker. But why do you want to hear this old story again?"

"Cuz it's a love story," Barney says. "And I love love stories."

Grandma kisses the top of his head. "Ooo. We shampoo your hair tomorrow night." Then she looks at her husband. "I guess we can tell them a seventh time."

"Boys, I will after I wash up. But Grandma's first." As she walks to the bathroom, he says, "Let's listen to the game 'til she gets out."

8:17. Grandma emerges from the bathroom in her cotton nightgown and bathrobe, her gray hair in a rolled ponytail beneath a mesh hairnet. She sits on the sofa, and Grandpa ushers the boys to her. As he washes for the night, for the fifth straight night, Grandma reads the Little Golden Book Barney brought from home, "Rin Tin Tin and Rusty."

8:25. Grandpa joins the trio who Mother Nature is keeping wide awake with bright flashes of lightning and loud booms of thunder. "What's the score?"

"Tigers four to one in the top of the fourth inning," Barney says. "Tigers are battin'."

8:45. The weatherman interrupts the game with another storm warning.

"It sounds bad." Grandma snuggles against her husband's left side. "Maybe we should go to the shelter?" A loud **BOOM** rocks the house, and the two small bodies nestle deeper into their grandparents' arms.

8:55. Unbeknownst to them, a tornado, later rated an F3, is violently twisting at a rate between 136 to 165 mph through Tonkawa, Oklahoma, destroying a few homes, barns, and granaries but injuring no one. It is fifty miles from Udall, Kansas.

9:27. The boys are lying in bed—the storm preventing them from sleeping—and their grandparents are listening to the ballgame. The tornado, later rated an F5, with winds exceeding 200 mph, sweeps through Blackwell, Oklahoma, killing twenty and injuring over two hundred. It is now forty-one miles from Udall.

10:03. As thunder, lighting, and driving rain grow more intense over Udall, KSCK, the Arkansas City radio station, intercepts an Oklahoma police radio broadcast stating that a tornado has hit Blackwell.

10:08. "I'm gonna see if I can get the weather." Grandpa turns the channel dial until the crackling fades to the sounds of a weather report. He has stopped at KSCK.

"…tornado has hit Blackwell, Oklahoma at 9:27 p.m. Wichita is experiencing heavy thunderstorms. Tornado warning includes areas east of a line from Winfield to Wichita."

Grandpa quickly rustles his wife from her sleep. "Bri. Bri! We're in a tornado warning. We should go to the shelter **right now**."

With wide eyes, she gently shakes her grandsons until they open their eyes. "Come. We need to go to the shelter. Put your shoes on."

"Is a tornado coming?" Kenny asks, following Barney off the bed.

"I hope not." She herds them into their bedroom and helps them on with their shoes and jackets as Grandpa puts on his shoes and a raincoat. He sticks his billfold in his coat pocket, grabs his wife's purse, and hurries into the living room, where the three are already at the front door.

A flash of lightning knocks out the electricity as thunder rumbles across the sky.

10:11. Holding the portable radio in one hand and Rinty in the other, Barney leans against Grandma. Kenny, holding his Teddy bear in one arm, hugs her leg with the other. She pats the backs of their heads.

Grandpa turns the knob off the front door, and instantly, the door flies open, knocking him back into his wife and grandsons. Howling like a pack of hungry wolves waiting to devour them, the wind drives cold rain through the screen door, spraying the four. The boys shiver in their grandmother's arms—and not from the cool rain. Grandpa unhooks the screen door, and the wind rips the knob from his hand. **BAM! BAM! BAM!** The door slams against the house, destroying the bottom third of the door. A second later, a blinding lightning flash precedes an earsplitting crash of thunder. The boys begin crying.

"Bri, carry Kenny. I've got Barn." Grandpa lifts Barney in his arms. "Hold onto the railing until we get to the shelter. Okay?"

"Oui! Oui! Go!"

With the flashlight in his left hand and holding Barney in his left arm, Grandpa steps into the pitch-black night and fights to grab hold of the wooden porch column. Quickly but steadily, he works his way down the five steps, firmly holding onto the handrail as the fierce wind tries to strip the clothing from their bodies while stealing even a fleeting breath. Using her husband as a windbreak, Grandma follows close behind, with Kenny's face buried in her neck to shield him from the stinging rain.

Lightning bolts crash into the earth with nerve-jolting sonic **BOOMS** as the four make their way along the lengthy porch to the shelter. There, Grandpa grabs the handle to the western door and pulls. It does not budge. He grabs the handle of the other door and pulls. Instantly, the wind rips it out of his hand. An excruciating groan bursts out of his mouth. But Mother Nature's loud roars drown it out. Pea-sized hail begins peppering them. With haste, he carries Barney down the steps, Grandma close behind. At the bottom, he drops Barney, then hands him the flashlight before helping his wife down the last steps, escorting her and Kenny to the far corner.

10:15. "**Everyone okay?**" a winded Grandpa asks, turning on the lantern. He looks at each boy. They nod, both crying. He looks at his wife. She nods. "Hail didn't hurt ya?" All three shake their heads.

Seeing his right arm hanging limp. "Chérie, you okay?"

"I think my shoulder's dislocated." Grandpa's breathing becomes labored. "Dang it. I forgot my inhaler."

Bri reaches into her raincoat pocket. "Here, Mon Amour," and hands him his medicated asthma inhaler.

He grins. He shakes the small canister three times and shoots a puff of mist into his mouth and into his lungs. With a couple of breaths, his breathing returns to normal—as normal as can be under the circumstances. "What would I do without you, my love."

"What can I do about your shoulder?"

"See if there's an Ace Bandage in the first aid box."

Bri opens the metal box, and Kenny exclaims, "There, Gammaw!" She picks up the elasticized bandage and wraps it around her husband's upper torso and right arm, stabilizing his arm against his body.

10:20. Less than eight and a half miles from Udall, the killer tornado hits Oxford, Kansas, killing five children in one home.

10:25. Inside the shelter, they hunker down in the far corner. "Barney, turn on the radio." He does. Grandpa finds a channel clear enough to hear. The KAKE announcer reports, "Tornado hit

Blackwell, Oklahoma at 9:27." Then, the weatherman says, "A tornado was reported on the ground one mile north of Oxford."

"Oh, mes dieu! Oxford!"

Suddenly, the temperature drops, rushing a chill through everyone.

Ping, ping, ping, ping-ping-ping—golf ball-sized frozen rain shatter on the steps, sending tiny shards of ice ricocheting in all directions as if performing some angry, pagan dance in homage to the black funnel of death approaching in the godforsaken night. The boys scream and cry as Grandma hugs them. "No. No. No cry. Nothing can hurt us down here."

Bolts of lightning sizzle across the black sky, giving light to the outside. Thunder rocks the earth.

10:35. Suddenly, the hail stops, then the wind and rain. Goosebumps erupt over Grandpa's body. He knows there is not a moment to lose. Hurrying up the steps, he grabs the door handle. **"ROSCOE!"** Lightning illuminates the sky. The crash of thunder drowns his second call. Another flash of lightning sends electricity up his spine, for in the light, he sees the thirteen-hundred-yard-wide black monster. It seems to span his entire peripheral vision. He slams the door shut and slides the latch home just before both doors start vibrating. "Please, God, make 'em hold." He backs towards the others and kneels in front of his family, shielding them from danger. **"Our Father, Who art in Heaven."** The rumble of the Santa Fe's 1104 approaches. But it is not 11:04, and it is not the train. Grandma joins him. **"Hallowed be Thy name."** The earth trembles. Louder and louder, the rumbling roars until it is deafening. Their ears pop. **"Thy kingdom come, Thy will be done, on earth as it is in heaven."** They cannot hear their words. But they do not need to. **"Give us this day our daily bread. And forgive us our trespasses."** Then, before Grandpa can beg for all of them to be delivered from evil, Evil pounces on them with fury. The cellar doors shake as if trying to break free of their hinges. The crackling of breaking glass and wood joins the horrific howl. They hold one another for dear life, trying to shrink deeper into the corner of the only place where they have a chance of surviving. The angry, ear-piercing growl of the beast continues as it scratches at their haven.

Then—quiet.

Grandpa takes another puff of his medi-haler. Then, his body relaxes. "I think it's over." He gives his grandsons a kiss on the cheek and his wife a peck on the lips then gets up and climbs the steps to unlatch the doors. He pushes on one. It does not budge. He tries the other. It, too, does not move. He gives it another good shove, but to no avail.

"We cannot get out?" Grandma voice quivers with concern.

"Nope." Grandpa sits on the steps and lets out a dejected sigh, tenderly hugging his arm.

Kenny rushes to him and hops onto his lap so Grandpa's good arm can continue protecting him. A crying Barney, on the other hand, rocks back and forth from one foot to the other while holding the wet crotch of his Roy Rogers pajama bottoms.

"No. No." Grandma comforts him as Kenny pees in the bucket kept for that purpose. "Don't cry. The tornado made you. Shame on that tornado."

Then, with everyone somewhat relaxed, Barney asks, "Grampa, will you tell us how you and Gramma met?"

"We didn't tell ya already?"

"No."

"Well, might as well. We're gonna be here for a while. I was a thirty-two-year-old captain in General Pershing's American Expeditionary Forces. We were in Verdun, France, when I spotted this beautiful mademoiselle in a bakery."

"Gammaw!" the boys exclaim.

"Oh no. It was another mademoiselle. Ooo-la-la."

"No, sir!" Barney objects. "It was Gammaw." He looks at the woman in question. "Right Gammaw?"

"Well, I hope so, or Grandpa has some explaining to do."

They both laugh—Grandpa with some pain—then he resumes. "Yes, it was Grandma, and she had some flour smudged on her forehead and cheeks. I knew only one line in French—."

"The one to pick up girls," the boys say, then chuckle like they had the other times.

"Thank you. You help me out anytime ya want." He clears his throat. "As soon as I saw her, I knew I should've learned more French."

"Gamma said it was love at first sight," Kenny says.

Grandpa puts the flashlight under his chin and, in a low, spooky voice, says, "Would you like to tell our story?"

The boys squeal as they burrow against their grandmother. She laughs.

"I wasn't there to get a girlfriend. I was there to win the war and go home. That part of the story will wait. I will say it was hard not to think of that brunette honey in the bakery who made the **best** French bread."

"I think he **very** handsome—and a gentleman. So, I give him biggest loaf every time he come in so he keep coming into store."

"When Germany surrendered, I ran to the bakery and asked Grandma if she would go to America."

"She said yes!" the boys exclaim and their grandfather stares at them—then grins.

He continues. "So, I gave her my parents' address and phone number and told her I'd be waitin' for her when she got off the ship."

"After we celebrate the end of the war, I kiss my parents goodbye and board the biggest ship I ever see and sailed and sailed and sailed. I think we never get to the U. S. of A. **Finally**, my heart jump when I see The Statue of Liberty. Oh, how beautiful! Then it jump again when I see Grandpa waiting at the dock." She chokes back a tear. "And I cried."

"Were they happy tears, Gamma?" Kenny asks.

"Very happy tears, my Chérie." She kisses the top of his head. "Very, **very** happy tears."

Barney yawns, and Grandma gently rubs his belly and chest. Then Grandpa looks at Kenny fighting to keep his eyes open. "I think the story's over," he whispers to his wife.

11:45. KAKE Radio learns of the Udall tornado. However, the station does not know the extent of the damage.

THURSDAY, 26 May 1955

Five thirty-eight a.m., a voice calls from above, "**Hello! Anyone down there?**"

"**Yes! Yes!**" Grandpa yells through the crack between doors, picturing the voice of God being more of a bass than a tenor.

"I'm Chief Pelzer, Sumner County Fire Department. Everybody okay?"

"Yes, we're okay."

"What's your name, sir?"

"Joseph Snodgrass, but call me Joe."

"Okay, Joe. Your oak tree is layin' across the shelter doors. We'll have to cut it up before we can get you out."

"I understand." He looks at his wife and grandsons. "We're not goin' anywhere."

"We'll use chainsaws, so there's gonna be loud noise."

"Chief, we already heard the loud noise."

"Yes, sir. Looks like you did. Guys, let's get these people outta there."

Seven minutes after seven, the firemen finally cut through the trunk of the hundred-year-old tree, and the cellar doors open to a world Joseph and Brigitte Snodgrass hoped they would never witness again.

"Mon Dieu," gasps Grandma, choked by the shock of what she sees. She staggers out of the hole, tears running down her sixty-year-old cheeks. It is a sight the woman born in a tiny town two hundred miles east of Paris had seen before. For nearly ten months in 1916, the German artillery had bombarded her countryside and town. What surrounds her now isn't much different, except for the stench of death is absent. And that is always a good thing.

Grandpa shakes his head in disbelief. To the south, he stares at the swath of dark earth where yesterday a sea of graceful green wheat had waved in the breeze. He looks at his old oak tree, the one his bride had fallen in love with the moment they saw it lording over the quaint farmhouse back in 1919, the one their boys almost climbed to the top one day before their mother discovered them and ordered them down, fearing they would fall. But the little monkeys had always been at home in that enormous tree, playing Tarzan or one of the other heroes their father had introduced to them through his favorite Edgar Rice Burroughs books. It is amazing how high the roots stuck out of the ground, another time as tall as Grandpa. It is as if a giant hand had plucked it from the earth, laying it like a dead beanstalk across what once was his home filled with love and years of memories. He gazes to the west. Gone are the chickens and their coop; not a feather is seen. The shed where the wagon, tricycle, and tools were stored is a pile of sticks, its contents gone. The house is a shambles. Only the radio and nightstand in their bedroom look untouched. A couple of wood studs lean towards the northeast as if pointing in the direction the merciless assailant had escaped.

As Joe and Bri hug and weep, she says, "We have lost everything, Chéri."

"Everything except what is most important." He gives her a kiss on the cheek. "We can rebuild a house. **We** are the home."

The man pulls the robe away. Blood squirts out of the gaping hole. At once, he applies pressure on the wound as a woman rushes into the living room carrying two red satchels labeled with a white cross above the words FIRST AID. "Linh, call an ambulance! **Wake up, Joe! C'mon! Open your eyes!**"

No response.

12:01:05.

"This tornado was the second time you faced death."

"Second? I don't remember another time."

"You wouldn't. It was during your birth. Your nuchal cord was wrapped around your neck. It could've shut off the blood flow to you. But you wiggled your way out of it in time, and the umbilical cord loosened, and everything came out normal."

"Wow. I never knew that. So, I have an excuse for the way I am."

"It didn't shut off that much blood." The angel grins.

"Are you prosecutin' or defendin' me?"

"Defending, of course. I love challenges." She smiles, then gets serious. "That tornado was the worst: an F5. There were one hundred ten tornados in those three days in May. This one cut a path of destruction

for fifty miles, from Blackwell to Udall, killing eighty-three people and injuring one-third of the citizens of Udall. Anyone would've been terrified."

"Busy day for guardian angels."

"It usually is when the night explodes."

"One good thing came out of it," Barnard says. "Roscoe limped home the next day. And by the looks of him, he hadn't been with his girlfriend unless she was a pit bull in heat."

"Come. We've fallen behind."

"I hope the next stop is better than this one."

"How about June 11th, 1955?"

Barnard shrugs, and the angel escorts him into the light.

5

The First Ballgame

SATURDAY, 11 June 1955

"Barn, you excited about your first baseball game?" Jim asks.

"Yeah."

"Don't sound like it. Nervous?"

He shrugs.

"Barn, you know who Marilyn Monroe is married to?"

"Joe DiMaggio," Kenny quickly answers, standing in the backseat between his mother and grandmother.

Barney, kneeling in the front seat between his father and grandfather, whips around and yells, "**Daddy asked ME!**"

Jim pats Barney on the seat of his husky jeans. "Hey. You know the rules. No yellin' in the car." Then he looks in the rearview mirror. "Kenny—when I ask Barn a question, you **do not** answer. Understand?"

"Yes, Sir. I'm sorry." His arms cross in front of him as a gush of air rushes over a puffed-out lower lip. Then he asks, "Wanna know when they got hitched?"

"I know you're dyin' to tell us," Jim says. "Go ahead."

"January 14, 1954."

"And—**Barney**—," Jim says, looking in the rearview mirror, "what position does Joe DiMaggio play?"

"He doesn't play any," Barney answers. "He retired in 1951. But he played center field for the Yankees. Now Mickey Mantle plays center field," he adds with a big smile.

64

"Kenny, his nicknames were…?"

"Joltin' Joe and The Yankee Clipper. And he had a fifty-six-game hittin' streak that no one broke."

"I'll break it," Barney boasts.

"Well, Barn, you have two games a week 'til the end of July. That's fourteen games. If you have fourteen games a year. And you need fifty-seven games to break DiMaggio's record. How many years will it take to break the record?"

Silence.

"I'll help ya out. It's a division problem. Divide fourteen into…"

"What's division?" the boys ask.

"Just tell them, Einstein," Dottie says. "Barney's not even in kindergarten yet."

"Mommy, Albert Einstein was a physicalist," Kenny says. "He died April 18. He was seventy-six years old. To do division, we need to be mathamagicians."

Dottie chuckles and hugs her baby. "At three years old, you certainly do."

Nose to nose, Kenny glares into her eyes. "Mommy! I'm three years old and nine months old."

"That old? Seems like only yesterday I was changing your diaper."

His eyes bulge. "Mommy! I don't wear diapers no more. Wanna see?"

"No, Sweetie. I know exactly what you're wearing." She kisses him on the cheek, and he returns to looking out the rear window and waving to the people in the car behind them.

"Anyway, Barn, it'll take ya four years to break his record. How old will ya be?"

"Nine," Barney says before Kenny says, "Seven."

"It's gonna take a while. But ya might as well start today."

While Barney warms up with Nick and his other teammates, Jim introduces his across-the-street neighbors, Dan and Connie Wainwright, to his parents. Then, the six sit together on their lawn chairs along with the other families. Kenny sits on the grass with Nicole playing with his soldiers and her favorite doll.

Barney trots to the mound and takes his eight practice pitches; all hitting the catcher's glove—not one does the catcher catch.

Jim shakes his head. "We're in trouble, Pops."

"Yep."

"Batter up," the teenage umpire says, and the first batter walks up to the plate.

Barney throws three strikes. The catcher fails to catch a pitch. The opposing coach and spectators yell, "**RUN!**" The batter gently lays his bat on the ground and trots to where the coach is pointing—first base. The catcher watches him run, but instead of throwing it to first base, he throws it back to Barney. Then, the runner runs to second base on Barney's first pitch to the second batter, which happens to be a strike, and the catcher fails to catch.

Two more strikes and the result of the second batter is the same as the first.

"That's okay, Barn!" Jim says, clapping his hands. "Keep throwin' strikes. That's all ya can do."

On the first pitch to the third batter, the runners advance. After the catcher cannot keep the third strike in his glove, the batter runs down to first base.

"Okay guys," Grandpa says through cupped hands as a megaphone. "Bases loaded. Just step on any base for an out."

"Keep throwin' strikes, Kiddo. One of 'em'll swing," Jim says.

No batter swings. And like a merry-go-round, they all round the bases, one strike at a time, no matter where the ball falls, because the catcher does not know what to do with it except throw it back to Barney, not even when the parents leap out of their chairs screaming at the top of their lungs, "**Tag him! TAG HIM!**"

"Yep. We're in trouble," Jim mutters. Then, when the opposing team bats around, he says, "I've had enough." He walks to the coach and sits down beside him. "Barn can catch the ball. Why not put him at catcher and let someone else pitch?"

"That's what I was thinking. Thanks." The coach calls time out and walks to the mound. "Barney, you catch and—Dick—you pitch."

As Barney dons the catcher's gear, his father says, "Just keep your eye on the ball. If a runner comes home, tag him out—just like we play in the backyard. And keep your right hand behind your back until you throw it to Dick. Okay?"

"Okay."

Jim pats Barney on the shoulder before returning to his chair. Then, he and the other fans watch Barney catch every pitch Dick throws and finally puts an end to the potential runaway.

"Maybe you oughta coach," a dad says to Jim.

Jim grins. "Thanks, but I'll be an unsolicited consultant."

Everyone in earshot chuckles.

The other team has the same problem until Barney comes to the plate with bases loaded.

"Okay, Slugger," Jim says. "Put one out there in the weeds."

For the first time in Barney Snodgrass' young baseball career, he steps into the batter's box. He watches two pitches bounce in front of home plate. The third pitch does not. He blisters a sizzling worm-burner into left-center field. The coach and parents of the opposing team scream at the squatting dandelion picker, who looks up to see why they are invoking his name, then returns to collecting the yellow 'flowers'—probably for someone special—probably for someone loudly encouraging him to "**GET THE BALL!**" And Barney lumbers around the bases for his very first grand slam homerun.

"**Good hit, Slugger!**" a clapping Jim says as Barney rounds third base, his broad smile seeming to push his ears to the back of his head. After he stomps on home plate, he returns to his jubilant teammates before getting more personal praise from his homegrown cheering section. "Well, Dan, let's see what Nick can do."

Of course, his son gets on base, as do every player on both teams.

"Can't kids play baseball?" Grandpa asks. "What the heck do they do at practice?"

"What do they do at home?" Jim whispers. "Don't the dads play catch with their sons—like we do?" He taps Dan on the arm.

"Hey," Dottie says. "They're five years old, not professionals."

"Well, that grand slam just cost us a buck."

"Besides, it's kinda cute to see a kid picking flowers for his girlfriend."

Jim, his father, and Dan groan and shake their heads as the women laugh.

The umpire calls the game at the one-hour limit, with both teams scoring in double-digits.

Barney's entourage congratulates him on a perfect game—batting. And he reminds them how much he earned with two homeruns.

Jim turns to Dottie. "And he's not a pro, huh?"

"**Wow! That was fun!**" an excited Barney exclaims. "I like hittin' homers better than pitchin'. Ain't no fun strikin' a batter out, and he runs to first. It's just not fair."

"How many did ya strike out?" Grandpa asks.

"**ALL OF 'EM!**" the frustrated five-year-old answers.

On the drive home, Jim suggests, "Maybe some Saturday you can have a couple of the boys over for a sleepover, and we can play catch in the backyard. Give 'em some practice."

"Yeah! When?"

"Well, that's up to Mommy." Jim looks in the rearview mirror and sees a disapproving glare as Barney turns around and almost begs his mother. "I'll barbeque some burgers and dogs. How does that sound?" His wife's expression does not change, even with the homerun hitter's sincerest begging. "And maybe, if you're extra good, Mommy'll make some of her **deee-licious** cupcakes." Jim smiles as he sees Dottie shake her head and grin.

"My son, the brownnoser," Grandpa mutters under his breath before chuckling.

Barney looks up at the gray-haired man. "What's a brownnoser, Granpa?"

Grandpa looks at his son, who says, "Hey. Don't look at me, Pops. I'm keepin' my—brown nose out of it."

Barney looks at his father. "Daddy, you don't have a brown nose."

The women chuckle. Then Kenny says, "Daddy, I know the definition of a brownnoser. Wanna hear it?"

"Well, I'd like to hear it," Dottie says.

"It's someone who has a brown nose."

"And what goes good with cupcakes?" Jim asks, and the boys scream for ice cream.

A block later, Jim turns the car into the Dairy Queen parking lot. He buys the boys chocolate Dilly Bars and the adults sundaes: a small Caramel for Grandma, a medium Pineapple for Grandpa, a medium Strawberry for Dottie, and for himself, a large Hot Fudge with nuts.

Everyone thanks Jim for buying the treats before digging in. Then, after a couple of bites, Grandpa says, "Son, you have some fudge on your nose."

The adults almost choke.

He pulls the robe's belt and ties a tourniquet around Joe's upper thigh, then pulls the limp body off the recliner, lays him on the floor, and elevates the wounded leg on the recliner as Linh calls 9-1-1 from her cell phone.

"**Damn!** It's through and through. **Linh, give me the QuikClot!**"

12:01.45.

"That first game was a rough one," Barnard says. "But by season's end, most of the boys could catch the ball. And even some of 'em started hittin', whether or not it went anywhere."

"At least you never stopped to smell the roses during a game." The angel chuckles.

"Nope. Baseball was all business with me—even at five. And you could tell who had the natural ability and who didn't—thank you very much."

"Or maybe one could tell whose parents played catch with their sons."

"That too. Where to next?"

"Might as well keep with the first-time events."

"At five, aren't most of the events the first time?"

"Ohhh, look who's the smarty pants. Wanna take a guess where to?"

*Barnard thinks for a moment. Then his eyes widen. "Well, at five, it must be **kindergarten**." He grabs the grinning angel's hand. As they skip, like kids, towards the light, he says, "This Reckoning ain't so bad—except for the last time.*

"Enjoy it now."

6

First Day of Kindergarten

TUESDAY, 6 September 1955

After parking the car in front of Schweiter Elementary School, Dottie looks at her two sons seated in the front seat. "Barney, you're going to love school. It's just like we play at home. And Miss Dominie is so nice—and **pretty**. You're really going to like her. C'mon." She and Kenny exit the car and walk to the passenger side. She waves at Barney to get out. He does not move. She walks up to the car and pulls on the handle, but the door does not open. She glares at him. "Barney, unlock the door."

With arms folded in front of him, he stares straight ahead.

"Barney."

He shakes his head.

"C'mon, you don't want to be late on your first day. And look at all the other kids going to school. Nick and Nikki will be in your class. You're going to have so many friends you won't know what to do with all of them."

He remains motionless.

"Don't make me unlock the door." She waits a moment. "Did I say Miss Dominie is really pretty? She reminds me of Snow White."

His eyes widen. *Snow White?* But he still does not unlock the door.

"Okay. We'll go back home. But Daddy's not going to be happy with you when **you** tell him you wouldn't go to school."

He unlocks the door.

Dottie escorts her two boys, one on each hand, up to the south doors of the one-story blond-brick building. "That's your room," she says as they walk straight to the first door. Just then, a tall, lanky woman steps out of the room, and Barney's eyes bulge. In a split second, he darts out of the school and sprints for the car.

Dottie and Kenny follow. Barney tugs on the door handle. "I locked it. C'mon. You're going to school."

With tears running down his face, Barney turns and glares at his mother. **"You fibbed!"**

"Fibbed? How did I fib?"

"You said my teacher looked like Snow White! She looks like the Wicked Witch of the West!"

Dottie bursts out laughing.

"It's not funny!"

"Oh, Barney. That's not your teacher. That's the principal. She's the boss. She's nice, too. C'mon. If you don't think your teacher looks like Snow White, I'll take you home, and you'll never have to go back to school."

"Promise?"

"Promise."

"You know what Daddy says 'bout promises."

"You never break a promise."

They walk back to the school, Barney refusing to hold his mother's hand—not so much being angry with her, but for a quicker escape—just in case. Inside, again, Barney's eyes bulge as his mother says, "Barney, this is Miss Dominie, your teacher."

"Hello, Barney." The young, raven-haired woman leans forward with her right hand extended.

Automatically, a starry-eyed Barney shakes her hand.

"I'm pleased to meet you. You want to come with me, and I'll show you our classroom?" Like in a trance, Barney walks into the room together with the woman who could be Snow White's twin. He never looks back.

Miss Dominie takes Barney to the rear wall. "This is your cubbyhole. See, your name is on it. You can put your lunch in here." Then she shows him the closet located behind the cubbyholes. Finally, she says, "I see you're wearing a medal. Are you in the Army?"

He smiles, shyly, and shakes his head.

"Whose is it?"

"Daddy gave it to me for saving Kenny's life."

Her eyes widen. "You saved your little brother's life?" He nods, and she asks, "What happened?" He tells her. "Wow. That was very brave of you—and smart. Would you like to tell the other children about what happened?" He shakes his head. "Okay. But if you change your mind, please let me know. I think the other children would really like to hear the story. And maybe it would teach them what to do if they get in that situation."

After the starting bell rings, Miss Dominie has the children sit in a circle on the floor and introduce themselves. There is Mikey, Bobby, David, Dick, Tommy, Barney, Nick, Nikki, and ten others. Each time, she repeats their name and welcomes them. "I'm very pleased you're all in my very first class." Then she asks, "Mikey, what did you do this summer?"

"We went camping at Lake Afton. Daddy and I went fishing, but we didn't catch no fish."

"Nikki, what did you do this summer?"

"We went to Disneyland in California."

"Wow! That must've been a lot of fun."

"It was, except for all the people. We rode a lot of rides, but we stood in line a long time. I got really, really tired."

"What was your favorite ride?"

"We liked the Jungle Cruise the best," she points to the boy next to her.

"Nick, you look like Nikki. Are you twins?"

They nod.

"Nick, did you go to Disneyland, too?" He nods. "What was your favorite ride?"

"I liked the Mad Tea Party the best."

"Yeah. He made the teacup spin really fast," Nikki says. "I thought I was gonna barf."

The children laugh.

The teacher continues getting the children to share their favorite summer experiences. Then she asks, "Barney, what did you do this summer?"

"I was at Granma and Granpa's when a tornado blew away their farm."

"**Really?** Where did this happen?"

"Udall. I lost Old Betsy."

"Old Betsy? Who's that?"

"Davy Crockett's musket. Granpa made it. It was my favorite birthday present, except for the bike Mommy and Daddy gave me. I left it at home." He swipes the back of his right hand across his forehead.

"Was everyone safe?"

"Yeah. Well, Granpa hurt his arm, and the fireman pulled on it, but Granpa didn't make a sound but made a really ugly face. I got to wear a fireman's helmet! That was really neat—but it was **really heavy**—not like my fireman's helmet."

"Wow. You had quite a summer. I'm glad no one was badly hurt."

"Well, Roscoe got hurt. But he came home after the tornado was gone. Him and Granma and Granpa live with us now 'til their new house is built."

"Who's Roscoe?"

"Granma and Granpa's dog. He's really nice. He looks like Lassie. But Lassie's a girl. He likes to play catch, but sometimes he won't give the ball back, and me and Kenny gotta run after him. Guess he likes to play Tag."

"That's the way my dog does," a girl says, grinning.

When everyone has shared their favorite summer activity, Miss Dominie asks, "Who has a talent you would like to share with everyone?" When no one raises a hand, she says, "Who can sing a song?" Still, no one volunteers. "Who can dance?" The kids are stone still. "Anyone know a joke?"

Timidly, Barney raises his hand. "I can do *Gertrude and Heathcliff.*"

"I love Red Skelton! Come stand here so everyone can see."

Barney stands beside the teacher, messes his hair, which gains laughter, puts his hands in his armpits, and flaps his arms, which gains more laughs. Then, in his best Red Skelton imitation says, "Heathcliff and Gertrude are seagulls, and they're flyin'. Heathcliff says, 'Ya know, I flap my wings 40,000 times a day.' Gertrude says, 'You're puttin' me on!' Heathcliff says, 'No! I flap my wings 40,000 times a day!' Gertrude says, 'Well, why don't ya use deodorant?'" Barney bows, and his laughing audience applauds.

"That was very good, Barney. Thank you. I hope you'll do some more when we have a talent show. Okay?"

He nods and hurries back to his place on the floor as Miss Dominie asks for others to show their talents. Seven hands wave.

After all the volunteers have had a turn, Miss Dominie says, "Now I think it's my turn to entertain you." She holds up a book showing a little girl holding a kitten and reads the title, "Mumpsy Goes to Kindergarten." She looks at her students. "Who do you think Mumpsy is?"

"**The kitten!**" the children yell.

"That's right." Then she begins reading, "Mumpsy was a little yellow kitten who wanted, more than **anything** in all the world, to go to kindergarten." When she finishes, she says, "Louise Lawrence Devine wrote this book. Who enjoyed it?"

Everyone raises their hand.

Before recess, the children go to the restroom, some requiring adult assistance, then play on the playground equipment until lunchtime. After lunch, they roll out their rugs and lie down as Miss Dominie reads another book, Dr. Seuss' *Horton Hears a Who!*

After thirty minutes of naptime, the teacher goes around the room to find out who can recite the alphabet and who can count to one hundred. Only Barney, Nick, Nikki, and Mikey did both.

Finally, they color pictures showing their favorite activity during the first day of school.

The final bell rings at 3:30. Miss Dominie makes sure each child has their belongings before they line up in two lines: boys to the left and girls to the right. Then, she leads them out of the building.

"See ya tomorrow, Miss Dominie," Barney says after hugging his teacher. Smiling from ear to ear, he runs to his mother, who is leaning against the passenger car door, Kenny sitting on the open window.

"Did you have fun?" Dottie asks.

"Yeah! This is my favorite thing I did today." He hands his artwork to his mother.

"Pretty picture. Swinging and playing on the jungle gym was your favorite activity?"

"Yeah! It was fun. And I made lotsa friends." Barney proceeds to name his classmates. "Nick and Nikki are in my class."

"I know. Mrs. Wainwright and I will carpool starting tomorrow." They get in the car. "So, how do you like your teacher?"

"Fine."

"Fine? Is she nice?"

"Yeah."

Dottie pulls out from the curb. "So, tell me everything you did today." And to her delight, her son enthusiastically tells her in more than one word what he did on his first day of kindergarten, including going to the restroom by himself and telling everyone about his Silver Star.

"I had forgotten Miss Dominie. She was beautiful—and nice."

"Just like how The Magic Mirror described Snow White. Lips red as the rose. Hair black as ebony. Skin white as snow."

"Well, her skin wasn't white. I wonder if she made herself look like Snow White or if it was by accident."

"Well, since she has already made the trip you're a step away from making, I can tell you Snow White was her favorite childhood fairy tale character. Whether it was a conscious decision or a subconscious one is something you can ask her—whenever."

"Oh, thanks a lot, ye of li'l faith in my brother and his wife."

"Well, he is doing the best he can with what he has to work with."

"What does that mean?"

Linh removes the QuikClot dressing from the package and packs the gauze in the wound—on top of the leg and bottom. The man whips off his overcoat and drapes it over Joe's upper body to keep him warm as Linh quickly puts an oxygen mask over Joe's nose and mouth, a pulse oximeter on his finger, and a blood pressure cuff on his upper left arm. She pushes the ON button, and the machine automatically monitors his vitals.

The man applies firm pressure on the through-and-through wound.

12:02:15.

"Well, you're the driver of this bus. So, where to, Angel?"

"Well, nuclear war was big back then." The angel takes a surprised Barnard's hand, and they walk into the light.

7

Sputnik, The Bomb, and the Fallout Shelter

SATURDAY, 5 October 1957

Jim sits at the kitchen table, crunches two Nabisco Shredded Wheat biscuits into his cereal bowl, and pours whole milk onto the fibers, finally sprinkling a teaspoon of sugar on top. He shovels a spoonful into his mouth before unfolding the morning newspaper. As he chews, his eyes widen, then he swallows the half-chewed cereal. "Oh my god. They really did it."

"Who did what?" Dottie asks, waiting for the toaster to eject two pieces of white bread.

He reads the front-page headline, "Russians Launch First Artificial Moon."

"Artificial moon?"

"A satellite. The article says it's twenty-three inches in diameter, weighs a hundred and eighty-five pounds, and is circling the Earth five-hundred sixty miles up."

"So?"

"**So?**" He glares at her. "So, the Russkies can spy on us and we can't spy on them. Hell, we can't even shoot the damn thing down if we needed to."

"Daddy said a bad word," Kenny announces as he and Barney enter the kitchen.

"How much can they see from that far up?"

"Well, that's the $64,000 question." Jim puts the paper down and resumes his breakfast.

MONDAY, 4 November 1957

4:55 p.m. The boys are sitting on the floor watching *The Mickey Mouse Club* on ABC when the front door opens.

"**Daddy!**" Kenny jumps to his feet and wraps his arms around his father's hips.

"Okay. What did ya do that Mommy's gonna tell me, and you'll be in trouble? Huh?"

Both boys look at their father and shaking their heads, answer almost in unison, "Nutin'. Promise." Then Kenny says, "We just don't want ya to be mad when ya read the 'paper."

"What's in the paper?" He hands his lunch pail to Kenny. "Take this to the kitchen, please."

As Kenny hurries to the kitchen, Jim picks up the evening Wichita Beacon and flops down in his easy chair. Dottie steps into the dining room from the kitchen. "Don't get worked up about this. You know what the doctor said about your blood pressure."

"Would the love of…." He looks at the front-page headline. "You've gotta be kiddin'! **Two of 'em?**"

"Two of what, Daddy?" Barney asks.

"Two satellites," Kenny answers. "Yesterday, the Soviets launched Sputnik II. It's the second spacecraft sent in orbit around the Earth. I made a report about Sputnik I. A dog is ridin' in Sputnik II. His name's Laika. I don't know what kinda dog. He's the first living thing sent in space. Sputnik II is shaped like an ice cream cone. Yum. It's thirteen feet high and has a base diameter of six and a half feet. It weighs about one-thousand, one-hundred pounds." He proudly grins at his father, who is staring at him.

"What did I say about you answerin' someone else's question?"

Kenny looks down at the floor and shrugs.

"Do you do that in kindergarten?"

Again, Kenny shrugs.

"And how do you know so much about Sputnik II? You a Russkie spy?"

"**No!**" Kenny pats the medal pinned on his shirt. "Russkies don't wear Purple Hearts."

"So, how do you know so much about Sputnik II?"

"I read the newspaper," a proud Kenny answers.

Then Jim looks at Barney. "Why didn't you read the article?" Barney shrugs. "After supper, you read the article and tell Mommy and me what it says—like you would in school."

"Daddy," Barney groans.

"Yes. You're seven. You've been readin' the sports page and comics for a long time. It's about time you read somethin' more important. And boys, the Russians up there," he points to the ceiling, "is **very** important."

"Jim, you're not suggesting…," Dottie says.

"No. I'm not suggestin'—anymore. We're buildin' a bomb shelter."

"**Really?**" The wide-eyed boys stare at their father. "Can we help?"

"I thought we discussed this."

"We did. But wouldn't you rather be safe than sorry? Now the Commies have two spyin' on us, and we have **nothin'**. And we live two miles from McConnell Air Force Base. Do you know how far the blast reached in the bombs dropped on Hiroshima and Nagasaki?"

Dottie shakes her head, and Kenny says, "We dropped Little Boy on Hiroshima on August 6, 1945. It had a blast of about 15 kilotons of TNT and had a blast radius of eight-tenths of a mile. We dropped Fat Man on Nagasaki on August 9, 1945. It had a 21-kiloton blast with a radius of one mile."

"Thank you, Mr. Brittanica," Jim says.

"So?" Dottie says. "We're outside the blast radius."

"Kenny, did Fat Man hit the bullseye?" Jim asks.

"No. It missed the target by two miles."

"And Dot, remember, McConnell trains B-47 Bomber crews, not to mention the ICBM silos scattered about. And with all these nuclear bomb tests, it's just a matter of time when some SOB pushes the button."

"We do *Duck and Cover* drills at school," Barney says, and instantly Kenny starts singing, "There was a turtle by the name of Bert." Barney joins him. "And Bert the Turtle was very alert. When danger threatened him, he never got hurt. He knew just what to do. He'd duck and cover, duck and cover. He'd hide his head and tail and four little feet. **He'd duck and cover!**"

Jim claps, then looks at Dottie. "And the best place to duck and cover is in uhhh…"

"**Bomb shelter!**" the boys yell.

Dottie glares at her husband. "So, how much is this going to cost?"

"About a thousand."

"**A thousand dollars?** Jim, we don't have that kind of money for a hole in the ground."

"How 'bout one that could save our lives—like Mom and Pop's."

Dottie walks back into the kitchen. "Your bread and water will be ready in ten minutes."

Barney looks at his father. "I thought we were havin' Goulash."

"Mommy's kiddin'. I hope."

"We gettin' a storm shelter?" Kenny asks and his father nods, holding his forefinger in front of his puckered lips.

*"Poor old Laika croaked in outer space because of an overheating A.C.," Barnard says. "That was a blessin' cuz if he had survived, the next step would've been Russians manning phaser weapons from space. **But—** three months later, January 31ˢᵗ, 1958, we launched Explorer 1 into space, our first satellite."*

"And the Space Race was on," the angel adds.

"In the Fifties and early Sixties, 'fallout shelter' was the buzzword in American homes. In the Spring of Fifty-Eight, when the ground thawed enough, they started diggin' the backyard next to the foundation. Three months later, we had an addition to our basement—and a hump next to our bedroom. Since Dad worked during the day, Grandpa supervised the whole thing. He sat out there in a lawn chair smokin' his pipe and takin' pictures of every step. Grandma treated the workers to her freshly baked chocolate chip cookies and lemonade or coffee. Mom was not too thrilled about the excavator driving over the garden. That was the only year we didn't have a garden, which was okay with me. Nick, Nikki, Kenny, and I had a blast playing with our little army men on the freshly dug dirt and clay when the men finished for the day. Wonder how many soldiers were left behind."

"Well, on the first day, you boys left five soldiers. On the second day, another…"

"Sorry I asked."

The angel grins. "The shelters were a civil defense initiative intended to reduce casualties in a nuclear war."

"So was the London Underground during the German Blitz in World War II."

"One big difference, engineers designed these bomb shelters to allow people inside to avoid exposure to radioactive fallout and its likely aftermath of radiation until levels were safe. We learned that lesson with the two bombs dropped on Japan to end World War II."

"Ike wasn't much interested in fallout shelters until November of '57 when a Gaither Report evaluated the nuclear capability and civil defense

efforts of the U.S. and the U.S.S.R. It concluded that the Russians would surpass us in all categories of nuclear weapons, and their civil defense preparedness was ahead of ours."

"Many Americans took the report seriously and started digging fallout shelters. By the late Fifties, the U.S. was promoting building these shelters. From 1958 on, the Office of Civil Defense published manuals and created videos with instructions on how to build home shelters."

"What shifted the building of bomb shelters to high gear was the Russians ending a three-year moratorium on nuclear testing in 1961 with a nuclear detonation over central Russia and a warning to the West that it would take very few multimegaton nuclear bombs to wipe us out."

"John Kennedy—he's one of mine," the angel says, "recommended that everyone should have a fallout shelter ASAP."

"So, I may be joining an elite group of souls?" Barnard asks.

A grinning angle shrugs. "If you're lucky. Now, getting back on track, John called…"

"John? You're on a first-name basis?"

"Jealous?" The angel grins seductively. "Remember, he was a lady's man. Even had a relationship with one of the most seductive women ever."

"Marilyn Monroe."

"She's one of mine, too. Now, without further interruptions, John called building the Berlin Wall in August 1961 'the great testing place of Western courage and will.' Then, the Cuban Missile Crisis shoved the entire world to the brink of nuclear war from October 16th to the 28th, 1962."

"The Russians installed nuclear missiles in Cuba, just 90 miles from Florida. Khrushchev authorized Russian field commanders to use tactical nuclear weapons if the U.S. invaded Cuba. Then Kennedy made a deal to remove missiles we had in Turkey if the Russians removed the missiles in Cuba. That prevented nuclear war."

"Building fallout shelters continued until the mid-sixties when three things happened: first, a ban on nuclear weapons testing; second, campaigns to disarm nuclear weapons; and third, Americans began thinking these shelters may not protect them from a nuclear disaster. So, they turned them into wine cellars, storage spaces, or just plain storm shelters, like your grandparents had."

"It saved our lives from that killer twister."

"And talking about saving lives…"

"Ken, BP 120/80, pulse 65, resp 20." Linh feels Joe's cheeks. "Skin cool, pale, sweaty. Stage 1 Hemorrhagic shock."

Joe's head bobs to the left, then right.

"JOE! Stay with me!"

The bobbing stops.

12:02:55.

"It did. And that convinced your mother to agree to the shelter. So, how would you like to go to Kansas City?"

"YOU BET!" A wide-eyed Barnard grabs the angel's hand and pulls her into the light, as he sings, "They got some crazy little women there and I'm… only **seven**. *Dang it!*

8

Meeting a Hero

MONDAY, 28 July 1958

Carrying a suitcase in one hand and the other holding Barney's hand, Jim walks with his father, who holds Kenny's hand, as they walk into the train station in Newton, Kansas, twenty-eight miles straight north of Wichita, on Highway 81. A few minutes later, they board the Atchison Topeka and Santa Fe passenger train and find their seats. The boys sit next to the window and eagerly await the start of their 215-mile journey to Kansas City, Missouri.

"Daddy, when are we goin'?" Through the train window, an impatient Barney watches the other travelers outside the train.

"We'll go when everyone's aboard. Let's play a little game."

"What?"

"You both read the newspaper in the last couple of days." Jim stares at his sons for confirmation. After Kenny nods and Barney's right shoulder shrugs, he says, "Good. Let's start. And only answer the question I ask **you**. Understand, Kenny?"

"Yes, sir," he says shyly.

"Barn, on Friday, a car company is stopping the manufacture of one of their cars. Which company and which car am I talking about?"

With a big smile, Barney says, "The Studebaker-Packard Corporation and the Packard."

"Very good. Two points for you. Kenny, Saturday, a satellite was launched into space. What is the name of the satellite, and what country launched it?"

With a big smile, Kenny says, "The satellite is Explorer 4 and the U.S. launched it."

"Excellent. Two points for you. Game tied. Barn, yesterday two people flew in something to an altitude of 82,000 feet, then landed somewhere. What did they fly in and where did they land?"

"They flew in a balloon and landed in—uh—in—Minnesota."

Smiling from ear-to-ear, Kenny quickly waves his hand.

"What?" Jim asks.

"Daddy, they didn't fly in a balloon. They flew in a closed up 'lum'num gon'ola. And they didn't land in Minnesota. They took off in Minnesota and landed in North Dakota." He snobbishly wrinkles his nose at his older brother.

"Very good. That's true—technically. But no one flies **in** a balloon. It's understood that they fly in a gondola that the balloon carries. So, Barn gets one point and Kenny gets one point for knowing where they landed."

"Pops, what's the score?"

"Three to three."

"Okay. Kenny gets the last question. We're still talkin' about the balloonists. What layer of the Earth's atmosphere did they reach? And what's the name of that layer?"

"That's easy. The stratosphere is the second layer of the Earth's atmosphere. The troposphere is the first layer. That's what we're in."

Jim looks at his father, then his youngest son. "That wasn't in the newspaper."

Kenny shakes his head. "It was in Barney's My Weekly Reader."

"Okay. Kenny wins five to three."

A smiling Kenny jumps off the seat and does a victory dance with hands raised while a pouting Barney's shoulders slump.

"Hey, both of you should be proud of how well you did. I'm proud of both of ya."

"Me too." Grandpa pats both boys on the legs. "And I'm most proud that both of you are readin' the 'paper. I bet your friends aren't reading the 'paper. Keep it up. It'll make ya smart."

"Daddy, will we be back for my game tomorrow?"

"Barn, you asked me that yesterday. What did I say?"

Looking downward, he says softly, "Yes."

"Things haven't changed just because we're on a train. As soon as we get to Kansas City, we'll go to the hotel, eat lunch, take a nap, and then go to the ballgame tonight, where we'll eat the best hotdogs in the world. Then, after the game, we'll sleep at the hotel, and tomorrow morning, we'll eat breakfast and get on the train back home. And…"

"We'll be in bed by nine o'clock," Kenny says, getting a glare from his father. "Well, you already told us twice." In a huff, he crosses his arms and stares out the window.

"Yes, I did. When you guys need to go to the restroom, let me or Grandpa know, and we'll take ya."

"They have a restroom on the train?" a surprised Barney asks.

"Sure." Then Jim sees his youngest staring at him. "What?"

"Where does the poop go?"

Jim glances at his grinning father, who is looking at him, eager to hear his answer.

After a moment formulating the answer, Jim says, "The same thing they do on airplanes. They flush it out the bottom of the train." The boys stare at him. "That's why you never, ever, walk on train tracks. No tellin' what you might step in."

"Ooo!" Kenny wrinkles his nose, then thinks for a moment before kneeling on his father's lap and staring into his eyes. "Daddy, I think that's a tall tale. Ain't it?"

Jim chuckles. "Yes. It's a tall tale. What really happens is everything is collected in a big tub. Then a truck comes by and sucks the tub clean for another train trip. That's the same as they do with passenger airplanes." He raises his right hand. "Honest."

Kenny looks into his father's eyes. "Promise?"

Jim smiles and nods. "I promise." He gives Kenny a kiss on the cheek. "You know you're gettin' heavy for a five-year-old?"

"In two months, I'll be six. You wanna know what I want for my birthday?"

"Why do you think you're gettin' anything for your birthday?"

Kenny grabs his father's cheeks and stares nose-to-nose into his eyes. "Because I've been really, really, REALLY good! Just ask Mommy."

Jim and his father burst out laughing. "Wow, that's pretty good. So, whadaya want for your birthday?"

"I want a Swept-Wing Interceptor, a Moon Space Ship, a Outer Space Ray Gun, a Disney Space Ship Set—you havta help me put it together, and a Adventures of Lassie Game."

"Does this game have any parts you can stick in your mouth?"

Making an X over his heart, Kenny stares into his father's eyes. "Daddy, I promise I will never stick anythin' in my mouth never again—except food."

Suddenly, the train jerks and Grandpa says excitedly, "We're on our way."

"All aboard." Kenny pretends to pull down on something as he says, "Choo, choo, choo, choo. Choo, choo, choo, choo. Chooooo. Choo, choo..."

Jim nods. "When we get home, you tell Mommy what you want. Then, we'll go to the store and look at these things." He gives him a kiss on the cheek before lifting him off his lap and setting him on the floor.

For the next two and a half hours, the men read the newspaper or a magazine they brought with them while the boys read one of their books, every now and then looking out the window at the flat farmlands. Then, they stop at the Great Overland Train Station in Topeka, KS, where everyone tests out the train's restroom. Thirty minutes later, they are treated to one of the Eight Wonders of Kansas Geography, the rolling hills of prairie tallgrass on the Konza Prairie, part of the Flint Hills in Northeast Kansas.

"Imagine cowboys and Indians riding in them thar hills," Grandpa says to his grandsons as they stare out the window.

A little over two hours later, the train pulls into the Kansas City Union Station in Kansas City, Missouri. They disembark and get into a taxi for the drive to their hotel. Ten minutes later, they check into their room and then go to the restaurant for lunch. After lunch, they hit the sack for a three-hour nap before going to the ballpark.

At the park, Grandpa buys the tickets, and Jim buys two programs. Then they walk up the ramp. As soon as they reach the top, a wide-eyed Barney stops and gawks at the field. "Wow! It's really, really big."

"Kiddo, that's why they call it The Big Leagues," Jim says. "Let's see if we can get a few autographs." They walk to the bottom of the stands and wait next to the visitor's dugout—along with a few dozen youngsters eager to get their favorite players' autographs. Then, about two and a half hours before game time, the Yankees walk out of the dugout. Barney's eyes bulge, and his heart attempts to leap out of his chest. He knows them all. The kids yell their names and wave whatever they want them to sign: programs, baseballs, Topps cards, caps on their heads, and the shirts on their backs. Barney's jaw drops as the players walk over to the fans and begin signing their names.

"Be sure to say 'thank you,'" Jim says in his boys' ears. Then, he watches as, one by one, the players sign Barney's program, then Kenny's. An ear-to-ear smile brightens his face as he hears, "Thank you, Mr. McDougald." "Thank you, Mr. Skowron." "Thank you, Mr. Howard." "Thank you, Mr. Kubek." "Thank you, Mr. Stengel." "Thank you, Mr. Mantle."

"You're welcome. Call me Mick," he replies to a gawking Barney, whose eyes bulge with delightful shock.

"Thank you, Mr. Berra." "Thank you, Mr. Ford." "Thank you, Mr. Larson." "Thank you, Mr. Turley." "Thank you, Mr. Richardson." "Thank you, Mr. Slaughter." Many reply, "You're welcome," like The Mick did.

As the players trot to the outfield to stretch, Jim gives his sons a kiss on their cheeks. "I'm proud of ya for sayin' 'thank you'."

"Mickey wants me to call him Mick," Barney says, almost in a dreamlike trance.

Kenny shakes his head. "Boy. I don't think I ever said 'thank you' that many times in my whole life—except maybe Halloween."

"Jimbo, you've trained 'em well."

"Thanks Pops. Wanna give me a kiss on the cheek?"

The wide-eyed boys look up to see, and the men laugh. Then Grandpa says, "How 'bout a beer instead?"

"Granpa," Barney says. "Kenny's too young."

"I tasted beer before," Kenny says. "It tastes yucky."

The men chuckle, then look for a vendor selling beer or soft drinks as Barney watches the players go through their warm-up routine.

"Daddy, these guys don't have good penmanship," Kenny says, studying the autographs.

"Well, they're in a hurry. What's important is that they stopped to sign their names for **you**."

Barney looks at Kenny's program and points to a signature. "That's Mickey's." He points to another. "And that's Yogi's." He identifies most of the names. "Ya think we'll get a chance at catchin' a foul ball?"

"All you can do is hope and be ready." Grandpa waves for the beer vendor.

For the next hour or so, the four wash down peanuts, Jim and Grandpa with beer and the boys with pop, as they watch the Yankees take batting practice. They "Ooo!" and "Ahh!" and "Wow!" as Mantle, Berra, Howard, and Skowron launch balls over the outfield fence.

"Boy, I sure hope The Mick hits a homer."

"I hope he fouls a ball into my glove," Kenny says, pounding his right fist into the dark leather.

"Yeah. Me too."

After batting practice, they go through infield and outfield practice, then leave the field; some resume signing autographs while others vanish into the dugout.

"Let's go over to the K.C. side and see if you can get some autographs from them." Jim leads the clan to the first base side for the arrival of the Athletics. They do not have to wait long. And to Jim's pride, he hears the boys thank Roger Maris, Bob Cerv, Hector Lopez, Hal Smith, and Ralph Terry for their signatures.

"We better find our seats." Jim leads his father and sons to the upper deck, where they sit on the second row from the front above the third base dugout.

A spectator sitting below them sees the boys' autographed programs. "Who did ya get?" The boys tell him, Barney pointing to Mantle's and Berra's. "May I see?" Barney looks at his father, who gives him a nod, and he halfheartedly hands the program to the man. As he looks through the program, the announcer says, "Ladies and gentlemen, please stand and join opera and recording star, Miss Adele Addison, in singing our national anthem."

The man returns the program to Barney as Jim and Grandpa stand and hold their fedoras over their hearts. Barney and Kenny do the same with their Yankee ballcaps. Then they all sing, 'The Star-Spangled Banner'.

The man sitting in front of them turns and says, "You've got a really good voice. How old are you?"

"I'll be six on September 11th. And thank you for the compliment."

"You're welcome. And you have very nice manners."

Kenny leans against his father's side as his dad pats his shoulder. "Thank you for sayin' that."

They all sit down to enjoy the game.

Top of the first inning, Hank Bauer pops up to the third baseman, and Gil McDougald grounds out second to first, bringing up Mickey Mantle. Barney, fit to be tied, stands as his hero comes to the plate. "Mickey's battin' right-handed."

"Why?" Jim asks.

"Cuz the pitcher's left-handed."

"That's right. Why?"

"Cuz it's easier to hit a curveball if it's breakin' towards ya."

The spectator overhears the conversation. "You really know your baseball."

Barney smiles and Jim asks, "Whadaya say when someone gives you a compliment?"

"Thank you," Barney says, never taking his eyes off Mantle as he steps into the batter's box.

CRACK! Barney jumps up as Mickey launches a line drive over the right field fence. He cheers as The Mick rounds the bases. "Boy! Did ya see that? Three hundred and fifty feet!"

Then Bill Skowron ends the top half of the first with a strikeout.

In the bottom of the first, Yankee pitcher Zach Monroe sandwiches a walk between a flyout and a groundout first to shortstop, with the batter, Roger Maris, beating the throw to first. Then the cleanup batter, Bob Cerv, sends a monster shot over Mantle's head for a 450-foot-two-run homer. Then Preston Ward ends the first with a groundout third to first.

Jim signals the hotdog vendor, who hurries to his new customers. "Eight hotdogs, please." After paying for them, he says, "If ya see the beer and pop guys, send 'em this way."

"Will do. Thanks."

Barney takes a big bite of his first ballpark hotdog, then looks at his grandfather who is smelling his dog. "What's the matter, Grampa?"

"Nothing. I just like to fill my lungs with the best smell ever."

"You're right, Pops. I wish I could make hotdogs as good as these."

Nothing exciting happens until the top of the fourth when Mantle walks, then steals second. Skowron flies out. Elston Howard singles; mantle stays on second. Andy Carey singles to left field, scoring Mantle. Howard advances to third. Norm Siebern walks, loading the bases. Tony Kubek scores Howard on a fielder's choice to second. Carey advances to third, Siebern to second on the shortstop's error. Zach Monroe strikes out, bringing up Bauer, who lines a shot to right field, scoring Carey, Siebern, and Kubek. Bauer, trying an inside-the-park homerun, is nailed at the plate on a perfect relay throw from the shortstop.

"Did you see how the right fielder hit his cutoff man?" Jim asks Barney, who nods, a big smile on his face as he looks at the scoreboard: Yankees 6, Athletics 2.

In the bottom of the fourth, Hal Smith sends a solo shot to deep right field bleachers for a six-to-three score.

The top of the fifth sees the Yankees score three more runs on a Mantle single, Skowron double, singles by Howard (Mantle and Skowron score), and Carey, a Siebern walk loading the bases, Kubek grounds out shortstop to second scoring Howard.

In the bottom half of the fifth, Bob Martyn triples to center, then scores on Bill Tuttle's single to left. Yankees 9; Athletics 4.

Before the top of the sixth inning, the voice of the announcer comes through the speakers, "Attendance for tonight's game is 19,984. The Kansas City Athletics thank you for your support."

Then the homerun derby continues after Bauer's single. McDougald's two-run homer scores Bauer. Then Mickey makes Barney go bonkers with his second homer, this one to left field.

But the derby is not over. In the bottom of the sixth, Monroe makes a trip around the bases after a boomer to deep left field. Then, Ward and Lopez single. Pinch hitter Whitey Herzog reaches first on an error, scoring Ward and Lopez. Yankees 12; Athletics 7.

Before the start of the bottom of the seventh inning, the announcer says, "Will everyone please stand and join one of the great pitchers of the American League, National League, and Negro American League, Leroy Satchel Paige, in singing, 'Take Me Out to the Ballgame.'"

"Oh, goodie!" Kenny exclaims. "I like this song." Then, he blurts out, "**Take me out to the ball game, take me out with the crowd.**

Buy me some peanuts and cracker jack; I don't care if I never get back. Let me root, root, root for the home team. If they don't win, it's a shame. For it's one, two, three strikes, you're out at the old ball game."

Athletics cannot score another run.

And the Yankees score a run in the eighth on a homer by McDougald and another run in the ninth on doubles by Siebern and Bauer.

Three hours after the first pitch, the scoreboard, bought from the Boston Braves, shows the first-place Yankees 14 and the fifth-place Athletics 7.

As they stand, an excited Barney says, "Daddy, seven homeruns! Wow! That was the best game I've ever seen!"

"Me, too," Kenny says. "Can I get a box of Cracker Jacks?"

"It wouldn't be a complete game if we didn't. Hope the stand's still open."

They follow the crowd down the ramp to the bottom level, where they find the concession stands still open. Jim buys two boxes of Cracker Jacks, then goes to the souvenir stand where Grandpa buys the boys each a Yankee and Athletics banner.

As they begin to leave, Barney says, "Boy, sure wish we'd caught a foul ball."

"We didn't even come close," Grandpa says. "But you sure got some good autographs."

"You know which one is my favorite autograph?"

"Oh gee, let me guess," Grandpa says just before Kenny blurts out, "Mickey Mantle." Then he proudly looks at his father, who is glaring at him. So is Grandpa. "Well, it was a stupid question. Everybody knows Barn's favorite player is Mickey Mantle."

"Kenny. I said I was gonna guess," Grandpa says. "When you don't take your turn, it spoils the game."

"I'mmmmm sorry."

"Okay. Try to let other people go first. Okay?"

Kenny nods.

On the way home, Barney says, "I'm gonna put my program with my Braves' trophies."

"Good idea. How many do ya have?"

"Three first-place pitchin' trophies and one second-place hittin' trophy and a third-place hittin' trophy."

"Did you read in the 'paper that this year is the last year for the Wichita Braves?"

"I did, Daddy," Kenny says proudly. "They're goin' to Fort Worth, Texas, to be the Fort Worth Cats. Stupid name."

Jim shakes his head, exasperated, then says, "That's good that you read the paper. Barn, did you read that article?"

Barney shakes his head. "Can we go see 'em?"

"Don't see why not. Just depends on your schedule."

Jim parks the car on the driveway and the boys run into the house, yelling, "Look what we got!" The excited boys give their mother and grandmother an earful covering the train rides to the rats scratching the hotel's alley wall six floors below their window, what they ate in the restaurant and stadium to the ballgame to getting up close to major league players—especially…

"Mickey Mantle told me to call him Mick," a very happy Barney says.

"You would've been proud of 'em, Dot," Grandpa says, walking into the kitchen. "They said 'thank you' every time a player gave 'em an autograph."

"That's what I like to hear. Anyone want BLTs and Grandma's coleslaw?"

She receives a resounding, "**Yeah!**"

"That was a trip to end all trips," Barnard says. "I wish I had shaken his hand, though."

The angel chuckles. "Well, an eight-year-old can't think of everything when they meet their boyhood hero for the first time."

"Guess not. Well, where to next?"

"To your fourth grade."

"Fourth grade?"

"C'mon." The angel takes his hand, and they hurry into the darkness.

"BP 110-75. Pulse 100. Resp 25. Breathing shallow. Ken, Stage 2 Hemorrhagic shock."

"More QuikClot."

Linh gives it to him and Ken sticks another sheet of gauze in the top and bottom of the wound, wrapping it with another pressure bandage. "That damn well better hold it."

Linh swabs Joe's lips with a wet gauze.

12:03:55.

9

New Kids in Class

TUESDAY, 8 September 1959

On the first day of school, Mrs. Dabir, the fourth-grade teacher, stands in front of the classroom with a boy and a girl. "Children, we have two new students. Please say 'hi' to Erika Andersson and Charlie Tyran."

"**Hi, Erika! Hi, Charlie!**" the twenty-eight, nine- and ten-year-olds enthusiastically yell.

"Thank you. Now, please stand. Barney, will you lead us in The Pledge of Allegiance?"

The children stand and face the American flag located to the right of the teacher's desk. With their hands covering their hearts, everyone says, "I pledge allegiance to the flag of the United States of America and to the Republic for which it stands, one nation, under God, indivisible, with liberty and justice for all."

"Thank you. Please be seated." After everyone sits at their desks, Mrs. Dabir says, "I would like to know what everyone did this summer. Let's start with our new students. Erika, would you like to tell us what you did this summer?"

"Yes, Ma'am." She stands. "My family spent the entire summer in Brazil. That's where my mom was born, and her family is there. We saw gobs of festivals. As soon as we got there, we went to the Festa Junina that goes on every day in June." She laughs. "All the kids paint freckles on their faces. Everyone dances, like square dancing, and the food is, wow, like my mom would say, 'deliciosa.' Then, we spent three days in June in Amazonia for the Parintins Folklore Festival. That was a party—singing, dancing, plays, great food. Finally, we saw the Festival de Cachaça in Paraty, a little town south of Rio de Janeiro. Adults like this celebration because they get to sample cachaça. It's the national liquor of Brazil and is made from sugar cane. My grandpa owns a sugar cane farm, among other businesses. And that's about it. Oh! We went swimming in the Atlantic Ocean." She sits.

"Thank you, Erika. That was very interesting. I would like you to make a report about Brazil when we study Geography."

A smiling Erika nods.

"Charlie, what did you do this summer?"

"Nothin'. Just hung around the house and smoked and went to the show and played ball."

"What shows did you see?" He shrugs as if disinterested. "Okay. Well, who wants to be next?" Many hands rise, and the teacher calls on each child. Finally, she calls on Barney.

"Mom, Dad. Gramma, Grampa, Kenny, and me went to Kansas City to watch the Yankees play." Most of his classmates boo. He smiles before saying, "They won, 14 - 7. I got autographs of the whole lineup!" He names every player who autographed his program. My favorite player, Mickey Mantle, hit two homers and a triple and knocked in most of the runs—six!"

"Sounds like you, Barn," a boy says from the other side of the room.

"David, is Barney a homerun hitter?" Mrs. Dabir asks the one who popped up.

"Sure is! He usually hits one every game—sometimes two."

"Wow! We might have the next Mickey Mantle right here." She looks at Barney, whose timid side suddenly emerges.

10:15. As the kids go outside to play Kickball, Erika walks next to Barney. "My favorite team's the Dodgers. Last year, when we lived in L.A., we had season tickets, and I got every autograph, including Don Drysdale, Sandy Koufax, Gil Hodges, Duke Snider, and Pee Wee Reese."

"Wow! Were you a fan when they were in Brooklyn?"

"No. I was born in L.A., but my dad's favorite team was the Brooklyn Dodgers. So, when they moved to L.A., he was still a fan, so I fell in—**HEY!**"

Charlie barges between them and glares at Barney. "I hate the Yankees. And I hate Yankee lovers."

"That was rude!" an angry Erika scolds.

Charlie glares at her. "I wasn't talkin' to you—Sweetie!"

"Don't call me **sweetie**! And I've only known you for two hours, and I don't like you."

He scoffs at the rebuke, shoves Barney, and runs to the ball diamond, where many of the children are waiting for the teacher to choose teams. Mrs. Dabir chooses Erika and Charlie as captains because they are the new kids in class. And since ladies go first, Erika chooses first. She picks Barney. He volunteers to be the pitcher. And the first kicker he faces is—the other new kid.

Barney rolls the ball toward homeplate. By rule, the kicker must wait until the ball reaches the plate before the kicker can kick it. However, Charlie does not wait. He charges the ball when it is ten feet from homeplate and slams his right foot against the ball. Like a rocket, it streaks toward from where it came, hits Barney in the chest, and ricochets fifteen feet in the air. It comes down in Barney's arms.

"**Out!**" yells the teacher, and his teammates yell, "**Good catch, Barn!**"

After three outs, Erika's team goes on offense. When Barney gets up to 'bat,' he launches the soccer ball between the gap. Charlie catches up to it, and instead of throwing it to an infielder, he runs it in—and directly at Barney, who is already standing on second base. With all his might, his right arm whips around to fire the ball point-blank at the baserunner. But the ball escapes his grip, and only an empty hand does Charlie throw. The children howl with laughter.

"**Charlie Tyran!**" Mrs. Dabir yells. "**Come here!**" He does, and a private conversation is seen but not heard. She watches his behavior closely.

FRIDAY, 11 September 1959

8:00 a.m. After Nikki leads the class in the Pledge of Allegiance, Mrs. Dabir asks, "Who would like to start Show and Tell?" She looks at all the waving arms beckoning her to choose the eager child extending it. After five children describe the items they have brought, the teacher calls on Erika.

She carries a box to the front of the room, removes a twelve-inch-tall doll, and holds it next to her head. "This is Carmen Miranda. She was born in Portugal—not the doll—the person and was a Brazilian singer, dancer, and actress. Her nickname was 'The Brazilian Bombshell' and she was known for the fruit hat outfit she wore in American movies. She died in 1955. My mom is teaching me Samba, which was Carmen's favorite dance. This doll is almost twenty years old. I collect dolls, and this is my favorite. Thank you."

"Thank you, Erika," the teacher says as her fellow classmates applaud.

3:30. The final bell rings, and the children line up in two rows: boys on the left, girls on the right—Charlie, a couple of boys behind Barney.

Nikki and her girlfriends stroll behind the boys as they walk along the sidewalk on the opposite side of the school. The boys talk about television cowboy shows: *Colt .45, Maverick, Lawman, Cheyenne, Sugarfoot, The Rifleman,* and *The Life and Legend of Wyatt Earp* on

ABC; *The Texan*, *Rawhide*, *Wanted Dead or Alive*, and *Have Gun Will Travel* on CBS; and *Tales of Wells Fargo*, *Wagon Train*, and *Bat Masterson* on NBC.

Suddenly, Barney takes a nosedive face-first to the ground. The others scatter as Charlie shoves the fallen with his foot. "**Give me your money, Barnyard!**"

Barney quickly stands. "I ain't got any money!"

"**Liar!**" Charlie punches Barney in the face, startling everyone and knocking Barney backward. Before he can steady himself, Charlie lays into him with a barrage of punches to the face and body, knocking Barney on his back. Suddenly, Kenny jumps on Charlie's back. A quick turn and Kenny tumbles to the ground. Charlie glares at Kenny. "Stay down, ya snotnosed squirt." He tries getting up but Charlie pushes him down. "**Stay down, or I'll hurt ya!**" He does. Then, Charlie scowls at the others. "Give me **your** money, or you'll get the same." They scatter like rats from a flood. Charlie lets out a belly laugh. "**Ya can't run from me! Monday money or else!**" He turns to find Kenny standing behind him with fists at the ready. Charlie scoffs at the much smaller foe. "Go home, Squirt. Next time, I won't be so nice." As he starts to walk away, he again shoves Barney with his foot. He tumbles on his side. "Dollar a week, Snottyass, or I'll give ya a knuckle sandwich you'll never forget."

As Kenny helps his brother to his feet, he says, "I'm gonna kill that sonofabitch."

A doubled-over Barney groans, "Nope. I will." As they limp home, he says, "Not such a happy birthday. Huh?"

4:00. "How did your first week of school go?" Dottie asks from the kitchen.

"You tell me." Barney walks into the bathroom.

As he gingerly splashes water on his face, his mother stops in the doorway. He looks at her in the mirror on the medicine cabinet door, and her eyes widen. "**What happened?**"

"Ya know that new kid?"

"Who's been bullying you?" He nods. "Why did you get in a fight with him?" He tells her. "Wait until Daddy gets home."

4:45. Jim walks into the house to find everyone in the kitchen, Dottie fixing supper, his boys sitting at the kitchen table, Kenny drinkin a glass of milk, Barney holding a wet ice-cube-packed rag to his cheek. "What happened to you?" Barney tells him. "You get any punches in?"

"Think so."

"C'mon. We need to put a stop to this before it gets any worse."

5:00. Jim parks in front of the Tyran address closest to the school and knocks at the front door.

"Yeah?" A man wearing a sleeveless wife beater undershirt stands on the other side of the screen door, a cigarette barely hanging from his lips.

"You have a son named Charlie who goes to Schweiter?"

"Yeah. Why?"

"He's been pickin' on my son, and I want it stopped."

"What did he do?"

"He beat up my son and demanded money. Like I said—I want it stopped." Jim turns and starts walking towards the car.

Tyran steps onto the porch. "What if he don't stop?"

Jim turns. "Then I'll be back, and you'll get to know me a lot better."

"Charlie didn't stop."

*"No, he didn't! Dad wanted to go over there every time we got beat up, but Mom stopped him. She said it would be better to pay the kid off than to fight. So, to keep peace in the family, Dad stayed home—no matter how many bruises and split lips **we** got."*

"But your father told you and Kenny to keep track of every cent you gave Charlie."

"Which we did. Every cent. And Kenny kept a notebook logging everything Charlie did to us—at school and goin' home. Enough of this. Let's go somewhere else. I'm sick and tired of that SOB."

"Talk about sick and tired. You're not doing so well."

Blood loss is four pints.

"Still bleeding." Ken grabs another QuikClot pack and sticks more gauze in the wound as Linh checks Joe's vitals. The automatic blood pressure monitor beeps.

"BP 90/50. Pulse 122. Resp 35. Stage Three. Ken—transfusion?"

Suddenly, the monitor whines.

"He crashing!" At once, Linh begins administering thirty chest compressions and two breaths as Ken puts a tourniquet around Joe's leg near his groin. **"C'mon Joe! Fight!"**

12:04:55.

The angel holds out her hand. As they walk into the blackness, the angel says, "You know we're not quite finished with that—you know what."

"Yeah. I know what."

10

The World Series Heartbreak

THURSDAY, 13 October 1960

11:30 a.m. "Class," the teacher says. "We'll go outside for some games, then we'll eat lunch and watch the seventh game of the World Series." Barney's 5th-grade class launches an excited cheer. Then, when everyone quiets, they line up at the door, boys to the left of the girls. Erika and Nikki briefly skirmish to stand opposite Barney. Give or take a few inches, both can claim victory. They smile at each other—snobbishly.

Charlie, standing behind Barney, whispers, "Don't smile at my girl, Barnyard Snottyass."

Barney turns around. But before he can respond, the teacher says, "Barney, face forward, please. Leaders. March your sides outside.

With a whistle in hand, the teacher positions the girls in a straight line. As they have done many times in the past years, as soon as the teacher blows the whistle, the girls sprint to the fence and back— about thirty yards each way. Erika beats Nikki by five yards. The rest trail a few yards behind her.

Then, it is the boys' turn. Barney glances to his right to see Charlie readying himself for the race. The whistle blows. Barney springs into action. But when his back foot comes forward, it hits Charlie's left foot, and he nosedives into the dirt. Then the laughing Charlie tries to catch the other boys. When the group races back, Charlie aims for Barney, who is running towards them. But instead of trying to avoid Charlie, Barney speeds up and rams directly into Charlie like a fullback blocking a linebacker. A stunned Charlie flies backward, his feet flailing above his head as he crashes to the ground. Barney proceeds to the fence. He turns to find a recovered Charlie waiting for him with hands in tight fists. Barney charges Charlie. But like a seasoned running back, he zigs and zags, leaving Charlie swinging at the wind. He gives chase, but the rippling shrill of the teacher's whistle slows his charge.

"**Charlie!** No fighting, or you'll miss the last game of the World Series. Now, stay clear of Barney. And I'll be watching you."

11:50 a.m. While everyone except Charlie goes to the restroom, the students return to the classroom. Then, the teacher allows Charlie to go. When he walks past Barney, he says under his breath, "After school, Barnyard."

Just before game time, Barney stands in front of the class and presents his Show and Tell item. Holding the plastic eight-inch color statute, he says, "This is Hartland's figure of the Yankee's center fielder Mickey Mantle." Most of his classmates erupt in loud boos. He smiles. "He's my hero. So is Willie Mays who plays for the San Francisco Giants. Both of 'em play center field. I have his figure, too. I have eleven baseball greats, including Babe Ruth." More boos. "Yogi Berra." Louder boos. "The Mick, that's his nickname, was born October 20, 1931, in Spavinaw, Oklahoma. That's in the far northeast corner of Oklahoma. He's a switch hitter. That means he can bat both right-handed and left-handed. He joined the Yankees in 1951. He won the Triple Crown in 1956, leading the majors with a .353 batting average—anything over .300 is really good, 52 homers and 130 runs batted in. That's the Triple Crown. Two years ago, I got The Mick's autograph when the Yankees played the Athletics in K.C. He doesn't write very good, but then, none of the players do." He sits down to a round of applause—except for Charlie. The teacher thanks him and Erika pats him on the back. "That was interesting—even if it was about a Yankee." She smiles.

As Barney shows Mantle to his friends, Charlie says, "Pass it down here." Barney shakes his head and puts the plastic replica back in the box.

Noon. The children stand as the television broadcasts the National Anthem, then sit and eat lunch. While watching the first pitch, Erika leans toward Barney and asks, "What did Charlie say to you?"

"He said you were his girl."

"**His girl?**" An outraged Erika leaps from her desk, glares at Charlie, and yells, "**Charlie, I am NOT your girl!**"

Their classmates burst out laughing before the teacher settles them down and admonishes Erika for the outburst.

After the first inning, the score is 2-0 Pirates, on first baseman Rocky Nelson's homer over the right field wall with left fielder Bob Skinner on base.

C'mon Mick. Hit it out. Barney holds the Hartland figure standing on his desk as the real deal leads off the second. On a two-and-one pitch, Mantle smacks a deep flyball to right-center for a long out. *DANGIT!* Left fielder Yogi Berra and first baseman Bill Skowron ground out.

At the end of the second inning, the Pirates scored two more times, bringing cheers to most of the students, especially Charlie, who shows Barney how big of a smile he can make.

Yankees 0. Pirates 4.

"Don't mind him," Erika whispers. "The game is far from over."

"I thought you didn't like the Yankees," Barney says.

"I don't. But I dislike Pittsburgh more since they're in the National League and beat my Dodgers."

It is not looking good for Barney and the few Yankee fans in the classroom until Bill Skowron takes Pirate right-hander Vern Law deep to right field for a solo home run, bringing those fans out of their seats.

New York 1. Pittsburgh 4.

The top of the sixth is even better for the boys in pinstripes. Yankee second baseman Bobby Richardson sends a line drive up the middle before shortstop Tony Kubek walks. Right fielder Roger Maris fouls out, and Mantle singles up the middle, scoring Richardson. Then Berra homers down the right field line, scoring Kubek and Mantle.

New York 5. Pittsburgh 4.

No one scores until the top of the eighth when Berra walks, Skowron and catcher Johnny Blanchard single scoring Berra. Then third baseman Clete Boyer doubles, scoring Skowron, and a broadly smiling Barney gives a fist-pump. *NOW WE GOT 'EM!*

New York 7. Pittsburgh 4.

Finally, it is looking good for the team who has won seven of the last ten World Series championships—until the bottom of the inning when pinch hitter Gino Cimoli, center fielder Bill Virdon, and shortstop Dick Groat single before the Yankees can get two outs. Then right fielder Roberto Clemente singles before catcher Hal Smith hits a three-run homer over the left field wall. Barney's shoulders slump as he stares at Mick standing on his desk.

New York 7. Pittsburgh 9.

In the top of the ninth inning, Richardson, pinch hitter Dale Long, and Mantle single, scoring Richardson. "**Yeah!**" Barney yells. Gil MacDougal pinch runs for Long who is at third, then scores on Berra's groundout to first base. Barney yells louder.

New York 9. Pittsburgh 9.

2:36. With the count of one ball, second baseman Bill Mazeroski hits right-hander Ralph Terry's second pitch deep to left field. Berra sprints to Pittsburgh's Forbes Field's vine-covered wall only to watch the ball sail out of sight. The hometown crowd and the Yankee-hating students erupt into cheers while Barney bursts into tears.

"Ha-hahaha-ha!" Charlie blares. "**Barnyard Snottyass loooses! Ha-hahaha-ha!**"

The teacher glares at her trouble-making student. "**Charles Tyran**, that's a poor sport. And shame on you for calling Barney names."

With his nose in the air, Charlie continues his hateful teasing.

Erika pats Barney on the shoulder. "Don't mind him. It was a great game, and someone had to lose." Then under her breath, she says, "Sorry, it had to be those damn Yankees."

Instead of seeing Mazeroski rounding the bases, Barney sees *the Devil's sexy red-head, Gwen Verdon's Lola, dancing in the Senators' locker room trying to seduce Tab Hunter's Joe Hardy.*

3:30. The final bell rings, and the students line up at the door. The teacher dismisses them in the orderly manner she has trained them. Some climb into their parents' cars. Others hop on their bikes. Still others walk in groups. The remainder walk alone. All go home to play or do their homework or chores. For seven, they have a date with destiny.

As Barney, Kenny, Nick, Mikey, David, Tommy, and Willie wait at the corner for traffic to pass, suddenly, Barney lunges into the street. **BEEEEEEEEEEEEP!** He jumps back just in time to avoid discoloring the driver's passenger-side headlight, not to mention what that corner and hood would have done to his body, mind, and soul.

Through the gasps and moans and groans of the rest, loud laughter turns everyone around to see who finds the near fatal situation hilarious.

"**Whadaya doin'?**" Barney growls.

"That wasn't funny, Charlie!" Dick admonishes.

"Wanna bet. Shoulda seen your face."

"He could've been killed," Nick says.

"Let me see your dolly—Snottyass."

"My name ain't Snottyass, and it ain't a doll, and NO!"

Charlie extends his hand. "Give me the doll, or next time, a car won't miss ya."

"I said **NO!**"

Charlie lunges for the haversack draped over Barney's left shoulder. Backing up, Barney turns to his left. But instead of grabbing the bag, he punches Barney in the face. Instantly, Barney's hands cover his stinging face. Charlie punches his midsection. Barney doubles over. Charley grabs the 'sack, jerks it away from the owner, and throws it to the ground before hitting Barney again. Barney drops to his knees. Charlie lords over him. **"When I want something—give it to me—or I'll take it!"** Jerking around, he glares at the others. "And that goes for you chickenshits, too." He takes a step towards the others who have failed to defend their comrade—except one—the one his buddies hold. Walking up to Kenny, he puts a stop to his kicking and squirming with a punch to his belly. Gasping for air, Kenny falls to the ground, curls into a fetal position, and cries. As a laughing Charlie and his goons strut away, he stomps on the haversack.

While the boys console their battered and bleeding friends, Nick carries Barney's books and Tommy his haversack while they discuss what Barney should have done and boasting what they will do if Charlie dares come knocking at their heads. For two blocks, Barney says nothing—until he has heard enough. "Thanks, guys. Six ta three. And you just stood there and watched—except for Kenny. Why didn't ya help?" With no answer, Barney takes his bag and books, and the battered brothers of Bassar Street walk alone.

Five until four, the boys walk up the driveway and into the living room. They drop their books and the haversack on the dining room table and go straight to the bathroom. As Barney dabs the blood from his face, Dottie steps into the doorway. Her jaw drops. "Charlie again?" They nod. "I'll make an icepack." After Barney cleans his face and stops the bleeding, he sits in the kitchen holding ice wrapped in dish rags to his bruised and battered face. "So, tell me what happened."

Barney tells her, especially the part on the street, and her eyes bulge. "**He tried to kill you?**" He nods. "I'm calling the police." Dottie dials 0. After telling the police officer what happened, she hangs up. "Someone'll be here shortly." She shakes her head. "Wait 'til Daddy gets home."

At four twenty-five, a patrol car parks in front of their house, and two uniformed police officers walk up to the house. Dottie greets them at the door. Inside, they note Barney's injuries and question him. He explains everything that Charlie has done to him and tells the officers the names of his thugs and the witnesses. From the school directory, Dottie gives them their names, addresses, and phone numbers. Since Charlie is new, his name is not listed.

Twenty minutes later, Jim hurries into the house. "**What's wrong?**" As soon as he sees Barney's face, he knows who did it. Then asks what happened. After Barney tells him, a red-faced Jim adds, "This Charlie Tyran is two years older than my son, so he's failed a couple of grades—in other schools. He's a juvenile delinquent. I met his dad about a year ago. He's a Nazi lover. And I hate Nazis."

"Mr. Snodgrass," one officer says. "Don't do anything to make things worse. Let us handle the matter. Okay?"

"Okay. But put this in your log book—anything less than attempted first-degree murder won't sit well with me."

After the police officers leave, Barney says between puffy lips, "Mom, I know ya want us to turn the other cheek. But I've run outta cheeks to turn."

"Me, too," Kenny says, rubbing his belly. "Even though Jesus taught to turn the other cheek in his Sermon on the Mount, in the Book of Exodus 21:23–27, it says an eye for an eye."

"I guess it depends on what you believe."

Barney stares at his broken Hartland figure. "Get the crap beat outta ya and see what **you** believe."

Jim picks up Mickey's plastic left leg. "Well, I know what to believe. C'mon, Boys."

"What are you going to do?" Dottie follows Jim and her sons out of the kitchen.

"What I should've done weeks ago."

Five o'clock, Jim turns onto the street where the Tyrans live. "Dang it." He drives past the house with one police car parked in the driveway and another in front of the house.

Barney stares at the patrol cars. "Is Charlie gonna get arrested?"

"He sure better." An unsatisfied Jim drives back home.

SATURDAY, 15 October 1960

Noon. While eating lunch in the living room, a knock at the door draws them away from watching *Watch Mr. Wizard* on NBC.

"Sorry to interrupt your lunch," the casually dressed young man says through the screen door. Dottie comes to the door. "Remember me? I'm Officer Jaeger. I took your report on Friday."

"Yes! Please come in." He steps into the house. "You know everyone." He nods. "Please sit."

"No, thank you. I wanted to see how Barney was doing." Barney nods. "Good. I also wanted to tell you, based on your friends' accounts, Charlie Tyran is in the juvenile detention center. Early next week, the Sedgwick County District Attorney should decide what charges he'll file."

Jim looks up at the young man. "Please tell the District Attorney, attempted—first—degree—murder. And tell him anything less, and he'll never get my vote again."

Jaeger looks at Jim. "Should I tell him anything else?"

"You can add anything you want." Jim returns to watching the educational show about the science behind everyday things. When Jaeger leaves, Jim says, "Good news, that li'l SOB's behind bars. Hope in the slammer'll give him time to think about his behavior."

Barney looks at the reconstructed Mantle. "Dad, I'm gonna buy another one. I don't want this one."

"Don't blame ya, Son. And I'll buy it. But don't take **anything** to school if this kid is there."

"I won't. Promise."

MONDAY, 17 October 1960

8:00 a.m., Barney's jaw drops as Charlie walks into the classroom. Before he sits in front of the teacher's desk, he scowls at Barney and runs his forefinger across his neck—mimicking Jim.

Erika whispers to Barney, "I thought he was in jail." He shrugs.

Ten o'clock, the class goes outside for Recess and immediately, David, Mikey, Tommy, and Dick rush over to Barney. "What's the deal?" Mikey asks. "Ya told us he was in jail."

"I don't know how he isn't. Why don't ya go ask him?"

"Ah, shit. Here he comes." The four not-so-much Musketeers distance themselves from Barney.

"Charley! Over here." The teacher points in front of her.

Before he turns about-face, he says, "It's Monday, Snottyass. You know what that means." He shows him a tight fist.

Three-thirty, the students exit the school in an orderly manner—except for one. Charlie sits at his desk and writes ten times the twenty Spelling words he misspelled.

Four-fifty, the boys greet their father as he walks into the house and tells him, "Charlie was in school."

His forehead furls and eyes glare at his oldest. "Did he do anything to ya?"

"No. Mrs. Dabir kept him after school. But he **was** gonna pound me."

"C'mon."

"Jim, what are you going to do?" Dottie asks.

"I'm gonna let Charlie's dad feel what my boys have felt for months."

"**Our** boys."

Five o'clock, Jim parks his car in front of the Tyran residence. "Stay here." He walks up to the front door and knocks—hard. A moment later, the door opens.

"Thought you might be by," a smug Mr. Tyran says.

Jim steps off the porch. "Your punk brat gave my sons a knuckle sandwich and almost killed my oldest. I'm here to give you a double-decker."

Tyran throws the screen door open, steps out of the house, and pulls out a knife from his jeans' pocket. With the push of a button, the six-inch blade swings out. "I see you're familiar with knives."

"Put it away, **or I'll** put it away. And you won't like where I stick it."

Tyran jumps off the porch and lunges at Jim, who steps to the side. Tyran staggers past~~sed~~. Abruptly, he turns and swings the knife like Errol Flynn swinging a sword in the 1935 swashbuckling pirate film *Captain Blood*. Jim retreats a step. Tyran follows until Jim grabs Tyran's wrist and twists his arm as he brings it over his right shoulder. Then, with Tyran at his back, he brings the arm downward. The elbow bends the wrong way—**CRACK**—snapping like a twig. A loud, shrilling "**OOOWWWW!**" fills the neighborhood. The knife sticks in the ground. Jim turns. As Tyran holds his broken arm, Jim lands a mighty punch to Tyran's solar plexus. He doubles over. Then Jim lands an uppercut, and Tyran's head jerks upward. His body slowly falls backward like a pine destined to be a lot of two-by-fours. Dazed, Tyran lies on his back. Jim stands over him and pummels his face with six left and right punches until his face is bloodier than his boys'.

"**DAD!**" two boys scream from the door. They charge out of the house but stop when Jim glares at them, his fist cocked for the knockout blow. "**LEAVE MY DAD ALONE!**"

Jim takes a step towards them. They took two steps to retreat ~~two~~. Jim points his fingers at the smaller kid. "If you touch either of my boys again—I'll be back to cut that fuckin' tattoo off your dad's arm. And don't think I won't—cuz I **hate** Nazis—especially American ones—you dirty, rotten, filthy traitors." Jim picks up the knife and looks down at Tyran. "Thanks for the souvenir. I collect 'em." He walks back to the car.

As he gets in, Barney exclaims, "**Boy, Dad! You kicked his ass!**"

Still fuming, Jim does not respond.

"Can I see the knife?" Kenny asks eagerly.

On the way, he adds, "After supper, I'll teach ya to fight."

"**Like a commando?**" a wide-eyed Kenny asks.

"Like a commando. And when you're fully trained, I want you boys to kick Charlie's ass so he'll **never—ever**—bully you again."

"And his pals," Kenny says.

Jim looks at his youngest. "And his pals."

As soon as Kenny rushes into the house, he yells. "**DADDY KICKED HIS ASS!**"

"Whose ass? Charlie's?" Dottie asks.

"**NO!** Mr. Tyran."

"Ya shoulda seen it, Mom!" Barney says. "Charlie's dad never laid a hand on Daddy. I think he broke that Nazi lover's arm."

"Jim, you didn't."

Out of his pant pocket he pulls out the switchblade and drops it on the kitchen table.

"What's that?"

"It's Mr. Tyran's Nazi knife!" the excited boys answer.

"You brought it home?"

On his way out of the kitchen, Jim says, "He's lucky I didn't give it back to him—in his heart."

During supper, Jim says, "Boys, when you train to fight Charlie, you DO NOT tell anyone. This is top secret. You do not tell Nick or Nikki or any of your other friends. **No one!**"

"Loose lips sink ships," Kenny says.

"Exactly. **Charlie's** the enemy. If the enemy gets wind of what you're doin', he'll beat the tar outta ya before you can defeat him. **Top—Secret.** Promise you won't tell anyone."

The boys promise, crossing their hearts and hoping to die.

Jim looks at Dottie. "Objections?"

She stares at him, then her boys. "Beat the hell out of him!"

The boys let out a resounding cheer.

After supper, Jim goes downstairs while the boys help their mother wash dishes. About an hour later, Jim calls them to the basement, where they find their father's army Barracks Bag hanging from a heavy-duty screw hook embedded in the master bedroom's floor joist. "It's stuffed with old clothes, sheets, and pillows," Jim says, landing a solid punch in the middle of the bag. "I think Old Charlie's soft enough for you guys to hit."

The boys laugh. "You called it Old Charlie," Kenny says.

"That's right. I want you two **focused** on who you're fightin'. Any time you're hittin' this bag, you're hittin' Charlie and his goons. Can you do that?"

The boys give him a resounding "**Yeah!**"

"Let's see ya make a fist." The boys make fists, and Jim checks Barney's. "Perfect." He checks Kenny's and repositions his thumbs, and straightens his wrists. "Make sure your arm is straight from the elbow to your knuckles." He taps the knuckles of their fore- and middle fingers. "When you punch, hit your target with these knuckles. Try it." Kenny hits the bag. "Good. Hit it again." Jim makes a tiny tweak, and Kenny punches the bag again. "Just like that, Kiddo. Now, Barn, let's see you punch." Barney hits the bag. "Very good. **Punch Charlie!**" Barney sends a haymaker into the bag. "No! You're not throwin' a fastball. You're hittin' a bully." Jim positions Barney's hands in a ready position. "There, you look like Joe Louis. When you punch, twist your hand. Doesn't have to be much. That makes your punch hurt more. Just a little twist can do a lota damage. And you **WANT** to hurt Charlie. **Now punch!**" Barney lands a right jab against the bag. "No. That was a love tap. Throw your weight behind the punch. Make the bag move like you want Charlie's head to move—right off his shoulders."

"Like my Rock 'Em Sock 'Em Robots!" Kenny lands a one-two punch to the bag's gut.

"Very good. Now watch this." Jim faces the bag and brings his fists in front of his face. "Stare at Charlie—right in his eyes. Show him you're not afraid of him. Show him you're ready to fight. Give him a chance to chicken out. But, if he wants to make the mistake to fight you, you're ready. Now, get ready to fight." The boys take their fighting stances, and Jim makes slight corrections. "Good. **Punch!**" The boys hit the opposite sides of the bag. "Excellent. Now, when you punch—**grunt**—like this." As he hits the bag, Jim lets out a loud grunt, startling the boys. "Scare ya?"

"Yeah," they reply, giggling.

"Good. You need to scare Charlie when you hit him—**and hit him—AND HIT HIM!** Don't just hit him once. Make him cry. Make him bleed. Make him run away. Make him **never** want to bully you again. **EVER.** Understand?"

The boys nod as their mother walks into the room. "Jim, you hurt?"

"No. I'm teachin' our boys to put a world a hurt on Charlie and his thugs. Okay. Hit him and grunt." Jim watches his boys punch and grunt. "No. I want a **LOUD** grunt and a **HARD** punch. I want you to **scare** him and **hurt** him at the same time. Now, do it again!"

Dottie and Jim watch their boys get ready to hit the dummy, then let out loud grunts as they punch the bag.

"**Louder!**" The boys comply. "Good. Now, do that ten times. Don't rush it. I want perfect stances before you punch. Watch your wrists and thumbs. That's it. Go."

The boys pummel the bag, making sure their thumbs are across the first two fingers, their wrists are straight, and they twist their fists as they contact the bag.

"Very good," Jim says. "Ten more times."

After the boys beat the duffle until their arms feel as heavy as iron beams, Barney asks, "When can we beat up Charlie?"

"After you learn to fight like a commando," Jim says. "This is only your first lesson. I want you pounding this bag for one hour every night all year."

"Daddy, what do we do when Charlie wants money?" Barney asks.

"Give him what he wants. He'll think you're chicken and won't fight back. But one day, when you fight like commandos, you'll kick his ass, then give him a bill and tell him you expect him to pay up."

"But what if he doesn't?" Barney asks.

"Then we put a world a hurt on him," Kenny says. "Right, Daddy?"

"Exactly right, Kiddo. Now, start punchin'! Twenty more. Both hands. Then you're gonna kick old Charlie in the balls."

"James!" Dottie glares at her husband, and the boys laugh.

"What? I'm gonna teach these two how to stop Charlie from bullying once and for all. And if that means crackin' some nuts, then so be it." The excited boys burst out laughing.

"Well, you could've put it differently."

"What? Testicles? This is commando training, Dot—not a school for sissies." He turns to his boys. "Hit him again! Ten more! **And mean it!**" Jim watches as Dottie leaves the basement. "Perfect stances."

An hour later, sweat stains the boys' shirts as their shoulders droop from the weight of their arms.

"Come here." They step up to their father. He wraps his arms around both boys and gives each a big hug and kiss on their sweaty cheeks. "You both did great. Go wash up, and I'll rub some Bengay on your shoulders."

After washing off the sweat, they go into the living room, where Jim rubs their shoulders and arms. "I know your arms and shoulders hurt, but a commando fights through the pain. It's almost seven-thirty. Kenny, turn on channel twelve." He does, and they watch *Father Knows Best* on CBS. "Tomorrow, I'll teach you how to kick old Charlie into next month."

The boys chuckle—too exhausted and sore to laugh.

That night, Barney wins the no-contest for sleep. As he relaxes in slumberland, *he rides his bike to the school. Just as he gets to the door, he hears a loud roar. Is it a lion? A tiger? Leopard? Grizzly?* His heart beats faster. *He looks to his left. Nothing. To his right. Nothing. Behind him. Nothing. Another roar. This time louder—or closer. Then, the ground quivers. Is it an earthquake? The thing making the loud roar? He pushes down on his top pedal as a gush of warm air rushes over him. His eyes water. He gasps. The stink almost takes his breath away.* Sweat beads on his forehead. *He looks behind him to see a huge trunk reaching around the corner. He slams on his pedals, and away he goes. But the hot air follows. He glances behind. The loud roar makes his ears ring. His eyes bulge as a giant albino Pachyderm, his burning red eyes glaring at him, his huge ears flapping like Dumbo's, his head turning, swiping his long, white, razer-sharp tusks at him. Around the corner he skids, his back tire slides out from under him. He quickly regains stability and races just ahead of the monster.* Sweat covers his body. *BOOM! A tusk crashes into the building. Bricks fly. RRRROOOOAAAAARRRR! The sound is deafening. Around and around, they race, trunk grabbing at him, the sharp tips of the tusks swinging only inches from his body.* Moans and groans and grunts. *BOOM! Another crash into the building. More bricks fly. He turns another corner. The trunk nudges his back tire. The bike skids out from under him. He slides on his back. The monster elephant lords over him. With trunk pointing to the sky, he releases a loud, triumphant RRRROOOOAAAAARRRR! Then…*

"Barney. Barney Honey. Wake up." He opens his eyes to see his mother staring at him. "You were having a nightmare. We could hear you clear upstairs." She feels his forehead. "Oh. You're all sweaty. Go take a shower, and I'll change your bed."

After taking a refreshing shower, he finds his mother sitting at his desk. "Tell me about your nightmare." Reluctantly, he does. "My goodness. No wonder you were sweating up a storm. Have you had this nightmare before?" He shakes his head. "Well, hopefully it's a one and done." She tucks him in, kisses him on the cheek, then turns the light off and leaves.

Barney does not close his eyes for the rest of the night.

"That was one heck of a nightmare," the angel says.

"Sure was. Too bad that darn thing wouldn't leave me alone. But at least I didn't dream about him every night."

"Let's talk about a more pleasant event—learning to fight like a commando."

"Every day after supper, Dad took us downstairs, and we beat the hell outta that bag. I mean, heck." The angel grins. "Kenny and I thought we were commandos from day one. Dad didn't. He drilled us for an hour, then rubbed us down with Bengay. The whole house stunk." He smiles. "Mom popped popcorn in hopes of overcoming the mentholatum smell, but all she did was stink up the house even more."

"You two paid Charlie every week."

Barnard nods. "Sometimes the SOB'd punch me even when we paid."

"And he extorted money from your friends."

"Friends that wouldn't stand up to him."

"Which was all of them. They were following your lead. If the biggest kid in school—except for Charlie—wouldn't stand up to him, how could they?"

"We outnumbered 'em— 'til Charlie and his gang'd catch one of us alone at school. We'd tell the teacher, but all she did was caution him." He shakes his head. "Caution him. Geez."

"Sometimes, he did get expelled. That did some good."

Barnard glares at the angel. "BULLSHIT!"

The light vanishes. Blackness. His body glows a fluorescent blue. Fingers and toes tingle as if asleep. Zap. His digits curl into painful knots. He shrieks. Flesh quivers. Hands and feet jerk in spasms. Arms and legs twitch uncontrollably. Finally, a groan gurgles in his throat, and his naked body lies silent. The blue slowly fades to black.

"Oh, man. Will I ever learn?"

Again, the angel shrugs. "Well, your brother and sister-in-law are doing pretty good."

The automatic blood pressure monitor beeps. "He back."

"Good. Better get the AED ready."

Linh sets up the automated external defibrillator, placing the two sticky pads on Joe's bare chest, one below his right shoulder and the other below his left nipple. The defibrillator monitors Joe's heart rhythm. She monitors his respiration. "Resp 38."

12:05:37.

The angel holds out her hand. "Enough of Charlie. Let's see who came to Wichita." They walk into the blackness.

11

The Next President in Wichita

SATURDAY, 22 October 1960

Dottie, Jim, his parents, and the boys find an empty area on the bleachers along the first base side about halfway to the top and carefully shuffle in front of the supporters already seated. As they sit on the hard, cold plank of metal, the man sitting to Jim's left says, "Pretty exciting seeing the next president."

"You sound like my wife."

"Democrat?"

"And Catholic."

"I take it you're not."

"Nope, on both counts."

"Kennedy'll beat Nixon."

"Well. Game ain't over 'til the last vote's counted in the Electoral College."

The man nods. "He coulda picked a warmer day. It's only supposed to be in the mid-fifties."

"Better hurry." Jim's steamy breath illustrates the mid-thirties temperature, even though the body warmth of seven thousand enthusiastic fans huddled in the stands of the Milwaukee Braves farm club, Wichita Braves' a place of business cannot chase away the nip in the fall air. But the crowd is not waiting for the start of their Triple-A team's post-season game. They are there to see the man who wants to be the thirty-fifth President of the United States. It is sixteen days before the general election, and he is hot on the campaign trail.

"The stage is very patriotic," Dottie says of the red, white, and blue half-circle banners hanging along the edge of the square platform positioned over the home plate area.

Jim nods as Barney asks, "Daddy, have you ever seen someone running for president?"

"I met Ike before he ran for president."

"**Eisenhower?**" a wide-eyed Kenny asks. "Before D-Day?"

Jim nods. "How did you know?"

"Encyclopedia and the patch with the eagle on it."

"Well, aren't you the li'l Sherlock Holms." Jim gives Kenny a one-arm hug.

10:00 a.m. The crowd begins to cheer as the dignitaries walk out of the third base dugout and to the stage, where they take their seats on the metal folding chairs.

"Where's Kennedy?" A wide-eyed Dottie searches each male on the stage.

"Maybe he realizes a Catholic doesn't have a snowball's chance being president and concedes Kansas." Jim gets a nasty glare from his wife. "Well, ask Mr. Britannica what chance he has in Kansas."

Dottie looks at Kenny. "Sweety…?"

Standing, he turns and takes his mother's face in his hands, then looks directly into her eyes. "Mommy, Kansas is predominately a Republican state. Since becoming the thirty-fourth state on January 29, 1861, Kansas has elected twenty-eight Republican governors and only six Democrats and two Populists. So, as Daddy says, they have a slim and none chance, and Slim is headin' outta town."

Jim chuckles the moment ear-piercing cheers drown out his amusement.

With Barney standing on the bleachers to see, Jim holds Kenny so he can see the infield over the standing crowd. But quickly, he sets the eight-year-old on the bleacher and rubs his left shoulder. "I didn't realize you've gotten so heavy. You stand with Barn."

"Daddy, I didn't get to see."

"I know. People'll sit down in a moment."

"Ladies and gentlemen," blares the exceedingly enthusiastic voice over the loudspeaker. "I'm proud to present the next President of the United States—**Senator—John—Fitzgerald—KENNEDY!**"

The crowd yells, cheers, and applauds as if this Kennedy fellow has just thrown the last strike of a perfect game. But he has not. Matter of fact, he has not done a thing except walk out of the dugout and wave. He steps onto the stage. It is quite a sight: the sides covered with red, white, and blue striped banners, the floor a blue field with white stars.

"Thank you. Thank you, ladies, and gentlemen. Thank you for such a warm greeting." The handsome man pretends, or not, to wipe his brow. The crowd cackles. "**It's wonderful to be in the great state of Kansas!**"

For the next ten minutes, they listen to the dynamic speaker's message, stand and cheer, sit and listen, stand and cheer, sit and listen. Finally, he concludes his speech with, "And remember—vote **Kennedy Johnson in November!**" He waves, and everyone begins chanting, "**Kennedy—Kennedy—Kennedy—Kennedy…**"

"Good lord," Jim growls. "I hope he doesn't do an encore."

Dottie chuckles, hoping he will. Then she looks at her beet-red husband. "You okay?"

He shakes his head.

"Let's go."

As soon as they reach the concourse, Jim heads for the water fountain. The water is cold. He drinks. He splashes some on his face and the back of his neck.

At the car, Dottie grabs the keys from Jim and orders him to the passenger side. He reluctantly relinquishes his place behind the wheel, knowing some battles are best surrendered without a fight.

11:10. At home, Barney asks, "Can I go play with Nick?"

"Are your chores finished?"

"Mom," he groans. She points to the boys' bedroom. Kenny runs to the room, not risking ruffling his mother's feathers.

12:45. After lunch, with their room passing their mother's inspection, Barney and Kenny are out the front door in a flash and heading across the street as fast as they can to Nick's house.

1:30. As the four ride their bikes to the top of the hill on Pine Tree Lane, they hear the whine of a siren. It sounds close—only a block or two away. The kids ride to the intersection in time to see an ambulance pass. They watch it head towards the hospital a block away. They continue home—four blocks to the north.

A minute later, Mr. Wainwright stops his car. "Get in, boys. Nick and Nikki, take their bikes home," he says with a sense of urgency.

"What's goin' on, Mr. Wainwright?" Barney asks.

"Your dad's been taken to the hospital."

Barney and Kenny jump into the backseat. Nick and Nikki wave at their best friend and his little brother as their father races to the Emergency Room.

Dottie, her hands covering her face, is standing in the hallway crying. Her sons run up to her. Already in tears, they wrap their arms around her waist.

"Mrs. Snodgrass?" asks the doctor. He introduces himself, then tells her, "Jim's resting comfortably." He hands her a pill and a cup of water. "Take this so you can relax. Can you tell me what happened?"

"We saw Kennedy. Jim didn't feel well. He ate very little lunch, drank lots of water, and complained of chills and stiffness in his left shoulder. He thought he pulled a muscle lifting our youngest on his shoulders. He watched TV for a bit, and the next thing I knew, he was slumped over in his chair. I tried to wake him, but he, uh—he wouldn't come around." She starts sobbing. "I called an ambulance."

The doctor looks at the paperwork a nurse handed him. "The EKG indicates his heart is acting up a bit. Any history of heart trouble?"

Dottie shakes her head. "He takes pills for high blood pressure."

"I want to keep him in the hospital for a couple of days."

"Of course. Can I see him?"

"Yes."

Barney tugs on her arm.

"Doctor?"

"Sure—if you're quiet. No excitement."

"Hey," Jim says sheepishly. After gentle hugs and kisses, he says, "Ya know, the last time I was laid up in a hospital was during the waning hours of the Battle of the Bulge. It was in an Army hospital near Bar-le-Luc, France, in the winter of '45. A nurse dug shrapnel out of my butt." The boys burst out laughing, then quickly remember the doctor's orders and the laughter abruptly stops. He points to Kenny. "You're wearin' the Purple Heart I received; and Barn, you have the Bronze Star."

"Did ya kill any Krauts?" Barney asks, and his mother gently whacks him on the shoulder.

"I think we need to let Daddy rest," she says.

"We'll be quiet." Barney puts his hands on his father's right arm. Where he touches him is not important—just as long as he can.

"Boys, see what happens when ya don't mind your mother. She'll lay ya in the hospital."

The boys chuckle, knowing their dad is joking—hoping he is joking.

"How you feelin', Daddy?" Barney asks.

"I'm ready to go home."

"Well, that's not going to happen today," Dottie informs him.

"I know. The doc already told me. I knew a Democrat would be the death of me."

Kenny points to the clear hose wrapped around his father's ears and running under his nose. "What's this?"

"Oxygen. It's so I can breathe easy."

Kenny points to the needle stuck in the back of his dad's hand. "What's this?"

"An IV. They're pumpin' helium in me, so I'll float around the room like a balloon."

The boys burst out laughing at the vision of a balloon looking like their dad zooming through the air. Barney covers Kenny's mouth with his hand. He holds his dad's hand and tries to look past the oxygen tube, the IV, and the bag of solution.

"Hey. Cheer up, Kiddo. I'll be fine. Promise."

"Never break a promise," Barney soberly recites the pledge they have given each other.

"I won't." He gives his son a reassuring wink. "I promise."

"That was a scary time," Barnard says.

"Not for me," the angel says. "I knew he wouldn't come over."

"How?"

"It wasn't his time."

"So, our destiny is predetermined?"

"That's one theory. The other is self-determination."

"So? Which is it?"

The angel shrugs. "Above my pay grade. But you'll find out—sooner or later. We all do. But no matter which it is, you were a great nurse when your father came home. Kind of like your caretakers. Oops! Wait!"

Again, the monitor whines and the AED indicates a shock is required.

"Stand back! Three, two, one, SHOCK!" Linh presses the shock button, and Joe's upper body lunges off the floor—then collapses. She checks his heart, then resumes CPR for another two minutes.

12:07:45.

"Wow! That was another close one."

Barnard shakes his head. "Well, at least I'm not throwin' a fit that they won't let me watch TV like I wouldn't let my dad listen to any sports on the radio—just easy listenin' music."

"It was so quiet in the house your mother thought she was living alone—or you boys were doing something you shouldn't."

"I think those three days Dad was recuperatin' were three days Kenny and me were as close to bein' li'l angels as ever—figuratively speakin', of course."

The angel grins. "Figuratively speaking. Why don't we pet a kitten."

*"Pet a kitten? We never had—**oh!**" His eyes widen, and he smiles. "A kitten!" He grabs the angel's hand and pulls her into the light.*

12

Smitten with the Kitten

FRIDAY, 5 May 1961

Eight thirty-three a.m., anxious hearts pound and fingers tightly cross as all eyes of the fifth-grade students stare at the teacher's RCA Victor color television showing the slender, black-and-white Mercury-Redstone rocket topped with the black upside-down ice-cream-cone-shaped capsule named *"Freedom 7"*.

A minute later, everyone joins the Mission Control announcer, counting down the moment of launch from ten to zero. Then, all quiet as the ten- and eleven-year-olds stare at the explosion at the bottom of the Redstone 3 rocket. Hearts skip beats or race. A moment later, the eighty-three-foot-high United States' spaceship begins leaving the ground. Cheers erupt from the thirty humans watching from the safety of the 5th-grade classroom at Schweitzer Elementary School.

However, the tension is not over as everyone watches the long, billowing contrail.

"Did it blow up?" a concerned Nikki blurts.

"No. It's the smoke from the rocket," Kenny says. "The Redstone rocket uses a propulsion system of liquid oxygen and alcohol and produces…"

"Kenny," Nikki interrupts. "You lost me after smoke."

Eleven minutes until nine, loud cheers erupt as everyone leaps to their feet as the black cone floats below three fully-opened parachutes.

Nine minutes after nine, another round of cheers rush from the classroom as a Sikorsky UH-34 Marine helicopter gently places the capsule on the deck of the Essex-class aircraft carrier, *USS Lake Champlain*.

Eleven minutes later, the first American in space is back on Earth. The teacher turns off the television and faces her students. "I don't think you've ever been quiet for a solid fifteen minutes before." The kids laugh. "Now that the fun is over, I'm going to introduce you to sex." Groans and snickers fill the room. Others swallow hard. Many heads begin heating. "At least I hope I'm introducing you to sex." A couple of chuckles. "This film shows that sex is a natural act—among animals. And animals have sex only to reproduce the species. Now, many of you are going through changes. This film addresses those changes, both in boys and girls. So, you'll understand what each other is going through. The main thing—don't be embarrassed. Every adolescent has gone through what you are going through—or will go through."

Charlie blurts out, "Did you have sex?"

"I gave birth to three children. So, what do you think?"

"Will there be a test?" Dick asks.

"No—unless I feel you're not paying attention. But you'll get a brochure explaining human sexuality that you can take home, read it, and understand what your body is going through. Okay. Nick, Tommy, will you please pull the shades down?" They do. The teacher starts the 16-mm sound projector. A quick, continuous click, click, click fills the room. It does not take long for the gasps and snickers to join the clicks.

As the film shows animals having sex, Charlie leans towards Erika. "That's what we're gonna do—wild animal sex." She ignores him. He reaches for her, but Barney, sitting behind her, grabs his wrist before he can touch her and slowly shakes his head. Charlie jerks his arm away, shakes a tight fist at the intercedent, and quietly snarls, "After school, Snottyass."

Erika glares at Charlie. "You're so vulgar and disgusting."

"You should use a word he knows the definition of," Barney whispers to her, but loud enough for his foe to hear.

Suddenly, the teacher is standing between the boys. "Are you paying attention? This is important."

"Snottyass should. He ain't had a wet dream yet." Charlie snickers.

"Either be quiet and watch the film, or you can sit in the principal's office. Up to you."

With arms crossed, Charlie turns his attention to the film and the teacher returns to the back of the room—but keeps an eye on the troublemaker.

Noon. As the students eat their lunches at their desks—except for one—who is eating his with the principal, Barney says, "Hey, Erika. Have you seen *The Absent-Minded Professor*?"

She shakes her head.

"Would ya like to go tomorrow—maybe to the matinee?"

She nods. "But I have to ask my mom. I'll call you tonight."

"Super! Uh, if ya want, I'll ride with ya to your house—if ya want."

Erika smiles. "Sure."

Three-thirty, the final bell rings, and the excited children rush out of the school, except for one student who the teacher holds back for a lecture on what she expects from him.

At the rack, the group hops on their bikes and hightails it towards the safety of their homes, at least two always looking back to make sure Charlie and his gang are not hot on their trail. They are not.

Before supper, Barney, Kenny, Nick, and Nicole don their fathers' Army helmets, caps, jackets, and ammo belts, grab their toy guns, and play a war against imaginary Nazis.

During one skirmish, Sgt. Anne Oakley and Capt. Bret Maverick lie in the bushes waiting for a German patrol to pass. Anne whispers to Bret, "You want to go to the show tomorrow?"

"Which one?"

"*The Absent-Minded Professor.*"

"I can't."

"Why?"

"Well, uh…" Suddenly, Barney jumps up and pulls the trigger of his 23-inch-long *Untouchables* Tommy Gun. Rat-tat-tat. Imaginary bullets shred the Nazis. Nicole joins the fight, picking off a few of the enemy running for cover.

Five o'clock, "**Barney! Kenny! Time for supper!**" Dottie calls a ceasefire, and the warriors walk towards the Snodgrass encampment. Nicole again asks, "Why can't you go to the show?"

"Well, I'm uh—I'm goin' with—."

"**Erika?**"

Barney nods, and Nicole runs home. ***Yikes!*** *What's got into her?*

With the battlefield washed off their exposed bodies, they sit at the kitchen table.

Dottie takes a sip of her coffee. "How did school go?" First, Kenny tells about the A's he got in Seventh Grade Algebra and Science and the sex film. Then, Barney tells her about Charlie threatening him, but had to stay after school, and Nicole running home after he told her he was going to the show with Erika.

"She's jealous."

"Why? I like her, too."

Dottie thinks for a moment. "Well, there could be a number of reasons. But I think she might feel Erika is threatening her close connection with you. I mean, you two have been an item since you were three."

"Mom. We've never been **an item**."

"You played with her and Nick almost every day. She's gone to almost all of your ballgames. She's gone with you to the movies—until Erika showed up."

"Oh."

"You do think Erika's prettier. Right?" He nods. "Maybe Nikki knows you think Erika's prettier." He shrugs. "Do you still talk with Nikki?"

"Sure."

"Well, I suggest you read that pamphlet you brought home about sex. Sometimes, the change in hormones can cause jealousy. My suggestion—if you want some motherly advice—is to be nice to Nikki, and before you ask Erika to something, you ask Nikki."

"Won't that make Erika jealous?"

"Well—it might—if she's the jealous type."

"The jealous type. How can ya tell if they're the jealous type?"

"If they're female, they're the jealous type," Jim interjects, quickly taking a bite of his grilled cheese sandwich as Dottie's glare takes a bite out of him.

At half past seven, the boys relax on the floor to watch *The Flintstones* on ABC while eating buttered popcorn their mother has made. She works on her sewing project.

Eight o'clock, the boys watch *77 Sunset Strip* on ABC.

An hour later, they are watching *The Twilight Zone* on CBS.

At nine-thirty, Dottie joins her boys to watch Walter Cronkite host CBS's public affairs program, *Eyewitness to History.*

At ten o'clock, Barney gives his mother a kiss, says, "Good night," and goes downstairs to his bedroom. While taking a shower, his budding genitalia responds to the slickness of his soapy hands. The blood vessels in his penis open and fill with blood. His heart pounds as his virgin member grows and hardens. As the warm, soothing water sprays over his body, a chill surges through his body. Suddenly, his erect penis spurts onto the opposite wall. ***Holy cow!*** He squats against the wall. Grinning, he says to himself, *"Wow! Dick was right. Masturbatin's bad, BAD, **BAD!**"* Then, the grin turns into an ear-to-ear smile. ***HOLY COW!*** He stares at the small globs of white ejaculate stuck on the wall and others the water is attempting to wash down the drain. *So that's semen. Hmmm. Wonder what it tastes like? The brochure didn't say.* And like curiosity killing the cat, it gets the best of him, too, and he wipes some off the shower floor and sticks his finger in his mouth. His eyebrows dip, then rise. *Hmmm! No taste. Well, maybe a li'l soapy. Hmm.* Then, the smile turns into a frown. *Dang. Now, I gotta clean that.*

After he wipes down the shower, Barney gets ready for bed. Lying in bed, he stares at the silhouettes of planes hanging above him. Then something draws his attention from fantasizing about piloting one of his model warplanes to his father's black army foot locker. Quietly, he stands, turns on his bedroom light, and steps into the utility room. Stealthily, he removes the three cardboard storage boxes stacked on top and stares at the faded and scratched two-inch tall white letters printed on the lid: Capt. J. B. Snodgrass U.S.A. above his serial number and APO address. Then, he releases the two latches and pulls up on the lock. CRE… Abruptly, he stops. *Dang, rusty hinges. **3 in 1 Oil!*** At once, he grabs the lubricant and drips a few drops on the back hinges. Then, he slowly lifts the lid. The silence brings a grin to his face. He glances at the items in the tray that he has seen before:

the 101ˢᵗ Airborne patch, the red-arrowhead FSSF patch, the ribbons on his father's Ike jacket and in black boxes containing their medals, a US Airborne Paratrooper wool garrison hat with the Army Airborne Glider Badge on the right side and the captain's double silver bars on the left, among other things. His eyes suddenly widen as he notices the difference in depth of the trunk versus the depth of the stuff he is looking at. He finds two holes on each side and with his fingers in them, lifts the tray. Before he can set the tray on the storage boxes, his jaw drops and eyes bulge, for there in front of him is the adolescent male's El Dorado—stacks and stacks of girlie magazines. Immediately, one grabs his attention.

After setting the tray down, he gently picks up the April 1954 edition of *Adam A Man's Magazine* and stares, mesmerized, at the scantily-clad woman gracing its green cover. ***Wow!*** *She's sexier than the centerfolds in Dick's dad's mags.* Suddenly, a twitch in his crotch lifts his eyebrows. His heart pounds as his watery eyes follow the tip of his forefinger as it moves slowly along every sultry inch of the enticing image, from the honey-blonde mane down to perfectly muscled, lightly-tanned torso, along the most dazzling legs he has ever seen to toenails painted red, as are the immaculately manicured nails of her fingers. *You're the most beautiful woman I've ever seen.* At her feet, which silver strappy heels encase, he quietly reads: "LILLY CHRISTINE Photos and Facts about THE CAT GIRL See page 6." With heart racing, he quickly turns to the desired page, and his wide eyes bulge as he stares at the four black and white photos. Another twitch makes the crotch of his pajamas jump. For someone who hates to read, he reads every word of the article titled, *"the girl with the golden torso."* Quietly, he reads, "…she's every man's dream of what a woman should be; because she has the power to bewitch men and arouse in them the desires of their animal instincts." The snake in his pajamas steadily grows until peeking through the fly, proving correct the author, Jim Long.

Barney reads that article and every word he can find about The Cat Girl in CABARET THE ADULT ENTERTAINMENT MAGAZINE, PIX, Jem, and SIR! among numerous others. He hurries to the bathroom and masturbates in some facial tissue.

When clean, he carefully puts everything away as he found them—except for the Adam magazine, which he hides below the files in his desk drawer. He sets the alarm clock. *Holy smoke! Twelve-thirty already.* He goes to bed, closes his eyes, and succumbs to the sandman. However, on this night, *The Cat Girl prowls in his head.*

With every sultry move she makes on his slumbering dancefloor, her description is eternally etched in his young, impressionable brain: *"Lilly is half cat… got tabbed the 'Cat Girl' from her slick interpretation of a cat dancing on a huge jungle drum… eyebrows arch over almond-shaped eyes…finger, long and sharply nailed as claws of a cat…breath-taking body …supple shoulders and upper arms…full, high and pointing breasts…flat and softly-muscled stomach…hips a sculptor couldn't equal…a leg not likely to be copied again…small and dainty feet…waist-long, silvery-blonde hair…beautiful and entrancing face…breath-taking, sun-bronzed torso…clad only in G-string and net brassiere… a dancer in the true sense of the word…five feet seven…Twenty-four…130 pounds…37-inch bust, a 24-inch waist, and 35-inch hips…near-perfect body…never married…didn't smoke or drink…didn't go out…didn't go running off to church every day…on a health kick… a nature girl…likes fresh air, exercise, sunshine (she sunbathes in the nude)…has one of the most supple and shapely torsos that ever weaved its way through an exotic dance…when she steps into a dance, something electric happens."* ZAP. Barney's eyes burst open at the electric shock nipping in his PJs. His new best friend sticks its head out of the fly to again see this modern-day Aphrodite. Instantly, the small head agrees with the big one, and he hurries into the bathroom and repeats his new favorite activity into a few facial tissues.

Then, lying in bed, he remembers, *"When she's not working, Lily spends most of her time reading and knitting socks for her dad. She also knits all her sweaters… parents are Swedish and Norwegian."* Wow. *Mom and Granma would like her. HECK! Dad and Gramps would love her.*

He looks at the clock. *Three-oh-five. Dang!* Then his eyes widen. *HEY! THIS IS SATURDAY!* He turns off the alarm and relaxes, spreadeagled on the bed.

Finally, he falls asleep again. But his mind is still a dancefloor. *"Langourously, she purrs love sonnets while her lithe form reveals the gentle pulsating motion of a wind-stroked wheat field… The phenomena! undulating of the muscles in her beautiful torso makes women gasp and…make[s] the blood rise in every man who sees her… Her every move signifies the meaning of love…"* The blood in the soon-to-be twelve-year-old body is certainly rising at the speed of a launched rocket. So is the ballistic missile rising on the launchpad in his pajamas.

"The Cat Girl's latest 'belly dance' creation…titled 'Harem Heat'… the story of an erotic sultana who worships strength… Because of this fetish, her lovers are kept in a constant exhibition of muscular display— ALWAYS—always ending in combat for her favors and – love! This rivalry never fails to send the sensuous queen into fits of passion and sextasy!"

The following morning, he wakes winded and in a cold sweat. He sits up in bed and wipes his face with the sheet, his heart pounding painfully hard. Then, he finds something electric has happened during the night—The Cat Girl's power to bewitch him and arouse in him the desires of his animal instincts has stuck to his pajama's crotch.

"DAMNIT!" In a huff, he jumps off the bed, rips the sheets off, and slings them and his damp pillow into the utility room. With the bedding scattered over the laundry room floor, he retrieves a dry set

from the cabinet and makes his bed. For the next two and a half hours, he sleeps. However, he is the only one.

Her long, wavy blonde locks flow over smooth, bare shoulders and down the small of a slender back like a mountain stream of gold. She smiles at her new admirer, full red lips gleaming, showing off sparkling white teeth. Her eyes—exotic, hypnotic—control him.

She is lean, trim, and curvy, with just enough muscle definition to make her body, on a scale of one to ten, a four zillion. Her lightly tanned skin glistens and her legs are perfectly muscled. If Barney had been a few years older, he would have known they were as smooth as silk. *Her body graces the sparkling silver, triangular-cupped brassiere straining to contain her more-than-ample bosom while the matching G-string enjoys a gentle, winding journey over finely sculptured hips, then dips seductively below her enticing, flat belly.* Barney's breathing grows rapid and labored. *From behind, she holds out, in a delicate grasp between the index and middle fingers, a dark diaphanous panel that is attached to the back of the scant G-string. It reaches her beautiful feet encased in silver, strappy high heels, which display her lovely ankles and tantalizing toes, their immaculate nails red, as were those at her fingertips.*

He tosses and turns. Beneath their lids his eyes quickly move right to left. Beads of sweat form on his brow. *Five-seven—twenty-four—130—long blonde mane—feline moves—slender, curvaceous body—37-24-35—perfectly muscled legs—beautiful toes.* His heart pounds, blood pressure rises. *Entrancing face—arched eyebrows—almond-shaped eyes—full, shiny lips—nails long and sharp like cat claws—brassiere—G-string—37-24-35.*

"Barney. Barney."

After blinking a couple of times, he opens his eyes and turns to see his mother standing at his bed. "I see you had an accident. Did you wet the bed?"

AH SHIT! I DIDN'T PUT THE SHEETS IN THE TUB. DAMNIT! He shakes his head.

"Oh! Is it time for you and Daddy to have the talk?" Barney shrugs. "I saw the brochure you brought home. Well, Daddy'll be home later this afternoon. You should ask him. Well, breakfast'll be ready in a few minutes." She leaves, and Barney gets out of bed with a burning head, suspecting The Cat Girl had danced in his head—again.

"Lilly had quite an effect on you. She was the woman you compared all other women to."

"I'm afraid you're right. But I couldn't have had a more perfect physical specimen as a standard."

"Sadly, a picture doesn't tell you her personality."

"She seemed to be a down-to-earth girl off stage—readin' 'n' knitin'. She may have been a good cook. Ya never know."

"I know. But that's for another time. We should move on. Things aren't looking so good right now."

"I'll take over. You get the DBT." Ken assumes CPR while Linh gets the Direct Blood Transfusion equipment. "When did they say the ambulance would get here?"

"She say snow makes it very difficult to travel."

"C'mon, Mother Nature. Help us out!"

12:10:02.

"Lead on, Angel. Where to?"

"The day before Mother's Day 1961."

*"Why there? **Oh!** It's comin' back to me."*

The angel holds out her hand. He takes it, and they walk into the light.

13

The Brazilian Beauty

SATURDAY, 13 May 1961

"Daddy! Daddy! Can we get a comic book?" Kenny asks, kneeling in the middle of the front seat as Jim parks the 1958 Olds 98 sedan in front of Duckwall's five-and-dime. He turns the ignition key to the off position, and the 371 cubic inch Rocket V8 engine silences. "Ya think ya were good enough this week to get somethin'?"

Kenny stares directly into his father's eyes. "Yes! I got Stars and OKs on all of my work. And I made my bed and kept my room clean **all** week. And I helped Mommy with the dishes when Barney said he had **too—much—homework**."

"Hey, Kiddo, watch the attitude. Brothers are supposed to help each other."

Kenny looks down. "Sorry, Daddy."

"Okay. Well, sounds like ya—**might**—deserve a comic book." Jim grins and then looks at Barney. "How 'bout you, Sport?"

"I was good," he says matter-of-factly. "I didn't get in trouble. I got all A's and B's. And Mrs. Lehrer told me she wants me to do the Pledge of Allegiance at the Fifth and Sixth Grade Spring Program."

Jim's eyes widen. "Really? Good for you! When did she say that?"

"Yesterday."

"Did ya tell Mom?"

"Not yet."

"Why not?"

Barney shrugs.

"You should be proud that she asked ya to do it. Just think. Out of all the kids in the fifth and sixth grades, she wants **you** to lead everyone in The Pledge. That's one heck of an honor, Barn."

He shrugs again.

"Well, I hope ya told your teacher 'Yes.' Did ya?"

He nods.

"Be proud of the honor." Jim looks at the dashboard clock. "Eight-ten. Better get our hair cut before it gets crowded." He gets out of the car. Kenny scoots off the seat with his shoebox in hand. Barney exits via the passenger door carrying two shoeboxes under his left arm. Jim shuts the door behind Kenny and the three walk down the sidewalk.

Barney stops and stares at the train traveling along the small oval track in Duckwall's window display. "That's what I want for Christmas."

"Ya just had a birthday a week ago," Jim says. "Why didn't ya say somethin' then?"

Barney shrugs.

As they get closer to the slowly spinning Marvy Barber Pole hanging in front of their destination, classical music begins to seep into their ears.

Kenny runs ahead and stops outside the barbershop. He peeks inside the open door where the music emanates. Then Jim and Barney stop and look at what so intrigues Kenny. Jim's eyes widen as he watches the raven-haired woman stand on pointe shoes, her arms and legs positioned in a croise devant. Then she twirls on the toes of her left foot, her thick black ponytail whipping behind her head.

As they watch the three boys and five girls of various heights and ages attempt to copy their teacher's stance and turn with different degrees of success, Jim bends over and quietly asks his boys, "Ya wanna be ballerinas?"

"**NO!**" they yell in unison.

The dance teacher and her students stop and look at the disrupters.

"I—I'm sorry," Jim says, starting to usher his boys into the barbershop.

"**Hi, Barney!**" one girl yells, stopping him in his tracks.

"Hi, Erika," he replies, head bowed sheepishly.

The teacher approaches them and holds out her right hand. "Olá. I am Calista Hor-ton."

Barney's heart pounds. *Calista. Wow. She's more beautiful than Lilly.* His eyes widen as he feels his budding adolescent cheat on The Cat Girl.

Jim shakes her hand. "Wow. Strong handshake."

She smiles. "You too."

He chuckles. "I'm pleased to meet ya, Miss Horton. I'm Jim Snodgrass."

"Nice to meet you, Jim. It is Mrs. Hor-ton. But please call me Calista. You enroll boys in dance class?"

Jim smiles. "Well, that's what I asked 'em when they so rudely interrupted your class."

"Oh." She looks at Barney and Kenny. "So, you no want learn dance?"

Barney shakes his head as Kenny says, "You're **really** pretty."

Sure is! She's got Lilly's eyes. Barney looks at the dark, sickle-shaped eyebrows that softly arch over almond-shaped hazel-colored eyes.

"Obrigado!" She holds out her right hand. "You muito handsome little boy. What you name?"

"Kenny Snodgrass, Ma'am." He shakes her hand as Erika hurries to them and excitedly asks, "Barney, you gonna enroll?"

He shakes his head.

"Ahh, c'mon. It's fun." Her brown eyes widen. "And we could be partners!"

He shrugs as his head begins to heat. "I gotta cut a hairget." He hurries into the barbershop.

Jim, Calista, Erika, and Kenny look at each other and chuckle.

"I think ya make him nervous," Jim says to Erika.

"He's funny," she replies. "We sit beside each other in school. He's going to lead The Pledge of Allegiance at the Fifth and Sixth Grade Spring Program next week and I'm going to sing The National Anthem."

"Well congratulations!"

"Thank you, Mr. Snodgrass."

"We're lookin' forward to seein' the program. Well, we better get our hair cut—or whatever Barney said. Again, my apologies for disrupting your class."

"Quite all right. Nice meeting you, Jim—Kenny."

"Nice meetin' you, Calista—Erika."

Jim and Kenny walk into Patrick MacAteer's Barbershop as Calista turns and claps her hands, restarting her dance class.

"Good mornin', Pat," Jim says, Kenny running to the back of the shop where Barney is looking through stacks of comic books, children's books, and newspapers. "Full house already."

"Day before Mother's Day," the red-headed barber replies, his scissors never missing a snip of his customer's hair. "Everyone wants to look nice. See you met my new neighbor."

Jim gently bites the knuckle of his right forefinger. "Her eyes are mesmerizin'."

Pat smiles as Jim grabs three round numbered disks from the peg above the shiny gold National cash register. "Betcha didn't even look at the rest of her."

Jim steps up to Pat. "Oh yes I did. She's drop-dead gorgeous. And her legs were the first thing that grabbed my attention."

"Oh yeah. She's definitely an eighteen-carat fox." Pat nods his head towards the door. "She drives that fifty-three Corvette parked in front of her studio."

"Really?" Jim looks out the window to see the white sports car with the bullet tail lights. "So, she has one of the first three hundred? Wow. And what accent does she have?"

"Portuguese."

"Portuguese? She's from Portugal? Wow. What's she doin' here?"

"No. She's from Brazil—some little town around Rio. Married the doctor whose office is across the street. She lives in that mansion on top of Pine Tree Lane."

"I wondered who bought it. Gorgeous place."

"She's only been there a year or so. Moved here from L.A."

Jim nods. "Well, better see what my boys are doin'. Later, Pat."

"It'll be about a quarter 'til nine."

Jim nods as he walks to the back of the barbershop where his boys are sitting at a children's table reading comics. "Hi Junior."

"Good mornin' Cap'n Jim. Beautiful day," replies the Negro seated on the stool shining Kenny's pair of brown dress shoes.

"Sure is. My boys haven't been botherin' ya."

"Nosa. Not a bit. Mr. Barney told me what he got for his birthday."

"Yep. Made out like a bandit."

Junior laughs.

"Did he tell ya what he's goin' to do at the school program?"

"No."

"Barn, tell Mr. Washington."

Still looking at the comic book, Barney reluctantly says, "I'm gonna lead the audience in The Pledge of Allegiance in the Fifth and Sixth Grade Spring Program."

"Wow! That's great! Congratulations."

"Thank you, Mr. Washington."

Jim rustles Barney's hair. "I just wish he'd be more excited about it."

"I am," he groans.

"Oh. So, you're humbled by the honor."

Barney shrugs.

Jim sits and picks up the newspaper. "Says here Khrushchev is gonna meet with Kennedy to talk about Berlin's future."

"I know. Quite a situation." Junior shows Jim Barney's shoes.

"Like a mirror."

Junior sets the shoes in their box and picks up Kenny's black pair of shoes. As he begins swirling polish over the leather, he asks, "You boys get your momma somethun special fo' Mother's Day?"

"Yes sir," they both proudly reply, almost in unison.

"We got her a ring and earrings with our birthstones. Barn's Emerald and mine's Sapphire. They're beautiful."

"Grampa helped us make a jewelry box. I stained it."

"I varnished it."

"I bet she's gonna love it.

"Hope so."

"What did your girls do for their mom?" Jim asks.

"The girls pooled their allowance and bought a dress their mom's had her eye on fo' some time."

"That was nice. And whadaya think they'll get you for Father's Day?"

Junior grins. "Don't know. They won't tell me."

"Loose lips sink ships," Kenny says.

Barney points to the wall behind Washington. "What ship's that?"

"The battleship U.S.S. West Virginia," Washington answers, his eyes glistening.

"The U.S.S. West Virginia was one of…"

"Kenny," Jim interrupts. "Mr. Washington knows all about the West Virginia."

Washington gives Jim a grateful nod. Then, for the next few minutes, the boys continue reading comic books while Jim peruses the rest of the newspaper, occasionally visiting with Junior, who continues polishing the three dress shoes the boys gave him. Then, Junior says, "Cap'n Jim, tell me if I'm outta bounds, but—."

Jim looks over the paper. "What Junior?"

"Well, you been comin' here for years and I always wonder how ya got that scar."

"You should've asked. In Italy, I got too close to a German bayonet."

"Oh my!" Junior shakes his head. "I'm glad ya didn't get any closer."

Jim nods. "Me too."

The boys look up from their comic books, and Barney asks, "You mean a Nazi cut your face?"

Jim nods.

"**I'LL KILL HIM!**" an enraged Barney yells, his head reddening with anger as the customers and barbers look towards the outburst.

"No need, Kiddo. The war's over. Some soldiers—and sailors," he looks at Junior, "lived to come home—and some didn't. The German who cut me didn't."

"You kill him, Daddy?" Kenny asks.

"Read your comic book."

"Cap'n Jim, I apologize for—."

"No need."

Junior nods as he polishes Kenny's last shoe, then says, "Almost done, Cap'n Jim. Just need to do yours."

Then, the loud roar of a Harley rushes into the shop. A moment later, a young man dressed in blue jeans, leather boots, and a white T-shirt with a pack of cigarettes rolled up in the right sleeve struts past the barber stations and sits on the shoe-shine chair. "Polish my boots, nigger."

Above the newspaper, Jim glares at the intruder, especially the tattoo on his right arm.

"I be with ya shortly, sir. I just…"

"Now, nigger. I'm in a hurry."

"Excuse me," Jim says. "Mr. Washington's polishin' my shoes. You just sit there and wait—with your mouth **shut**."

The guy glares at Jim. "What if I don't shut my mouth—**scarface?** Scarface?" He stares at Jim, his eyes squinting, nostrils flaring. "I remember you!"

Jim stares at the young man. "And I remember that tattoo. Why don't you leave and not come back?" Jim returns to the newspaper— but only for a second.

"You a nigger-lover?"

Jim calmly folds the newspaper as the man says, "I think you're a nigger-lover." Jim lays the paper on top of the many magazines and comics as the man says, "I hate niggers, and I hate even more **nigger-lovers.**"

"And I hate Nazis, and I hate even more Nazi-lovers. Why don't ya join me outside?"

The guy jumps off the shoeshine stand and rushes out the back door.

"Cap'n Jim. I don't…"

Jim steps into the restroom. A moment later, he returns with a bar of soap in his left hand.

"I'll be back in a minute."

"Daddy! Can we watch?" an excited Kenny inquires. Then his shoulders slump as if magic from the tip of his father's pointing forefinger causes his disappointment.

Jim joins the young man outside, closing the door behind him. A minute later, Jim returns, picks up the newspaper, sits, and turns to the sports page. The boys look at the back door. It does not open. A smiling Kenny looks at Barney. "Daddy kicked his ass!"

"Read your comics."

"Cap'n Jim, ya didn't havta do that."

"Yeah, I did. I don't like the word, and I hate Nazis. Like the old sayin': I killed two birds with one stone."

"**YOU KILLED HIM?**" the wide-eyed boys yell, and everyone in the shop looks.

"No."

Suddenly, the loud rumbling of a Harley chopper rushes into the shop. A moment later, it is gone, and Calista Horton steps into the shop. She says something to Pat, then walks to the back.

"What happen?"

Jim and Junior stand as Kenny eagerly answers, "Daddy kicked that bad man's…!"

"Hey!" Jim points to Kenny's comic and then looks at Calista. "I doubt if he'll be back."

"Obrigado, James. He muito bad man. He alway have bad look in his eye when he look at my girls—especialmente Kaelah." She holds out her right hand, and Jim shakes it. "Obrigado, again, James." She walks out of the barbershop, every eye following her every graceful step—except Kenny, who returns to the color pages of his comic. However, Barney looks.

After the pleasant interruption leaves, Jim resumes reading the newspaper while Junior finishes putting a high-gloss shine on his favorite customer's Sunday footwear. Then, he presents the shoes to Jim.

"Perfect, like usual." He stands, reaches into his pant pocket, pulls out two dollars, and hands it to Junior in a handshake. "Thank ya, Junior."

"Oh, this is too much!"

"Not for the job ya do." He picks up the three boxes and then smiles. "Ya think after five years in the Army, I could polish my own shoes." The two veterans laugh. "Oh. Before I forget, I owe ya for a bar of soap."

Junior smiles. "On the house, Cap'n Jim." He nods for his next customer to take a seat on the shoeshine stand.

"Boys, it should be about our time." Jim carries the boxes towards the front of the shop and sets them down on the chair beside the cash register, then sits and resumes reading the paper.

A minute later the boys sit beside their father and resume reading the comic books they brought. Then Kenny says, "Daddy, you know who that guy was?"

"Yes."

The barber next to Pat calls out a number.

"Daddy, that's us!" Kenny jumps up from his chair, digs the disks out of his father's shirt pocket, and hands back the higher two numbers.

"Guess you wanna be first?"

"Yeah!" Kenny waits for the barber to take the money from his customer, then hands him the disk before running to the barber's chair. He waits for the barber to sweep off the hair from the chair and then hops up on the booster seat.

"Just trim the sides off the ears," Jim says, and the barber nods.

Five minutes later, Kenny jumps off the chair and returns to his father, who inspects his haircut.

"Very nice. Mommy'll love it." Jim gives the barber a thumbs-up as he offers Kenny a sucker or a package of nine 2.5 by 3.5-inch baseball cards with a slab of bubble gum.

"Take the bubble gum," Barney urges before sitting on the chair without the booster seat.

"Same with him," Jim says as Kenny takes the package, saying, "Thank you."

Then Pat removes the sheet from his customer and they walk to the register. "You're up, James." He takes payment from the customer and thanks him.

Jim sits on Pat's chair. He looks at the clock. "Pretty good guess at the time, Pat."

"I was hopin' I'd get ya before nine." He gently secures the sheet around Jim's neck.

"Why?"

"You'll see." Pat starts to clip Jim's white hair. "So, what did ya think of Alan Shepard's space flight last week?"

"I had hoped he'd fly longer than Gagarin. But I like the name—Freedom 7."

"Yeah. Patriotic." Pat combs and cuts, then stops and stares out the window. "There ya go, James."

Jim looks out the window. "Wow."

"What Daddy?" Kenny asks as the boys hurry to the window. "The dance teacher?"

"That's the dance teacher and her three daughters. Kaelah's next to her mom. She's the oldest and looks just like her mom. Then Galiena's in the middle. She's a year younger. And Erika's walking in the lead. Barney, I think she's your age."

Barney nods. "We're in the same grade."

They watch the four walk across the street—all wearing leotards, shorts, and sneakers.

"She's got some gorgeous gams," Jim remarks.

"What are gams, Daddy?" Kenny asks.

"It's another name for a woman's legs."

"What makes 'em gorgeous?"

Jim looks at Pat, who is looking at him with great anticipation. After some thought, Jim says, "Well, uh, see the back of her legs?"

"Yeah."

"See how they kinda smile at ya?"

Kenny looks for a moment and then chuckles. "Yeah! Neat."

Pat and Jim chuckle. Then Jim adds, "Well, if the backs of a woman's legs smile at ya, then they're gorgeous."

"Daddy, all their legs are smilin' at me."

Pat and Jim chuckle. "Well then—all of 'em have gorgeous gams."

Pat says. "Barney, Erika's a pretty li'l lass. Have ya taken her to one of your ballgames?"

He shakes his head. "We went to see a movie last Saturday."

"Good for you. When ball season starts, you should take her to a game."

Don't know about that. Nikki's still mad about the movie.

"Did ya know her favorite team's the Dodgers?"

"Yeah. Nobody's perfect."

Jim, Pat, and Barney's barber burst out laughing as Calista and her daughters vanish inside Dockum Drug Store.

"Whadaya think of Khrushchev and Kennedy discussing Berlin's future?" Pat asks.

"I hope that Catholic doesn't give Berlin to the Russkies for some other deal. Ya just can't trust 'em Reds."

"Cincinnati Reds?" Barney asks, watching his father get his hair trimmed.

Jim chuckles. "No. The Russians. They're called the Reds."

Pat hands Jim a mirror, and he looks at the back of his head. "Good." Then Pat turns the chair around, and Jim looks at himself in the mirror. "Good job, Pat, like always. Thank you."

"And here they come." Pat turns the chair around to the front so Jim can see.

Jim and the boys look. "Man-o-man, they all look like sisters."

"I know. Her oldest, Kaelah, is thirteen and the spittin' image of her mom. They're all gonna be heartbreakers." He and Jim walk to the cash register.

"How old's Calista?" Jim pays for the three haircuts. "She doesn't look a day over twenty-five."

"I know, but she's gotta be thirty or so because Kaelah's thirteen," Pat replies as Barney walks up to them. "I don't know why I'm going to ask this, but sucker or baseball cards, Barney?"

Like usual, Barney picks a pack of baseball cards. "Thank you, Mr. MacAteer."

"You're welcome, Barney. Have a good season this year."

"Thanks."

As they walk out of the barbershop, they take a final peek into the dance studio. Erika sees them and waves. Barney returns the wave.

Jim looks at Barney. "I think she likes ya."

Barney shrugs. *Oh great. What do I do with two girlfriends? But she's a lot prettier than Nikki—and nicer. Maybe we should take dance lessons.*

Jim and the boys lay their shoeboxes in the car and then go inside Duckwalls, where they each search for the perfect comic book—and another pack of baseball cards.

On the way home, Jim says, "Ya know Boys, Mommy doesn't need to know we think the dance teacher has gorgeous gams."

"Why?" Kenny asks.

"Well—sometimes women get jealous of other women even when they don't need to be. So, we don't need to give Mommy any reason to be jealous—especially before Mother's Day. Okay?"

The boys shrug and nod.

"Just remember: Loose lips sink Daddy."

They chuckle.

"Promise and I'll show you what that guy gave me."

"**What?**"

"Promise."

"I promise not to sink Daddy," Barney says, and Kenny repeats his brother's promise.

Then Jim pulls something out of his pocket and pushes the button. Instantly, the stiletto blade swings out. Gasping, the boys' eyes bulge. Jim returns the blade to the handle before giving the slender pocket knife to Barney. "Do NOT touch this button."

"Daddy! It's got a Nazi Swastika on it—like the other one! Is that guy a Nazi?"

"He's Charlie's brother." The boys' eyes bulge, and their jaw drops. "He's a Nazi lover, and that's a traitor. You know what a traitor is?"

"Like Benedict Arnold was in the American Revolutionary War," Kenny answers.

"Exactly right."

"Ya gonna put it with those other knives?" Barney asks.

Jim nods. "I never told ya about that long one. Have I?" They shake their heads, and he taps the scar on his face. "That's the bayonet that did this."

The boys' jaws drop.

"It's not like this one," Barney says. "That one's long."

Jim nods. "About fifteen inches. Very sharp—like this one. So, you DO NOT touch 'em without me bein' there. Understand?" They nod. "Promise." They promise. "And we don't tell Mommy about this knife. Okay?" They nod and promise without their father prompting them.

Then, as Jim pulls into the driveway, he says, "And remember, we shouldn't mention the term 'gorgeous gams' to Mommy. Okay?" They nod.

As Jim and the boys walk into the kitchen, Kenny rushes up to his mother, who is setting the dining room table for dinner tomorrow. "Mommy, how ya like my haircut?"

She stops and inspects it. "Very nice. Barney, let's see yours." He walks up to her, and she turns him around. "Very nice. You boys are very handsome."

"**Muito** handsome," Kenny says.

"Muito?"

"Yeah. That's what the dance teacher said about me. She said I was **muito handsome**."

"Dance teacher?" Dottie looks at Jim as he picks up the newspaper.

"Yeah," Barney says. "She's Erika's mom. She's gonna sing The National Anthem at the Fifth and Sixth Grade Spring Program. Can I see if Nick and Nikki can play?"

"Until lunch."

"Mommy," Kenny says, standing behind his mother, "you have gorgeous hams, too."

"What? Gorgeous hams?"

Jim looks over the top of the newspaper. "We havin' ham tomorrow? Sure hope so. I can't remember when we had one of your delicious, juicy hams. **Right son?**" He glares at his youngest whose wide eyes indicate he has received his father's message loud and clear.

Dottie has too. With hands on hips, she inquires, "So, what's going on?"

After an impatient pause, Jim says, "Well, I happened to mention to Pat—ya know, the barber, that uh, that the dance teacher had gorgeous gams. That's all."

"Daddy said a woman has gorgeous gams if they smile at ya when she walks away," Barney says. "Yours kinda do."

"Thank you, very much. You set the table." Dottie marches into the kitchen.

"Way to go, blabbermouth," Barney whispers as he begins setting the table. Then he asks, "Daddy, can I still go to Nick's?"

"Better git while the gittin's good," Jim whispers. "And take that traitor with ya."

*The angel shakes her head. "So, at eleven you learned to keep things from **the** woman in your life."*

"Oh, it wasn't that bad, besides, Kenny spilled the beans. And Dad was right—Mom got mad for no reason."

*"Keeping secrets from your mother **is** bad. It's a bad habit to get into."*

"But there's no need to unduly upset someone you love. Right? And that's what Dad was tryin' to do—not upset Mom. And is it really that wrong to do the right thing for the wrong reason? Or is it the wrong thing for the right reason?"

"Keep talking. The noose can get only so tight."

Barnard's eyes widen. "Noose? For what? Trying to protect my mom's feelings?"

"Well, since you put it that way." She takes his hand. "C'mon, let's explore your humanitarian side." They walk into the bright light.

The AED whines. Linh says, "Stand back! Three, two, one, SHOCK!" She presses the shock button, and Joe's upper body again lunges off the floor—then collapses. "Weak pulse."

"We've gotta MTP now!"

12:12:25.

14

The Good Samaritan—Part I

FRIDAY, 30 June 1961

The coach waves his arms to the six outfielders. "Hey guys! Come on in!" After his players gather around, he says, "Great practice. Eat a good lunch, drink lots of water, and keep cool this afternoon. This heat feels like the middle of August."

"Yeah. But the pool's opened!" Dick announces, and the others cheer.

"We won't have practice until the Fifth. We'll practice at ten here. So, have a fun and safe Fourth. And if ya blow off any fingers, you're still gonna play—bandages and all."

The fifteen boys laugh.

"All right. It's almost eleven and it's gettin' hot. But before we split, I want to tell ya about a nine-year-old boy in California that was hit by a pitch in the chest and died."

"You're kiddin'?" Barney exclaims.

"No, I'm not. That's why it's **so** important for the batter to turn his back to the pitcher and duck when you're getting out of the way. **Got it?**"

"Yeah." The boys' reply is subdued. Then, Dick says, "Duck-n-cover. Duck and cover."

"Okay. Let's pick up the gear, and don't forget to listen to my Senators beat the Yankees tonight at seven."

"Those Damn Yankees!" Dick blurts to get Barney's goat. The boys cheer, except Barney. Instead, the seductive redhead, Señorita

159

Lolita Banana, the devil's best homewrecker, dances seductively in the locker room of his mind.

They laugh, then stick the bats and catcher's equipment in one bag and the baseballs in another. Barney tosses the ball bag into the trunk of the coach's car and then runs to his bike, where the gang is waiting.

"Hey, let's take Davy Crockett Trail," Bobby suggests with a wry smile.

"Yeah!" everyone exclaims.

"Maybe they're washin' the Corvette."

"Or the Lincoln," Tommy says.

"Who cares about cars?" a wide-eyed Mikey asks. **"Bikinis!"**

"Yeaaaaah!" the boys yell.

"Kaelah!" Willie exclaims.

"Yeaaaaah," the boys gush.

"Galiena!" Dick says.

"Yeaah," the boys gush.

"Erika."

"Yeah."

"How 'bout Mrs. Horton?" Barney's heart pounds as he secures his glove under the front carrier before tying his Louisville Slugger across the handlebars.

"Oh yeaaaaah!" the boys exclaim.

After putting on his mirrored aviator sunglasses, Barney moves the kickstand up with his right foot, swings his right leg over the red and white 1960 Schwinn bicycle, and steps down on the top peddle. **"Let's roll!"** The back wheel's spokes rapidly slap the four old playing cards clipped to the fender braces, making the Panther II sound almost like its motor-powered brothers.

They start their half-mile trip along the four residential streets until they reach the foot of the one-hundred-yard-long gravel road. Then they stop. Staring at the road's fifteen-degree incline, the trek looks insurmountable. But they have traveled these gradual curves that wind through the mature pine trees. So, with deep breaths, they forge upward past the dozen properties leading to the top of the highest point in The Air Capital City.

With grunts and groans, they trudge forward, bike tires slipping and sliding on the small loose stones, pinecones crunching beneath the inflated rubber. The boys huff and puff as they trek upward, sweat flowing down their faces, dripping from noses and chins, their goal pumping the needed adrenaline through their veins.

"Man, I hate this part," Bobby says.

"It'll be worth it," Dick replies.

"Only if they're there," Mikey gasps.

Finally, the top of the spire appears, and David announces, "Halfway there!"

Groans erupt from the exhausted boys.

As more of the roof of the two-story, six-gabled mansion appears, Bobby voices what most of the boys are thinking—and hoping, "They sure better be home."

"Yeah." Barney huffs and puffs. *If she wasn't so dang beautiful, I'd be home eatin' a fried egg sandwich and chips.*

Then they see the largest house in the city lording over a plush green fescue lawn lined with beautiful flowerbeds and huge trees.

The boys stop at the entrance to the long cobblestone driveway and, with jaws dropped, stare at what is outside the garage.

"Holy smoke," a wide-eyed Mikey says in an excited whisper, "She's wearin' a bikini!"

"Yeaaaaah," the boys gush.

"It's an itsy bitsy teenie weenie yellow polka dot bikini," Tommy sings dreamily.

"Yeaaaaah," the boys gush as the lyrics to Brian Hyland's 1960 hit single flow through their minds.

"Wow. What a classy chassis," Bobby says.

"Yeaaaaah," the boys gush.

"Man, she's got gorgeous legs," David says.

GAMS! burst into Barney's mind.

"Yeaaaaah," the boys gush.

"She's definitely a hot mama," Mikey says.

"The hottest," Tommy says.

"Yeaaaaah," the boys gush.

"I think Kaelah's hotter," Willie says.

"She's the queen. Have ya seen her knockers?" Dick asks.

"Yeaaaaah!" the boys gush.

"She's gotta be a D-cup," Willie says.

"She's got a rack, alright," David admits. "But they ain't D's."

"D cup?" Barney asks.

"Yeah," David says. "Bra size. A, B, C, D according to how big their boobs are."

"So, how ya know what size they are?"

"Don't ya know anything about boobs?" David criticizes. Barney shrugs, and David explains, "Okay. Now listen up, you virgins. An A-cup is like a flat golf ball. A B-cup is kinda like an egg on its side—like Bobby's." The boys laugh.

"Ain't funny, Buttwipe," the plump Bobby replies.

"Fried or poached?" Dick asks mockingly.

"Don't be a dick, Dick," David scolds, and the boys chuckle, except Dick. "Okay. Get back in the ballgame. A C-cup is the size of a tennis ball, and a D-cup is like a baseball."

"So, every time you pick up a baseball," Willie says, "think about Kaelah's boobs."

David lets out an exasperated sigh. "I'm tellin' ya, she ain't that big."

"How you know? You give 'em the ol' palm test?" Dick asks, and the boys hoot.

Barney stares at Mrs. Horton, her hands firmly planted on bare, curvaceous sides, as she glares at the riding mower standing outside of the garage.

"Mrs. Horton's are definitely tennis balls," Bobby says, "and Kaelah's ain't no bigger."

"Well, I think…Hey Barn, where ya goin'?" Tommy and the boys stare at Barney as he slowly rides his bike past the black wrought iron gate along the driveway, finally stopping a few feet from the mower.

"Hi, M-mrs. Horton." His heart pounds as he helplessly stares at her toned body and long, straight black hair pulled back in a tight ponytail, a yellow bandana circling her head. *She kinda looks like a Comanche—a **gorgeous** Comanche.*

She stares at him. "Barney. Yes?" He nods. "Girls no home. They at dance class."

"New m-mower?"

Above the snug bikini top caressing her bosom, her chest heaves then collapses, expelling a frustrated breath. "No. Dr. Hor-ton pull mower out here to mow, then he go to hospital—leave here. It no start!" Disgustedly, she glares at the machine.

"M-my dad has m-me and m-my brother inspect our m-mower before we m-mow. But we ain't got a rider." He shrugs. "I can look at it if ya want m-me to."

She stares at him, then shrugs. "No can hurt. It have petrol and oil."

Barney grins. *Petrol. That's funny.* He gets off the bike, kicks the kickstand down, and steps to the mower. After looking at the engine, he sees one problem. "The sparkplug wire ain't connected." He pushes the wire onto the sparkplug. "Ya wanna try it—or I can."

"You. I mad at it." She stands with her arms folded under her breasts.

Barney engages the choke, then pulls the cord, and the engine roars to life.

Mrs. Horton screams with elation. With a broad smile, she claps and yells, "**Muito obrigado!** Thank you! **Thank you! THANK YOU!**"

Barney smiles. *It was just the sparkplug wire.* "I'll m-mow your lawn for ya—if ya want."

She stares at him. "Okay. You mow lawn. I pay you ten dollar. Yes?"

Barney's eyes bulge as his face lights up in a broad smile. *TEN DOLLARS?* Then he shakes his head. "Oh. No. I—I can't take any m-money. I volunteered to m-mow."

She stares at him. "I insistir! You fix mower. You mow. You take money." She waggles her index finger at him. "I no take no for answer. Compreendo?"

Compreendo? Understand. His eyes widen, and then he shrugs and nods. "Okay. Deal."

"You watch grass bag. It get half full you drive to backyard and dump grass in compost. Come. I show you."

He turns off the mower and follows her into the backyard. "Wow!" Barney exclaims, seeing the enormous patio, in-ground swimming pool, and flowerbeds. "This is like Better Homes and Gardens."

She smiles. "Obrigado, Barney. It take muito work keep yard nice." She points to an enclosed area. "This is compost. Put grass here."

"Whew! It stinks." He fans the area in front of his face. "Yeah. We have one at home. But it don't stink like that."

"I add cow estrume."

"Es-true-me? Manure?"

"Yes. Ma-nu-er. Make garden belíssimo."

"Belíssimo? Beautiful."

She nods. Then, as they walk back to the mower, Barney thinks, *at least there ain't much to mow back here.*

He sits on the mower, steps on the brake, and restarts the mower, then moves the gear lever to the forward position and slowly eases up on the brake. The mower begins its trek down the driveway and onto the perimeter of the half-acre front yard. *Alan Shepard Jr., the first American in space, piloted the mighty Mercury Redstone Spacecraft, Freedom 7.*

As he continues towards the street, he sees his pals watching, their eyes bulging and mouths open. He carefully mows along the one-hundred-foot-long driveway to the flowerbed paralleling the street, turns left, and stops. With a swelled chest, he yells over the roar of the mower's engine, "I'm gonna mow Mrs. Horton's lawn."

David puts his hands to his face and, like a bullhorn, yells, **"Lucky dog!"**

Barney's face beams. *You got no idea. TEN BUCKEROOS! YEEHAW!* As the boys head off in the direction of their homes,

Barney continues mowing along the curvy, hundred-fifty-foot border of the flowerbed, the ear-to-ear smile never leaving his face. Again, he turns left and begins mowing along the second flowerbed towards the house. *Man, I'd hate ta weed this sucker.* He glances up to see Mrs. Horton sitting on the steps to the front porch watching him, the flip-flops lying at her left hip, her glistening golden gams parted and outstretched, her hands applying suntan oil to her bare abdomen. Barney's heart pounds, his loins tingle. *Man, she's be-lís-si-MO.*

At the end of the second flowerbed, he turns left and mows along the sidewalk in front of the house. As he passes, she gives him a nod. He smiles. *Mr. Horton's the luckiest man in the world.* ***And I'm the second luckiest!***

On the third lap, he stops. "I'm gonna empty the bag."

Mrs. Horton stands. "I go with you." She follows Barney as he rides the mower to the rear of the backyard. With the mower silent, she watches Barney disconnect the catcher and lift it over the fence of the compost. As he shakes the grass out of the catcher, she says, "You strong boy. Look like it no-thing for you empty catcher."

Barney grins. "Thanks. It's not really heavy. It would be if I filled it up."

"I watch. You do muito good job. After you finish, I make lunch. Girls be home then."

"Oh, I can't stay. My mom's probably wonderin' why I'm not home by now."

"I call her—tell her where you are. It be okay." She turns and walks towards the house as Barney reattaches the catcher. However, instead of concentrating on what he should be doing, he cannot resist watching Mrs. Horton's graceful, confident, and arousing walk: head up, back straight, shoulders back—*Bet she'd win Eraser Tag every time*—her beautiful legs seem to toss her bare feet in front one another, arms, hips, and ponytail swaying freely, almost hypnotically.

And her calves—perfectly muscled calves grin at him with every step. She steps into the house.

Finally, with the catcher in place, Barney restarts the mower and mows the remainder of the backyard before returning to the front. Thirty minutes later, he empties the catcher for the last time, then drives to the garage, where he automatically begins sweeping the grass clippings off the deck. He sees three girls' bicycles parked against the wall.

"Oh! You clean mower. Obrigada, Barney." Mrs. Horton steps into the garage. "I inspect lawn. Maravilhoso!"

"You're welcome."

She hands him a ten-dollar bill. "You park mower there." She points to an unoccupied area next to a wall as Erika comes into the garage.

"Hi, Barney."

"Hi, Erika."

"Mom called your mom. You're going to eat lunch with us. Hope you like BLTs and homemade potato salad. Mom makes the best."

"Sounds great."

Erika shows him where the mud/utility room and Barney washes the dust and sweat off his face and upper torso.

"Barney, I like you meet Mrs. Johansson and you know her daughter, Mina." They exchange greetings. "Mrs. Johansson my partner at dance studio." Then she turns to the tall, brunette woman. "How class go, Sonja?"

"Everyone did very well," she replies. "The girls were a great help with the beginners."

As soon as Barney walks into the kitchen, a glaring Dottie says with a hint of displeasure, "It's after two and Daddy and your brother did the yardwork, so you get to clean the house."

"Don't be mad. Mrs. Horton called ya. She insisted that I eat lunch there."

"I'm not mad about that. Your friends have been calling every five minutes for the last hour."

Barney hurries to the wall phone.

"Oh no you don't. You finish your chores before you do anything else."

"I can't even call 'em back?"

"No."

As Barney begrudgingly begins dusting in the dining room, Dottie leans against the opening between the kitchen and dining room, her arms folded comfortably in front of her. "So, what did you have for lunch?"

Barney tells her, smiling. "Mrs. Horton calls it B and L and T."

"Good?"

"Delicioso! That's Portuguese for delicious." Barney moves to the table as his mother's eyebrows rise. "She uses thick bacon and Texas toast, and she butters one side of the toast and grills it. Mmm. We should do that."

"Hmm," Dottie grunts through her nose. "Okay. From here on you make the BLTs." She watches her eldest clean the first chair. "So, Mrs. Horton's Portuguese?"

"No. She's from Brazil. But she speaks Portuguese—but not all the time—just some words. You'd think she'd talk better English, bein' in the U.S. for over eleven years."

"It's **speak** better English," Kenny corrects. "Geez. You'd think you'd **speak** better…"

"Hey," Dottie interrupts, giving her youngest a disapproving stare before he returns to the newspaper.

"You seem to know a lot about Mrs. Horton."

Barney shrugs.

"So, just you and her ate lunch together?"

"No." Then Barney tells her everyone who was there.

"**Even Kaelah?**" a wide-eyed Kenny blurts.

"Well—you should've called before you started mowing. I was worried about you until David called just before noon asking if you were back from Mrs. Horton's. I asked him what you were doing there, and he told me. Did ya do a good job?"

"Yeah. She said the lawn was belíssimo. That's Portuguese for…"

"Beautiful," Kenny interrupts.

Glaring at Kenny, Barney says, "Yeah! Beautiful." He steps into the living room, pulls from his pocket the bill sporting the face of Alexander Hamilton, and waves it toward his little brother.

"**She paid ya ten bucks?**" A wide-eyed Kenny's jaw drops.

"Yep!" Barney sticks the bill back in his pocket. "And I got to ride her mower and didn't havta rake or trim."

"Wow. Guess it pays to work for the rich," Dottie says.

"Yep!" Barney sticks his tongue out at Kenny as he thinks *rich and belissimo*. He returns to dusting another dining room chair.

"Don't expect a pay raise here," Dottie says.

As Barney moves from one chair to the next, the phone rings. Before he can take a step towards the phone, Dottie, putting away the dishes, says without looking at him, "Don't even think about."

Kenny answers the phone. "Hello. Yeah, he is. No. He's doing his chores. He'll call ya when he's finished. Bye, Willie."

During the next forty minutes, Barney dusts and vacuums the dining room, living room, and master bedroom while Kenny arrogantly tells Bobby, Mikey, Dick twice, Tommy, and Nick the same message.

Then, just when he thinks he is finished, Dottie says, "Don't forget to clean Kenny's room and yours."

A loud sigh gushes out as Barney marches into Kenny's bedroom. And with shoulders slumped, he cleans, all the time thinking, *I'll never get ta call 'em back.* Then, with the room clean, he stomps downstairs. As he opens the basement door, he hears his mother say, "And don't forget your bathroom."

"Don't forget your bathroom," Barney says mockingly, under his breath, as he shuts the basement door. "Geez. She's gonna make me work all day." *What does she think I did for the past two hours?*

In his bedroom, he stands on his bed and carefully swishes the feathers over the 1:32 scale WWII airplanes hanging from strings over his bed: the P-38 Lightning and P-51 Mustang, the type of fighters his late uncle flew over Europe, a Focke Wulf Fw-190 and Messerschmitt Bf-109 like the ones his uncle had shot down. As he dusts the last one, he makes the sound of machinegun bursts, imagining *the Lightning's four M2 Browning machine guns riddling the Messerschmitt's tail for Lieutenant Snodgrass' fifth kill, making him the newest ace in the U.S. Army Air Corps.*

Next, he takes down, dusts, and lays on his bed the Hartland Horse and Riders: Sergeant Frank Preston riding Rex, Roy Rogers riding Trigger, Dale Evans riding Buttermilk, Marshall Matt Dillon riding Buck, Jim Hardie riding Jubilee, Paladin riding Rafter, Josh Randall riding Ringo, and Nick Adams, Cheyenne Bodie, Bret Maverick, Captain Chris Colt, and Wyatt Earp riding nameless horses. He shakes his head. *Why did I tell Gramps and Gramma I wanted to collect these?*

Then, he dusts the Hall of Fame Baseball players: a new Mickey Mantle and Willie Mays, his baseball idols, Yankees Babe Ruth, Yogi Berra, Roger Maris, and Milwaukee Braves Hank Aaron, Eddie Mathews, and Warren Spahn.

Finally, he polishes the four walnut shelves his grandfather made for him before placing the Hartland figures back on display. Then he puts the polish, duster, and rag on the desk, winds up, and pitches an invisible ball, thinking *Barney Snodgrass throws a heater to Berra. The Mick swings! IT'S A DEEP DRIVE TO CENTER FIELD! Mays heads for the wall. HOLY SMOKE! HE MAKES AN OVER THE SHOULDER BASKET CATCH for out number three sealing the first perfect game in All-Star HISTORY!* With his arms raised in triumph, Barney trots in a small circle between the bed, desk, and two walls.

After cleaning his desk, Barney cleans his shower, sink, and toilet, then throws the rags into the pile of soiled whites as his mother enters the utility room.

She pulls a drenched sheet from the washer and inserts it through the wringer, then guides it into the tub containing rinse water. She continues with all the washed items until the washer is empty. Then she puts in another load before inserting the rinsed items back through the wringer, finally laying the wringed-out items in the laundry basket. "Would you be a dear and carry this basket outside for me?"

"Can't Kenny do it? I still gotta mop my room."

"Did you complain when Mrs. Horton asked you to mow her lawn?"

"I volunteered," pops out of his mouth. His mother's glare encourages him to be a dear.

At the clothesline, they start clamping the damp items over one of three wires strung between two T-shaped iron pipes spaced about forty feet apart. "What else do ya want me ta do after this?"

Dottie grins. "After you finish with your bedroom, you can go play."

Never have clothes been hung out to dry so fast—and to Dottie's satisfaction. Then, Barney hurries downstairs and mops the linoleum floors of his bathroom and bedroom.

"I believe that was the first time you ever volunteered to mow the lawn. My goodness. What a great pair of legs will make you do."

Barnard just shakes his head. "It was a curse."

"One you relish."

"Okay. Okay. So, I'm gullible or shallow or—I don't know what you'd call it."

"Oh my. There are so many. I'd call it exploitable, ripe for the picking..."

"Okay. I get it. I was easy to succumb to the power of a shapely pair of legs."

"So, you do know what to call it. Well, let's see how deep you fell under that power." The angel takes Barnard's hand, and they walk into the light.

Linh retrieves the telescoping IV pole from the Massive Transfusion Protocol items as Ken monitors his brother's vitals. She extends the pole before getting one bag of Ken's low-titer, Group O blood type, from the storage bag and hangs it on the pole. After cleaning Joe's arm with povidone-iodine, she inserts the needle into the vein in his right arm and starts the transfusion at a rate of one pint every fifteen minutes.

"I'm gonna see what's keeping the EMTs." Ken takes Linh's cellphone and dials 9-1-1.

12:13:59.

15

The Good Samaritan—Part II

SATURDAY 22 July 1961

"Hey Barn', you see *Liberty Bell 7* launch yesterday?" Nick asks as they leisurely ride their bikes towards the Boulevard Plaza shopping center.

"Yeah. But it sure was early—six-twenty. I was glued to the tube. Man! I bet bein' an astronaut's outta sight."

"In more ways than one."

They laugh, and then Barney says, "Glad it only lasted 15 minutes, 37 seconds—I had my stopwatch on it."

"Dad said we might go see Cape Canaveral this summer."

"Ooo! That would be **bad**. I'll try talkin' Mom into it. If I can convince her, I'm sure Dad'll go for it since he inspects planes." *Or maybe I should ask Dad first.*

"At least we're ahead of the Soviet Union, two to one."

"Yep. Yuri Garagin vs. Alan Shepard and Gus Grissom. I just wonder when they'll start orbiting the Earth."

"You wanna come over after supper and make a spaceship in our attic?"

"Sure! Oh! I forgot. I gotta mow the lawn."

"Have you seen *The Fiercest Heart*?"

"Uh-uh."

"Want to? The girl in *Can-Can* and *G.I. Blues* is in it."

173

"**Juliet Prowse?**" Barney's heart skips a few beats. "Man! She's definitely a fox! Yeah! When?"

"How about tomorrow?"

"I'll ask Mom."

"I'd love to have a girlfriend like that. She's **so** cute."

"Sure is! She's got gorgeous gams." *But not as gorgeous as Lilly's and Mrs. Horton's.*

"Gams?"

"Yeah. Legs."

"Sure does. And I really dig her accent."

"Oh yeah." *About as hot as Mrs. Horton's.*

They pull into the parking lot, hop on the sidewalk, and slowly proceed along the side of the brick building, finally stopping in front of Dockum Drug, where they park their bikes.

Nick starts toward the entrance, then seeing Barney staring across the street, stops. "You coming?" Then, he sees what controls Barney's attention. "Okay. Well…" He hurries inside.

Barney continues sitting on his bike while he looks across the street. *Hmmm. Erika and her sisters ain't there.* But the main attraction controls his attention. *Man, she's so graceful.* He watches her long, coal-black ponytail whirl behind her in unison with her body as she pirouettes on her left foot. *Wow. She looks like a ballerina in a jewelry box.* His heartbeat increases.

The children follow suit, some with the teacher's assistance. Then Mrs. Horton claps her hands, and the children stop. They give her a hug before leaving the studio, some with their parents, others on their bikes parked outside. A moment later, Mrs. Horton steps outside and locks the door as the barbershop clock hanging in its window reads 4:30. She waves at Pat, who is cutting a customer's hair, before walking down the sidewalk to the other end of the shopping center. His breathing increases as he admires the rhythmic, almost hypnotic sway of her hips and her thigh-high wrap skirt's slow-flowing wave with every resolute step her shapely legs take. *Wow, she's so beautiful.* She vanishes into Duckwall's. He quickly looks in the drug store's window. *C'mon Nick! What the heck's takin' ya?*

A few very long seconds later, Nick steps outside carrying a paper sack.

"Let's go to Duckwall's." An impatient Barney starts riding.

"Okay. But just for a minute. I gotta be home by quarter 'til five."

They walk their bikes across the street and park them outside the five-n-dime. Inside, the boys head straight to the magazine rack, where Nick grabs the latest *Tales of Suspense* comic book. Barney takes the May issue of *Our Army at War* while nonchalantly glancing around to find Mrs. Horton. Without success, he looks down at the cover. "Hey Nick, he finally made lieutenant."

"Who?" Nick asks, flipping through his pages.

"Sergeant Rock." Barney takes the comic and casually walks away. He looks down each aisle. Then, at the far end of the third aisle, his skipping heart leaps into his throat—for there she is—looking at dolls. *Wow, she tans good.* He admires the contrast between her dark flesh and the skin-tight, cream-colored, spaghetti-strapped body tights. She bends over and picks up another doll. *Man, that dress sure is short.* His eyes widen, a twitch exciting his loins.

"May I help you, young man?" a female voice loudly interrupts Barney's spying.

Quickly, he turns, red-faced, to find the middle-aged clerk glaring at him, her arms crossed over her chest. Hastily, Barney looks back to see Mrs. Horton staring at him. *Oh god. She caught me. Dang that old...* Mrs. Horton smiles, giving him a four-finger wave. Shyly, Barney waves back as the dance teacher returns to looking at doll items. "No, Ma'am," he replies before hurrying back to the magazine rack.

"Where'd ya go?" Nick asks. "I gotta make tracks."

"Okay. Let's go."

The boys carry their comic books to the cashier. As they wait for the clerk to arrive, Barney keeps looking for Mrs. Horton. Then he sees her walking towards him. He quickly turns to the register as Nick pays for his comic. A couple of seconds later, Mrs. Horton says, "Olá, Barney."

With his head heating from embarrassment, Barney replies, "H-hi, M-mrs. Horton."

She grins. "You find what you look for?"

SURE DID! He shows her the comic as Nick says, "Hey, Barn. C'mon!" He looks to see the cashier waiting for him. "You can go before m-me."

"Obrigado, Barney. You real gentleman." As she steps past him, her sensuous perfume glides into his nostrils. *Wow, she smells good.* She places the black-and-white swimsuit-clad blonde Barbie Doll sporting the Titian bubble-cut hairdo on the counter with three packages of doll clothes.

As the clerk rings up Calista's purchases, she says, "You have the cutest outfits. I love the short skirts."

Calista thanks her and then tells her where she can buy the clothing.

I love her accent. Barney's heart pounds as he helplessly stares at her. *Wow, she looks like a movie star.* She turns and grins at him, sending his heartbeat into overdrive. *She's prettier than Juliet Prowse. HECK! SHE'S MORE BEAUTIFUL THAN LILLY!*

"Thank you, Calista." The clerk hands the bag to her. "My husband and I are looking forward to class tomorrow evening."

"Good. I muito happy you enjoy dancing." Then she looks at Barney. "Nice see you again, Barney."

He swallows hard and nods. He watches her walk out of the store and back towards her studio.

"Would you like to buy that comic?" the clerk barks, jarring Barney back to the store.

"Oh. Uh. Yes, Ma'am." He lays the comic book on the counter. "And I'd like two packs of baseball cards, please."

She rings the amounts up in the register. "That'll be twenty-one cents."

Barney hands her a quarter, and she gives him change. She places the items in a paper sack and hands it to her distracted customer. "She's beautiful. Isn't she?"

"Gorgeous," he replies, almost trancelike, as he walks out of the store.

"Ready?" an annoyed Nick asks as Barney swings his right leg over his bike. "We gotta hit the road, or I'm gonna catch it."

They hop the curb and peddle the way they came. As they get close to the end of the shopping center, Barney says, "Hold up," and stops at the white 1953 Corvette and its owner standing beside it, arms akimbo, staring downward. He stops. *Uh-oh. A flat.* M-mrs. Horton, I-I'll change it for ya."

"You know to fix flat tire?"

"Sure. Me and my dad rotate our tires in the spring and put on snow tires in the winter."

"Well—okay." She steps to the rear of the car, leans forward, and unlocks the trunk; all the while, Barney stares helplessly at the back of her legs, how the skirt rises in back almost to her derriere, and how her calves faintly smile at him through the semi-opaque body tights.

His heart flutters. *Oh man. She's got the most beautiful—*. The trunk pops up, jolting him out of his trance.

"Okay." Mrs. Horton steps aside.

"Hey Barn, I really gotta split!"

"Just help me loosen the lugs, and I can do the rest."

"Alllll right."

Barney grabs the tire iron and carefully pries the Chevrolet Bel Air wheel cover off the steel wheel. Then he inserts the wrench over the top hexagon lug nut, grabs the crossbar, pushes down, and pulls up.

The nut does not budge.

"Nick, I'll push down, and you pull up."

Nick grabs the bar on the right side and pulls up with all his might as Barney pushes down on the left bar with all his weight. Ten seconds later, the nut surrenders its tight grasp of the bolt, hurling the boys to their left—Nick tumbling on top of Barney, who crashes face first onto the hot pavement only an inch from hippy-inspired, hand-painted, psychedelic-designed sneakers.

"**Oh, meu Deus!**" Calista exclaims as Nick sits up. "You hurt?"

"No!"

"You, Barney?"

"No, Ma'am."

She helps him to his feet. "Oh, Barney, you scrape you forehead."

He wipes the back of his left hand across his forehead, then looks at the streak of blood. "I'm okay. It doesn't hurt."

"No matter." Calista grabs her purse and pulls out a white handkerchief. "Look at me." He stares at his reflection in the dark lenses of the thick white oval sunglass frames as she dabs a corner of the 'kerchief on her tongue before dabbing it on his scrape. "Maybe tire too much for you boys."

"No Ma'am! We can do it. Right, Nick?"

"Barn, I really gotta get."

"Just four more nuts. M-mrs. Horton, I'm okay. Really. Thanks." Barney turns and puts the wrench on the second nut, and the boys proceed to loosen that nut with much less effort. He looks up at Calista. "See? Told ya we could do it!" Then, with success-induced adrenaline, the boys tackle the third and fourth nuts. They surrender with little resistance.

But, the fifth is a stubborn nut, and the boys grunt and groan and huff and puff as they push and pull with all their might until finally, the nut surrenders its grasp on the bolt, throwing the boys. Even though they brace their collapse, Barney's head slams on the pavement. He sits up and quickly rubs the back of his spinning head.

"Oh, meu Deus! You hurt you head. Look down." Bending his head forward, she gently combs her fingers through his sweaty hair, searching for any injury. Barney's eyes gawk at her bare chest above the curved front, barely allowing a hint of cleavage. *Yep. Baseballs for sure.* Then, his eyes bulge as two fingertip-sized protrusions make their appearance at the front of her chest. TWITCH. He swallows hard. She puts her right hand under his chin and gently lifts his head up. "You no bleed," she says. "But you get bump. You sit in shade. I get ice from food store." She waggles her index finger at him. "You no touch tire." Barney watches her walk down the sidewalk and vanish into the barbershop. Then, he jumps up. "Okay. Let's get this nut loose before she comes back!"

"You heard what she said," Nick says as Barney quickly returns to the tire.

"C'mon! We can put the tire on before she gets back."

"Hey, I gotta go, Barn. Sorry." Nick hops on his bike and pedals down the street.

As Barney starts jacking the car up, Calista returns with Pat MacAteer. She shakes her finger at him. "You no mind."

"You said not to touch the tire, so I didn't. I just jacked the car up."

With head cocked to the side, she stares at him.

"Calista, take him in the shop and put a bottle of pop on his head while I change your tire."

"Obrigado, Pat. Come Barney." As soon as she escorts him inside the barbershop, she exchanges greetings with the other two barbers and their customers. Barney sits while Calista buys two cold bottles of pop, which he holds one to his forehead while she holds the other to the back of his head. He thanks her. "You muito red. How you feel?"

"Fine. I can change that tire for ya now."

"No! You rest. Pat change tire." She looks around. "Where you friend?"

"He had to go home. His parents are really strict, and if he doesn't mind, they take a switch to him—if they can catch him."

"No!" She shakes her head in disbelief, and Barney nods.

"What his name?"

"Nick Wainwright."

She reaches into her purse and pulls out a dollar. "You take to him. Yes?"

"Yes, Ma'am." Barney sticks the dollar in his pocket and then shivers from the bottle's cold sweat running down his face.

"You sick?" a concerned Mrs. Horton asks.

"No."

She pats him on the shoulder.

"I'm okay," Barney says and stands. "I can change the tire by myself. Really."

"No. You stubborn boy. Stay." She walks outside and watches Pat change the tire. A moment later, she returns. "Now you drink."

Barney takes a couple of big gulps and gasps.

"Go to head?" Barney nods. "Drink slow—hold in mouth. Not cold to swallow."

You tellin' me! He shakes his aching head. *Wow. That hurts!* He takes another swig, but holds it in his mouth for a few seconds as he watches how her full lips pucker as she takes a sip. *I bet she kisses like that.* Another twitch in his crotch widens his eyes. He quickly names some of the American League All-Stars: *Luis Aparicio, Yogi Berra, Jim Bunning, Rocky Colavito, Whitey Ford, Nellie Fox...* He slowly swallows.

"Go to head again?"

Barney shakes his head. "I—I'm sorry I didn't change your tire."

She waggles her finger at him. "You no sorry! You do maravilhoso! I muito grata you try, especialmente **so hot**." She removes a cigarette from a pack, lights it, and takes a deep drag. Barney stares at her puckered lips as she slowly blows a narrow stream of light-gray smoke away from them. "You think about take dance lesson?" He shrugs. "It muito fun." Again, he shrugs. "You and E dance together. She excelente dancer." His head cocks to the side. "I think she like you. You like her?" He nods timidly. "She say you play baseball." He nods. "Why you no ask her to you ballgame?" He shrugs. "Cat bite you tongue?" His eyes widen. ***Does she know Lilly?***

A few minutes later, Pat walks into the store and wipes a wet towel on his sweaty face. "Calista, you're all fixed up."

"Obrigado, Pat." She gives him a kiss on both sweaty cheeks.

"The flat's in the trunk. It has a cut on the sidewall. I hate to say this, but I think it's a knife cut." Her eyes widen and jaw drops. "I'll make some flyers to see if anyone saw anything."

"Obrigado, Pat. I no think I had enemy." She shrugs. "Guess I do. I see you and Mary tomorrow in class. Yes?"

"We can't wait."

Mrs. Horton and Barney walk to the car. "Muito obrigado, Barney Snodgrass."

"Huh?"

She smiles. "I say 'thank you very much' in Portuguese."

"Oh." He smiles. "It's p-pretty how ya s-say it."

She smiles. "Portuguese is Iberian Romance language."

"Sounds romantic—the way ya talk—speak."

She smiles and pulls out her billfold from her purse, opens it, and brings out a five-dollar bill.

"No m-ma'am. I can't t-take any m-money. I offered to c-change the t-tire."

"You work muito hard. You take money."

He shakes his head. "T-thanks, M-mrs. Horton, but my dad'd be very disappointed in me if he knew I t-took m-money when I volunteered to help."

She stares at him for a moment, then nods. "You father be **muito** proud of you." She puts the money back in her purse, takes out a business card and pen, places the card on her right knee, and writes something, then stands and hands the card to Barney. "I teach you dance—free—eight lesson." She waggles her index finger at him. "I no take 'no' for answer." She plants a soft but firm kiss on both flushed cheeks. Then she looks into his eyes. "Muito obrigado, Barney Snodgrass."

"You're w-welcome, M-mrs. Horton." His eyes bulge, and his lips curl into a blushing ear-to-ear smile. His heart rate soars into the stratosphere faster than Alan Shepard's Mercury-Redstone 3 rocket as he watches her sit on the bucket seat, swing her legs under the steering column, and close the door. She looks up at him. "We start first Saturday after school start. I teach you Twist, Stroll—**Watusi**." She wiggles her upper torso. "We have muito fun." She cautiously backs out of the space and waves at him as she drives away.

Barney waves back, his heart still pounding. *She kissed me! TWICE!* He excitedly hops on his bike and starts peddling. ***Wow! She kissed me!*** For most of the way home, Barney shouts to the world, "She kissed me. She kissed me! MRS. HORTON KISSED MEEEEE! **MRS. HORTON KISSED MEEEEE!**" *I'm in love. Wow. I'm in love with the most beautiful woman in the world.* That thought and the rotation of his peddling legs produce a spasm in his crotch that grows into an unwanted bulge. *Oh no, NO, **NO!*** "Clete Boyer third base, Tony Kubek shortstop, Roger Maris right field, Mickey Mantle center field, Yogi Berra left field, Bill Skowron first base, Johnny Blanchard catching, Bobby Richardson second base." He repeats the Yankee lineup five times until he finally gets Mrs. Horton's image out of his mind—but not the feeling of her soft, pouty lips pressing against his cheeks.

Finally, he rides up his driveway, parks his bike on the side of the house, and walks into the kitchen.

"You're late," Kenny says between chews, his half-eaten hamburger sitting on his plate.

"Don't talk with food in your mouth." Dottie turns her attention to the new arrival. "It's nearly five o'clock. Where have you been?"

"Mrs. Horton had a flat tire, and I changed it for her—well, almost."

"Mrs. Horton? You mowed her lawn?"

Barney nods as he starts to walk into the dining room.

"Answer your mother," Jim says.

Barney stops. "Yeah. She's the dance teacher and Erika's mom."

"And Kaelah's!" Kenny eagerly interjects.

Barney hands his mother the business card and she looks at it, then her son's face. "She's going to give you free dance lessons?"

"I wouldn't take any money 'cuz I volunteered to change her tire."

Jim nods his approval as Dottie hands him the card. "Did ya fix it right?"

"Yes, sir. Just like ya taught me. But Mr. MacAteer finished 'cuz Mrs. Horton thought I was gettin' too hot. But I wasn't! I coulda finished on my own."

Jim grins as he looks up at Barney, then reads the note. "Well, she must've been happy with your work."

"Well, she drove away okay."

"Go wash up and put a Band-aid on your scratch. I'll fix you a burger. Remember, you have a ballgame at six-thirty."

"Okay." Barney hurries into the bathroom.

"Grilled onions?"

"Yeah." Barney scrubs his hands, and then, just before he begins washing his face, he looks in the mirror and sees what his parents were staring at. His head burns with embarrassment—and then his face slowly lights up in a proud ear-to-ear smile as he stares at the bright red imprints of puckered lips on his cheeks. *MRS. HORTON KISSED ME!* He leans towards the mirror and turns his head to get a closer look at her lips. *I love her. **WOW!*** His breathing becomes shallow. *I'm in love with the most beautiful woman in the world. Calista Horton. God, what a sexy name. What a sexy voice.* Instantly, the twinge returns. *Clete Boyer third base, Tony Kubek shortstop…*

Okay. Please hurry!" Ken turns the phone off. "They can't risk getting stuck. Almost twelve inches on the ground." He shakes his head. "Don't understand. We got here." He gently combs his fingers through his brother's damp hair. "Why didn't ya wait 'til Spring to clean the fuckin' revolver—**AND DRINK?**" He shakes his head. "Dad taught you better."

"You think accident or suicide?"

Shrugging, Ken again shakes his head. "He's always had the uncanny ability to miss a gimme."

12:14:42.

"I was beginning to wonder how many different things you could fix for this Brazilian bombshell," the angel says.

"Brazilian bombshell? She was a very nice lady."

"Okay. She was a very nice Brazilian bombshell."

"I think you're jealous."

"Do you want me to show you when I'm jealous?"

"No, no! That's okay. I really don't need to see."

*The angel's lips curl into an evil grin. "It would be more—**feel**—than see."*

"How 'bout let's move on," Barnard suggests. "Please?"

"Of course. This is your reckoning." She takes his hand and leads him into the light.

16

The Job Offer

After lunch, Jim and the boys sit down to digest their barbequed hamburgers and watch the Boston Red Sox host the New York Yankees on CBS. A knock at the door interrupts the bottom of the fourth inning. Kenny jumps up and answers the door. His jaw drops as he stares at the visitor. "Dad. It's Mrs. Horton!"

Jim stands. "Well, ask her in."

"Olá James, Barney, Kenny," she says after she steps into the house.

The three say, "Hi."

Dottie walks into the living room, and Jim says, "Dottie, this is Calista Horton, the dance teacher. Calista, this is my wife, Dottie—Dorothy."

"Hello, Mrs. Horton."

"Call me Calista, por favor. I muito please to meet you, Dorothy."

"Calista. Please have a chair." She sits. "Is there something wrong?"

"No. No. The opposite." She smiles at Barney. "I want ask you if I may employ Barney two or three day a week to help me in the yard and around house."

"Oh!" Jim and Dottie blurt at the same time.

"I pay him one dollar per hour and feed him lunch."

"Well, he plays baseball," Dottie says.

"That okay. I have three daughter and know how importante their activity. So, he no work when he have baseball or some other activity. Just let me know."

Jim looks at Barney. "Well, it's really up to you, Barn. Whadaya think?"

"Yeah! Thank you, M-mrs. Horton!"

"De nada. Uh, you are welcome. I muito happy you accept. Let me know you baseball schedule and we work around it."

"Okay."

"You start tomorrow?" Calista asks.

Jim looks at Dottie, then says, "Sure."

"Excelente!" a smiling Calista looks at Barney. "I see you tomorrow at seven o'clock. We work in flowerbed."

"Okay," Barney says eagerly. Then his eyes widen. *Holy smoke. Hope she ain't talkin' 'bout **all** her flowerbeds.*

"James, Dorothy, muito obrigado. I apreciar you allow Barney work for me."

"That's quite all right," Dottie says, and Jim nods.

"I no bother you more." Standing, she looks at the television. "Who play?" Barney tells her. "What the score?"

"Tied two to two."

"You know Erika favorite team is Dodgers."

Barney nods. "Mine's the Yankees."

She smiles. "She tell me."

"We'll walk ya to your car," Jim says.

The four escort Calista to her car. Barney quickly opens the door. "Obrigado." She gets in. "See you tomorrow. Tchau."

"Bye." They wave at each other as she drives away.

187

"Goodness," Dottie says, looking at Jim. "You didn't tell me she was so beautiful. And she certainly does have gorgeous gams."

"Boys, the game's still on." He heads to the house, Dottie following as she continues her interrogation about the dance teacher.

"Bet they're gonna argue," Kenny says after their parents vanish into the house.

"Yeah. Don't know why. So what if Mrs. Horton's beautiful? Mom and Dad are married, and Mrs. Horton's married." Barney shrugs as he shakes his head as they enter the house and sit on the floor, relieved that their father is sitting in his chair and their mother is sewing.

Barney glares at the television. "Dang it! The Sox scored a run."

After the fourth inning, Jim goes to the bathroom, and Kenny asks, "You gonna take dance lessons?" Barney shrugs. "If ya did, maybe Mom and Dad would, then all of us would, and Kaelah can teach me."

Barney laughs. "I can see you two dancin' together—Popeye and Olive Oyl—or Mutt and Jeff."

"C'mon Barn. Please. If you do, I'll do all your chores for as long as the lessons last. Please."

Barney stares at Kenny. "You **promise** to do **all** my chores for as long as the lessons last—which I think are eight or ten weeks?"

"I promise." He makes an X over his heart. "Hope to die."

"You will if you break your promise."

Jim returns, and an eager Kenny says, "Daddy, Barn has something to tell you."

Barney glares at his little brother as their father asks, "What?"

"I guess I'll take dance lessons."

Jim stares at his firstborn. "Really? Dottie. Better come here."

She enters the living room. "What?"

"You want to take Calista's offer?"

"About dance lessons?"

"Yes. Barn, you want to tell your mother?"

"I guess I'll take dance lessons. **And Kenny said he'd do all my chores as long as the lessons last.**"

Jim and Dottie stare at Kenny. "Really?" He nods emphatically. "Pray tell me why you'd do all of Barn's chores for maybe two or three months?" Jim asks.

"I wanna dance with Kaelah."

"Isn't she like three or four years older than you?"

"So?"

"Well—uh…" Jim looks at Dottie, who turns and walks into the bedroom. Then, he looks at the game. "Who's ahead?"

"Daddy, you believe in love at first sight?" Kenny asks. "Grampa said he fell in love with Gramma the first time he saw her."

I fell in love with Mrs. Horton the first time I saw her.

"So, are you sayin' you're in love with Kaelah?"

"Yeah! She's the prettiest girl in the entire world—and really nice."

"How do ya know she's nice?" Barney blurts.

"She smiled at me the Saturday before Mother's Day. And that's the first time I saw her."

Jim walks into the bedroom, and Kenny asks, "What if she doesn't like me after we dance?"

"Ya know what Daddy says—you'll never know unless ya try."

A moment later, Jim returns to his chair, and Dottie walks to the phone. They watch her dial, then step into the kitchen. They point an ear towards the kitchen but cannot make out a single word.

After a minute or so, Dottie hangs the phone on the hook and walks into the living room.

"Boys, I just called Mrs. Horton." Barney's face transforms from happy to concerned. *Now what? She better not have changed her mind or…* "We're goin' to take dance lessons."

"You kiddin'?" a stunned Barney says.

"**YEAAAAAA!**" Kenny yells.

"We need to learn some new dances," Dottie says. "Polka is getting old."

"So is the Waltz," Jim adds. "Besides, Barn has free lessons—."

"And we think it would be fun for all of us to take lessons," Dottie finishes the sentence.

"So, will Kaelah be there?" a wide-eyed Kenny inquires with a mouthful of cookie.

"Don't talk with your mouth full. Mrs. Horton said that her daughters help with the kids' lessons."

A wide-eyed Kenny's jaw drops. "So, Kaelah teaches dance lessons?"

"All of her girls do."

Jim, Dottie, and Barney stare at Kenny. Slowly, a huge ear-to-ear smile curls his lips.

"We'll be Fred Astaire and Ginger Rogers in no time."

Barney points to Kenny. "Is he gonna be Ginger?"

They all laugh, except for Kenny. Then Jim says, "Knowin' you two, you'll probably be Laurel and Hardy."

"Better not be," Dottie says. "You do **not** give Mrs. Horton any trouble, and you learn to dance. Girls really like guys who can cut a rug."

"Cut a rug?" Barney blurts out. "What's that got to do with dancin'?"

"Cut a rug is another term for dancin'," Kenny answers nonchalantly.

"How do you know that?" a surprised Dottie asks.

"Thesaurus. Cut a rug is under dancing."

Jim and Dottie look at each other and shrug.

By three o'clock, the boys are mourning the Yankees' five to four loss to the BoSox.

Ken and Linh look at the blood bag hanging on the IV pole. Then they look at each other. "That's it. He's still bleeding." After Linh pulls out the blood-soaked QuikClot gauze, Ken quickly stuffs more gauze into the wound. "If that doesn't do it, then we'll need to hook me up."

12:15:01.

"Why don't you tell the jury how your dance lessons went."

"Thank you for not callin' me Fred, Gene, or James."

*"I've seen you dance, and believe me, I would **never**. They'd pluck my feathers for sure."*

"You don't have any feathers."

"Yet! I'm sure you'll get me at least one wing. I think instead of boring the jury with your dancing prowess, why don't we see how you worked for Calista?" The angel takes Barnard's hand, and they walk into the light.

17

Working a Real Job

"I'm proud of ya, Son," Barney hears his father say. *"Keep up the good work,"* he hears his mother's encouraging words as he shifts his bike into third gear. Without sitting on the seat, he eagerly pedals the six blocks to the house on top of Pine Tree Trail. As he turns onto the long driveway, he looks at the pristine flowerbeds. *Had no idea you guys were so darn long.*

After parking his bike against the wrought iron fence, he opens the gate to the backyard and walks to the patio door.

"Bom Dia, Barney," Calista says, sitting at the table.

"Bom Dia?"

"Yes. That mean 'good morning' in Portuguese."

"Oh! Bom Dia, Mrs. Horton."

"Excelente! Sit. You want orange juice—or coffee?"

"No thanks. I had breakfast. And I don't drink coffee. It smells like dirty dishwater."

She laughs as he sits across the table from her. "Brazil coffee the best. Meu pai send me one can every month."

"Moo pie?"

"My papa."

"Moo pie."

"See, you know four Portuguese word, and it barely seven o'clock. You smart boy." She takes a drag of her half-smoked cigarette and slowly blows the gray fog to her left.

"Is Erika here?" Barney asks.

"Yes. Girls sleep in—have very busy day—gymnastic lesson at nine, cheerleading at ten, and ballet at eleven."

"Wow! All I do is play baseball."

"You hear on news Russia launched a man into space?"

"Yeah. Gherman Titov. He's gonna be the first person to sleep in outer space. I'd like to be an astronaut."

"I no want be astronaut. Enough fly to Brazil. Take two or three day to feel normal." As she takes a sip of coffee, her eyes bulge, and her right arm abruptly extends in front of her. She hastily swallows and blurts out something in Portuguese.

A faint, high-pitched yelp draws Barney's attention to the door as it closes. His eyes widen as he sees the back of a girl, wearing only a bra and panties, sprinting away, her brown ponytail fanning her bare shoulders.

"You see E?"

Barney shrugs.

"Ahh, I think you do. She forget I tell her you be here today. She no want you see her in her pijama."

Looking down, Barney shakes his head and grins shyly. "I promise I won't tell." Then he shrugs. "It kinda looked like a bikini."

"You good boy, Barney." Mrs. Horton takes a last drag of her cigarette and snuffs it out in the metal ashtray. "You do maravilhoso job in front. So, we work in back today." She stands and starts to pick up the paper and saucer.

"I'll take 'em in."

"Obrigado, Barney. You take paper."

As they walk into the kitchen, two other girls walk into the kitchen, look at Barney, and burst out laughing.

"What so funny?" their mother asks.

"We were wondering why E almost knocked us over, running to her room. Now we know." Kaelah chuckles again.

"Fix you breakfast while I show Barney what to do." Mrs. Horton walks back outside, Barney following, closing the door behind him. As she hands him a wicker basket, she looks at the thermometer hanging on the wall. "Ahh. Sixty-eight degree. Perfeito work outside." Walking to the opposite end of the backyard, she says, "We harvest onion, pepper, squash, and tomato. You mother say you do this before. Yes?"

"Yes, Ma'am. We grow all of 'em except squash."

"I make best salsa." She kisses the tips of her fingers. "Ooo-la-la. Delicioso! I give Flower Club women some and my best friend. You take home, too."

"Okay. Thanks."

"Show me how you harvest onion." With arms crossed, Mrs. Horton stands at the edge of the garden and watches Barney dig up a few onions, their green stems lying on their sides, gently removes the loose soil, and lays them in the basket. "Perfeito, Barney. Harvest onions with lazy stem. Yes?"

"Yes, Ma'am." As he digs another onion, he watches her walk to the bell pepper plants and begin snipping the fruit, some green, some orange, and some red. Then he watches her take a full basket of peppers into the house. *Man-oh-man, she's beautiful. How lucky can I guy get to be workin' for her?*

About twenty minutes later, she returns to find all the desired onions lying neatly in the basket. "Muito good! You finish. Now you clean onion and I pick tomato."

With the cleaned onions and tomatoes on the kitchen counter with the peppers, Mrs. Horton shows Barney where and how to weed her backyard flowerbeds. Then, she goes into the house to start making salsa.

At noon, she walks up to Barney and inspects his work. "Excelente! You do maravilhoso. Come. Time eat lunch." As they walk towards the house, she says, "E say she like you." He smiles. "You like her. Yes?" He nods. "She like baseball."

Barney smiles. "I know."

"You ask her go to you ballgame. Yes?"

Barney pauses, then says, "Well—I'd like to."

Stopping, Mrs. Horton looks at him. "You no take girl to you game?"

"Uhhh. Well…"

"Oh! You have girlfriend."

"No! Uhhh. It's just that, uh, well, my best friend, Nick, is on my team, and he has a twin sister, Nicole, who kinda likes me. And she goes to the games."

"I remember Nick. So, Nicole, no, you girlfriend?" He shakes his head. "So, what the problem? E like you. You like E. You no have girlfriend. You ask E to game. Maybe she like be you girlfriend. Maybe you like be her boyfriend."

Barney digs another onion from the ground. *Erika **is** the prettiest girl in school!—and really popular. **And Nicole ain't my girlfriend.** Just because we invite each other to our birthday parties don't mean we're girlfriend and boyfriend.* "You think Erika would go to my game if I asked?"

"You no know if you no ask." She places an onion in the basket. "When you next game?"

"Tomorrow at six-thirty."

"When they return from dance, you ask. Yes?"

Grinning timidly, he nods. "Thanks for tellin' me she likes me."

"I like play Cupido."

"Cupido? Cupid!" He chuckles.

Barney and Mrs. Horton join her daughters for lunch on the patio. "This is homemade potato salad, and this is a Brazilian Roast Beef Sandwich call Bauru. It have cheese, lettuce, and fresh tomato from fresh tomato from the garden. Tell me if you like."

"Wow." His wide eyes stare at the two-inch-tall sandwich. "It's huge."

"You work hard. You need a big sandwich."

As they eat lunch, he listens to the girls tell their mother how their classes went and their plans to go swimming in the afternoon—after they clean their rooms.

Then, when the girls finish, they take their dishes inside. As Erika stands, Mrs. Horton says, "E, I take you dish inside." She takes Erika's and Barney's dishes, stops at the door, looks back at Barney, and winks, then goes inside.

"Lunch was really good."

"That's one of my favorite sandwiches—right behind Mom's BLT."

"Oh yeah! That's my all-time favorite." He looks at the yard, takes a deep breath, then finally asks, "Uh—you like baseball."

"You know I do. Why?"

"Well, uh, uh, I was wonderin' if ya, uh—would like to come to one of my games."

"Sure. When?"

"I have a game tomorrow at six-thirty."

"Okay. I'll ask Mom." Erika jumps up and hurries into the house. A moment later, a smiling Erika returns. "She said I could! What time do you want me ready?"

He thinks for a moment. "I better call Mom." He does. "Five forty-five."

TUESDAY, 8 August 1961

At supper the next day, the phone rings. Barney answers. "Hi, Mrs. Wainwright. Sure." He hands the phone to his mother and then tries to listen to her side of the conversation. She hangs the phone up and looks at Barney. "The Wainwrights can't go to the game, so she asked if we could take Nick and Nicole."

"What did ya say?"

"I said, 'yes'."

"Mom! What about Erika?"

"This should be interesting," Jim says before tossing a French fry into his mouth.

"They like each other. Don't they?" Dottie asks.

"They won't after this game," Jim says under his breath.

"You're not helping matters." Dottie looks at Barney. "You treat both of them the same. It'll be okay. Just concentrate on the game."

"Should I call 'em and tell 'em who's gonna be goin' with us?"

"That would be a good idea," Jim says. "That way, one can opt for another day—without the off-the-diamond competition."

So, Barney gets on the phone with Erika. He hangs up. "It's okay with her."

"Well, ya know, one isn't the jealous type." Jim takes another bite of his burger.

Then, Barney calls Nicole. He hangs up. "**DANGIT!**"

Jim chuckles. "She's goin' too? Wow. Two girls who aren't the jealous type. How lucky can I guy get?"

5:35. With Kenny sitting between his parents, Nick and Nicole climb into the backseat of Jim's 1955 Oldsmobile 98 with Barney—Nicole in the middle—close to Barney. Then they pick up Erika. As a gentleman, Barney gets out of the car to let Erika in. "I like your uniform," she says before sitting—next to Nicole. Each extends a curt "Hi" to the other. As they drive to the ballpark, Dottie turns around and initiates a conversation with the girls. Erika joins in. Nicole, usually talkative, says but a word here and there. It is surprising that in the first week of August, the inside of the windshield did not frost over.

As Barney hurriedly joins his teammates in warming up, a wide-eyed David eagerly says, "You brought Erika to the game?" Barney nods, and David asks the obvious, "With Nikki?" Again, Barney nods and David again asks, "So, how did that happen?" Barney tells him, and David says, "Man, I know how Nikki can be. I would **not** like to be in your cleats."

"Believe me, I don't wanna be in my cleats."

Then, Dick trots over. "Hey Barn. You bring Nikki **and** Erika to the game?" Barney answers in the affirmative, and Dick says, "They don't look too happy," seeing Kenny and his parents sitting between the girls. "Man, I wouldn't wanna be in your shoes."

Mikey, overhearing the conversation, asks, "Well, how many of us have two girlfriends?"

"How many of us have one?" David asks.

"Nikki isn't my **girl**—friend." Barney throws the ball back to Tommy—with some heat. "She's my best friend's sister."

"Who has a crush on ya," David says.

"Since kindergarten," Mikey adds.

"**Guys, come on in!**" the coach yells. *THANK YOU, GOD!*

The first time at bat, Barney hits a double. At once, he looks over at his cheering section. Everyone is standing and cheering—except Nicole. She sits with arms crossed, glaring at him. After scoring, Barney sits on the bench next to Dick, who says, "Ya feel the pain in your back?"

"Whadaya mean?"

"From the knife Nikki's stabbin' ya with."

"Real funny."

David adds, "I'd love to be a fly in your car goin' home."

"I'll trade ya."

"I think Barn's gonna be the bug on the windshield," Dick says with a chuckle.

After the game, everyone enthusiastically congratulates Barney on the win and his homer. But the range of enthusiasm is as wide as the Grand Canyon, with Erika standing on Point Imperial and Nicole at the bottom of the Colorado River.

Per tradition, they stop at the Dairy Queen and Jim pays for everyone's favorite ice cream choice. With most stomachs happy, they arrive at the Horton's. Barney gets out of the car, then Erika does. "Thank you for inviting me, Barney," Erika says, then shocks everyone with a kiss on his cheek. "Bye. Good night, Mr. Snodgrass, Mrs. Snodgrass." She runs to the front door, waves, and vanishes in the house.

The silence is deafening as Jim drives home. He stops in his driveway. Nick and Nicole get out of the car. Nick trots across the street. Nicole runs. "Thank you for taking us," Jim says sarcastically. Then he turns to his sons. "If I ever hear either one of you not thanking someone when they do somethin' for ya, I'll thump ya black and blue. Get me?"

"Yes, sir," the boys answer. Then Kenny says, "We thanked you for the ice cream."

"Yes, you did. **They—didn't**. That may be the last time we take 'em."

"Erika said 'thank you,'" Barney says.

"She sure did. I like her."

"Well, Barnard, you cured the dilemma of having two girlfriends."

"Yeah, but I started a fissure between our two families. After that game, the Wainwrights never accepted our invitations to eat barbeque or come over on Sunday evenings to watch Mom's and Mrs. Wainwright's favorite TV program, The Ed Sullivan Show. Mom was really hurt. And they never went with us on Halloween again. But then, that was only for a year or two—since we had to quit when we turned thirteen."

*"For the record, **you** did not start the divide. Nicole did. She could've gotten over having female competition for your attention—and affection. She didn't. **And**—she brought her family into her hurt feelings. Shame on her. Second, the ill feelings of the Wainwrights only lasted that one year. Then things went back to normal. Third, despite Nicole's objections, you and Nick remained best friends. And between you and me—I **would not** handle her reckoning for all the feathers on **two** wings."*

Barnard chuckles. "Well, on one hand, I'm glad someone else is gonna have a rough reckoning, too. On the other, I'm sad it might be Nicole."

"You know, I don't think your reckoning is going so badly."

"You don't?"

"No. But then, we're not finished. And the way your brother is working, we might get to the end."

Barnard sighs. "That gives me a warm and fuzzy…"

Linh sets out the apheresis pack of PLTS as the last of four units of blood transfuse from the bag into Joe's body. Suddenly, the AED whines. "Stand back! Three, two, one, SHOCK!" Linh presses the shock button, and Joe's upper body lunges off the floor—then collapses. "Weak pulse."

"Hook me up."

12:15:44.

18

The Sexy Witch from South America

TUESDAY, 31 October 1961

4:53 p.m. Dusk is setting in the Midwest as Jim arrives home from work.

"Daddy! Why are you so late?" barks an impatient Kenny.

"I'm not late, Robin. Besides, you're not going anywhere until we've had supper.

"But Daddy…"

"But Daddy nothin'. You know what we said. Besides, no other kids are Trick-or-Treatin' yet. They're probably eatin' supper, too. Take my lunch bucket to the kitchen, please." Kenny takes the black metal container, and Jim says, "Thank you."

"You're welcome," a begrudging Kenny replies under his breath.

"Come here," Jim orders. Slowly, his son walks up to him, head bowed like a puppy knowing his tail end is destined for a date with a rolled-up newspaper. "I want you to have a better attitude when you go Trick-or-Treatin'. What are you goin' to say…?"

"Thank you."

"That's right. And I don't want to hear one time that you or you, **Barn**, don't thank those who give you somethin'. Understand?"

"Yes," the boys reply sheepishly.

"And there'll be plenty of treats for you guys whenever you get goin'."

5:00. Jim watches the news. He shakes his head when the newscaster says, "Yesterday, the Soviet Union detonated a 58-

megaton yield hydrogen bomb known as Tsar Bomba. It is the largest man-made explosion to date—more than three thousand times more powerful than the Hiroshima bomb and almost four times larger than the U.S.'s largest blast."

"Good—God!"

"What Daddy?" Kenny asks.

Jim tells him, finally saying, "Thank God we have a bomb shelter." Then, under his breath adds, "Hope it's deep enough."

5:15. The family sits down to a dinner of grilled cheese sandwiches and tomato soup. And before the first bite can be taken, a knock at the door launches the boys out of their chairs.

"Hold it," Jim says. "Barn, that's for you. Kenny, you get the next knock."

"See Daddy. Kids are already Trick-n-Treatin' and all the candy'll be gone by the time…" another knock stops his complaint. He starts for the front door, but Kenny yells, "My turn!" and runs past him.

"When you finish your supper, you can go." Jim watches Barney stuff half of his sandwich triangle in his mouth. "Make sure you chew it good. You don't want to puke when you're out with your friends."

5:30. After five interruptions, everyone has finished their supper. The boys take their dishes to the sink, then say, "Thank you for the dinner, Mommy. It was really good."

Dottie chuckles. "You're welcome. Batman and Robin have very nice manners."

"You're the best cook in the whole wide world," Barney says, "except for maybe Granma. Her meatloaf's really, **really** good. But I like your Red Velvet Cake the best."

Another knock launches Barney ahead of Kenny to the front door to find Dick Tracey and Popeye. "**Trick or Treat!**"

"C'mon in, guys," Barney says. "Dick and David are here."

"How'd you know it was us?" Popeye asks, talking from behind the hard-plastic mask.

"Dick said what you guys were gonna be."

Popeye whacks Tracy on the shoulder. "They were supposed to guess."

"He did," Tracy says, rubbing his shoulder.

"Mom fixed up a special bag for ya." Barney places a small paper lunch sack into their Halloween bags. "There's a caramel apple with nuts and three cookies, so be careful you don't put somethin' heavy on 'em, or they'll break."

"Wow. I love caramel apples," Dick says, his mask on top of his head.

"Thank you, Mrs. Snodgrass, for the treats," David says, and Dick follows suit.

"You're welcome. You kids have fun and watch both ways before you cross the street."

"You have school tomorrow," Jim adds. "So be home by nine."

"We have to be home by nine-thirty," Dick says to Barney.

"Dad? Dick and David can stay out 'til nine-thirty."

"Good for them. You be home by nine sharp. So, you better git."

5:35. The four are out the door and hitting house after house, saying the first set of magic words, receiving treats, then saying the second set of magic words, and feeling good that their father would not hear that they failed in showing their gratitude.

As they work their way west, Barney says, "We need to meet Erika at the ball diamond."

"She's going with us?" an annoyed David blurts.

"She wants to. Why? Don't ya like her? She's nice."

David's no answer does not slow the group from hurrying to the next house.

Along the way, the four meet up with Mikey, Bobby, Willie, and Tommy. Then, at the sandlot, they hear a girl yell, "Hey Batman! Over here." They see two girls standing under the streetlamp.

"Hi, Erika." Barney hurries up to her. "You make a good Snow White." She thanks and compliments him. Then he looks at Galiena. "Wow! You make a **really** good Catwoman."

"Meeeeeow! Mom made it. Kae wanted to be Catwoman because of Robin, but I won Rock, Paper, Scissors. And Catwoman isn't good." She scrapes the air in front of Barney. "She's very, very bad." *Not as bad as The Cat Girl.*

"Is Kaelah here?" an eager Kenny inquires, looking all around.

"No. She's helping Mom hand out candy," Erika says. "But she told me to tell you she's waiting to give you a **very** special treat. And she's got an **awesome** costume!"

"**Really?** You know what it is?"

"Yes. But I can't tell you. It's a surprise. Those are neat bags. Did you decorate 'em?"

"Yeah. It's fingerpaint, so I'm glad it ain't rainin'. I like your buckets," he says of the plastic poison apple and the black cat head.

"They get filled up pretty fast," Erika says, putting her arm across Kenny's shoulder, "so we'll have to stop at my house pretty soon."

"**Really?**"

She chuckles. "Really. About another block or two."

"Well, let's go!"

6:30. Snow White's apple and Catwoman's cat head buckets are heaping with treats with candy, Halloween-decorated cookies, popcorn balls, caramel apples, even money as they make their way to the mansion on top of Davy Crockett Road. With the yellow cape floating behind, Robin runs up the porch steps and rings the doorbell. The door creaks open, and white smoke billows out. When it clears, the boys' jaws drop as they gawk, beguiled, at an angel in black. Only the girls can utter the customary "**Trick or Treat!**" Then, the sisters go inside to dump their loot while their captivating sibling steps onto the porch. Nervous, the boys step back. Suddenly, the black wings unfold and flap. The startled boys jump. Again, they retreat, only the rail stopping them from plunging onto the bed of dormant flowers. A devilish laugh explodes from her mouth, then the wings retract, and she drops candy in everyone's container—except the Dynamic Duo. "Come in, Caped Crusaders, and get your—very—special—treats." She turns, and the beguiled souls follow the red heart at the end of her curly tail.

"Wow," Kenny says, trancelike, as Kaelah leads them into the house. At the stairs, she turns to Barney and points her pitchfork at him. "Stay." A wide-eyed Barney watches Robin follow the angel wearing the black garter sporting a sparkling 666 around her left thigh as they ascend the stairs and walk across the open hall, finally vanishing behind a bedroom door.

A moment later, as if on cue, through the smoke billowing from the dining room walks a witch in black, her pointed hat leaning to the side, a dark mesh veil hanging from its wide brim. Below the hat, long black locks swirl over bare shoulders as if pointing to the deep V-neck, showing cleavage so mouthwatering that even pubescent males drool—in two places. His eyes stare at the spider necklace adorned with diamonds, emeralds, and rubies.

With heart pounding, a lightheaded Batman gawks at the spaghetti-strap minidress with high scalloped slits tickling her hips, showing more leg—legs he sees in his wet dreams. Then, grabbing his attention is the sheer garter of a Black Widow weaving its elaborate web around her left thigh. Strappy high-heeled shoes encase otherwise bare feet with toenails painted blood red.

"Ahhh. Just what I need for my love potion—a delicioso **bat**." Suddenly, a wicked laugh explodes into the house, sending shockwaves through Barney's and the boys' tense bodies. Then, with fingers slowly curling into a soft fist, she beckons Barney to follow. "Come, my little bat." She turns, and with the broom's black wood handle between her thighs, he follows as if helpless to resist the black straw bristles through the white smoke to the living room. There, a dozen champagne-drinking, costumed adults are mingling, laughing, and dancing around a large, black pot to Glenn Miller and His Orchestra's "That Old Black Magic."

Stopping at the bar, she says to the man dressed as Satan, "Mmm. I love to ride a long stick." She fills the house with another blood-curdling laugh, then asks Barney, "You want trick or you want treat?"

"Tr-treat, p-please," a nervous Barney answers, meekly.

"Good decisão, Batman." She lifts the black sheer nylon veil over the floppy wide brim. His eyes bulge as he stares at the grotesque green face with cheeks and chin dotted with white puss-filled sores. Slowly, she leans forward. The long, slender, crooked nose of soft rubber bends to the side. Her puckered lips softly press against his cheek. The touch of her soft lips excites his crotch. **BOING!** Looking into his wide, dilated, watery eyes, she lightly strokes her long fake fingernails along Batman's left cheek. "Happy Halloween, Barnard." She hands him a medium-sized paper bag, stuffed and stapled closed. "I hope you like you treat."

With his right hand touching his cheek, he says, "I will, Mrs. Horton. And you're the prettiest witch I've ever seen." She lets out a wickedly loud laugh before saying, "Obrigado, Barnard. And you a delicioso bat! Now, go get more treats. And take girls with you, por favor."

"Yes, Ma'am. And obrigado for the treat," then adds, shyly, "and the kiss."

"You sweet boy, Barnard." She escorts him to the door. "See you Saturday."

"Yes, Ma'am!"

"I'm—jealous!" the angel growls.

"Why?"

"She had wings! And she isn't even a real angel!"

"But she was a fallen angel."

"Angels are angels. They happen to play for different teams."

"You know, I had forgotten that night. It was really nice goin' back."

*"I do know, and it should've been nice. You got another kiss from your dreamwoman—**WHO WAS THE MOTHER OF YOUR NEW GIRLFRIEND!**"*

*"Well, don't forget—**she kissed me!**"*

"That's your defense?"

Barnard shrugs. "Ya gotta follow your heart?"

"We better celebrate Christmas before the hole gets any deeper."

"Always liked Christmas—well—almost always."

"C'mon." The angel takes Barnard's hand, and they walk into the light.

Linh cleans Ken's left arm before inserting a needle into the artery. Then, she draws his blood into the apheresis machine, which separates the platelets from the blood, then returns the remaining blood back to Ken. The platelets form clots in Joe but diminish the clotting ability in Ken. The rate of transfusion is one pint in fifteen minutes without the donor suffering side effects. However, in a person who is rapidly losing blood—like Joe—the rate of transfusion must be faster.

12:33:00.

<h1 style="text-align:center">19</h1>

The Last Joyous Christmas

MONDAY, 25 December 1961

Barney and Kenny peer out the picture window. Kenny yells, **"Mom, when are they supposed to be here?"**

Jim glares at his youngest. "Hey. Don't yell in the house." He places the last silverware on the dining room table as Dottie answers, "Any time before noon."

"Make sure you go out and help 'em with any packages they bring," Jim says.

A few minutes later, Kenny exclaims, "Grandma and Grandpa are here!"

The boys hurry outside and greet their grandparents with "Merry Christmas," and a hug and kiss, then take the gifts from their car and carry them into the house.

"Merry Christmas, Momma," Jim says, she replying, "Merry Christmas, Chérie." They exchange hugs and kisses. Then he takes a long whiff. "Oh wow! My mouth is watering."

"Merci, Chérie." She takes the rolls into the kitchen and swaps greetings with Dottie.

The boys come into the house and lay the four packages under the very crowded tree as their grandfather enters the house. "Merry Christmas, Jimbo."

"Merry Christmas Pops." They hug each other.

Fifteen minutes later, a black four-door 1960 Lincoln Continental Limousine pulls up at the curb.

"**Kaelah's here!**" An excited Kenny hurries to the front door. With a big smile, he runs down the snow-free driveway to the car as Calista and the girls get out. Barney is close behind.

"Feliz Natal Kenny, Barnard," Calista says. "You boys look muito handsome."

"Thank you, Mrs. Horton," the boys reply. "Merry Christmas to you."

Then the boys and girls exchange "Merry Christmas" before Barney asks, "Is there anythin' we can help ya with?"

"You can carry these," Kaelah says.

Immediately, Kenny runs up to her and grabs the presents. "Your hair's really pretty."

She smiles. "Thank you, Kenny. I like your sweater and bowtie. **Very** dapper."

He beams as he escorts her up the driveway and into the house, the others following, Barney carrying more gifts, Calista and Galiena carrying covered bowls.

Jim greets everyone at the door with, "Merry Christmas. Welcome to our home." Then, with all the guests in the living room, he asks to take their coats. As the boys carry them to their parents' bed, Mr. Stanley Horton introduces himself, as does Jim, and then he introduces Calista and her girls to his parents.

"Yes, I remember you," Grandma Bri says. "Two years ago, you danced at the school's Spring program." She kisses the fingertips of her right hand. "Magnifique! You still dance?"

"Yes Ma'am," Kaelah replies. "Mother teaches dance, and we all help."

"We took dance lessons from Calista and the girls," Jim says. "She's an excellent teacher. And Kaelah is an excellent teacher, too. All the girls are very good ballroom dancers."

"Thank you, Mr. Snodgrass," the smiling girls reply.

Jim looks at Calista. "Dottie and I have been talkin' about learnin' some other dances."

"That would be maravilhoso," she replies as her three girls chuckle.

"What? I wasn't that bad, was I?"

They shake their heads, their smiles quickly turning to grins from their mother's stare.

"Girls," Calista says, "take bowls to kitchen, por favor."

As the boys and girls are admiring the presents under the tree, Dottie stands at the dining room table, taps a wine glass with a butter knife, and announces, "Lunch is served."

The adults take their places at the dining room table according to the small, decorative, handmade Christmas tree tents standing on their plates: Jim and Dottie at the ends with Calista and Grandma flanking her, Grandpa and Stanley flanking Jim.

In the kitchen, Galiena sits at the end with Barney and Erika sitting on one side. Kenny pulls the chair out, and a smiling Kaelah sits. Then, Kenny sits beside her. "Thank you for volunteering to eat in the kitchen," he says.

"You know I want to sit beside you."

He beams.

"Jim, would you please say Grace?" Dottie asks.

"I will!" Kenny quickly volunteers.

"Okay," Jim says.

Everyone holds hands and bows heads, and then Kenny says, "Lord, thank You for the feast You have provided. And thank You for bringing together these very special people to celebrate Your son's one thousand, nine-hundred, and sixty-first birthday. Amen."

"Oh, Kenny! What maravilhoso prayer!" Calista says.

"Yes, it was," Dottie says, smiling. "I thought he was going to say a much shorter prayer."

Jim, Grandpa, Kenny, and Barney chuckle.

"What's so funny?" Erika asks. And just before Barney opens his mouth to answer, Jim says, "Maybe he should save that prayer for supper."

"I want to make a toast," Grandpa says, holding up his glass of Mogan David wine. "You ladies outdid yourselves. To you."

Just before everyone takes a sip of their purplish drinks, Dottie says to Calista, "Don't worry, the kids have grape juice."

"The platter's kinda heavy, so if you'll pass your plates to the left, I'll dish up the ham." Jim places a slice of Dottie's brown sugar and pineapple glazed ham with a helping of her ham and pineapple bread cube stuffing, then hands the plate to his father. They pass the plates clockwise until every plate is full of ham, stuffing, Calista's Brazilian potato salad, and Vinaigrette Salsa, and another dish.

"Mmm, this is delicious," Dottie says. "Calista, what is it?"

She sees what Dottie is referring to and replies, "It is call *Farofa. It muito popular in Brazil. It have* bacon, raisin, sweet corn, chop bell pepper, onion, and green olive. But you can put almost anything you want in it."

"It is very tasty," Bri says.

"I made the potato salad," Erika whispers to Barney, but not quiet enough to escape Galiena's ears.

"**We** made the potato salad," she clarifies, staring across the table.

Erika nudges Barney. "They helped a little."

Barney smiles. "It's delicious. I like it with chunks of potato in it."

"Me too. If it's smooth, it's like mashed potatoes."

After everyone has had their fill of the main course, Dottie and Bri serve the dessert and everyone's eyes widen with excitement.

"This is called Chocolate Bûche de Noël. It is a favorite French dessert," Bri says. "It is a yule log cake made of vanilla genoise cake and covered in chocolate buttercream and sprinkled candy."

"I live for this dessert," Jim says. "Mom's made it ever since I was little."

Dottie and Bri return to their chairs and everyone digs in, chasing the first bite with a collective "Mmmmmm!"

After finishing the meal, the men sit in the living room, visiting while Dottie shows Bri and Calista her sewing projects. The children put the leftovers in the refrigerator and clear off the table, taking the plates and silverware to the sink. Then, Kaelah and Kenny wash the dishes, and Erika and Galiena dry them while Barney puts them away—since he knows where everything goes.

"Jim, get your camera! You have to take a picture of this."

"What's so special?" Jim says, walking into the kitchen with his 35mm camera. "Oh! I should say so! Say cheese!" The kids look at him and CLICK.

"Thank you for cleaning the everything," Dottie says. "Girls, that was very nice of you to help."

"You're welcome, Mrs. Snodgrass," they say. Then, Kaelah adds, "We thought it may need a woman's touch." Dottie, Bri, and Calista laugh.

"I think I hear presents calling," Dottie says.

"Let's go!" Barney leads the stampede into the living room.

The adults sit on the sofa, recliner, and rocking chair while the children sit on the floor, anxiously eyeing the gifts lying under the festively decorated Christmas tree whose red, white, blue, green, and yellow lights flicker in the eyeglasses of Stanley, Jim, and his parents.

"Well, I don't think those presents are going to open themselves," Grandpa says.

"Barn, you do the honors," Jim says. "Serve our guests first. Make sure everyone opens a gift before you give 'em another. And Kenny—don't spoil anyone's surprise."

An eager Barney finds one and hands it to Calista, then Stanley, his grandparents, the girls, and finally his parents and Kenny. As Erika starts to rip off the wrapping paper, Barney says, "Your mom said you collect dolls."

"I do!" She eagerly uncovers a Barbie Doll. "I don't have this one! Thanks, Barney!"

Then, Galiena unwraps Mattel's Charmin' Chatty Doll Stewardess with Travel Set. "I love her! Thank you, Barney! Thank you, Kenny!"

"You're welcome," the boys reply.

Kaelah unwraps *Where the Red Fern Grows* by Wilson Rawls. "I've wanted to read this book, but it's always checked out at the library. Now it's mine! Thank you, Kenny."

"You're welcome." He discovers four Match Box vehicles. "**All right!** Thank you, Kaelah. I don't have these."

Barney opens an Etch-A-Sketch from Erika. And before he can thank her, Erika says, "You like to draw so I thought you'd like this."

Barney nods. "I love it. Thanks, Erika."

Jim and Dottie give Calista a bottle of Brise de France Merlot. She says, "Oh, Merlot is my favorita wine. Obrigado Jim, Dorothy! This is muito expensive. How you get it?"

"I picked up a few bottles in the summer of '45 during a leave at Languedoc, France. That's where the Resistance in Languedoc prevented the Nazis from increasing their stranglehold on France."

"Muito interesting. Muito obrigado," Calista says. "I save it for especial ocasião."

"Mother—English, please," Kaelah says very politely.

"That's okay," Dottie says. "I'd like to learn some Portuguese."

"I be muito happy teach you."

"Maybe your mom'll teach her English," Kaelah says to Kenny under her breath. He grins.

The grandparents give Barney a Duro Pattern & Mold Co. Space Bank, and after thanking them, Barney tells Erika, "I collect banks."

"After we're finished here," Jim says, "you'll have to show her your collection."

Jim and Dottie give Grandpa Joe a chisel set, which lights up his face with an ear-to-ear smile. And they give Bri a set of handmade doilies and scented candles.

The grandparents give Kenny a chess set. Kenny stares at the pieces then begins to cry.

"What's wrong?" Grandpa asks. "Don't you like it?"

Kenny stands and walks to his grandfather and wraps his arms around his neck. "I love it." He cries.

Grandpa chuckles and rubs Kenny's back. "Hey. I'm glad you like it, Kiddo. We'll have to play a game later. Okay?"

Sniffling, Kenny wipes his eyes, nods, then returns to his place on the floor. Kaelah pats him on the back. "I'll play ya a game, too."

He timidly glances at Kaelah. "You play chess?"

"Uh-ha. And I'm pretty good, too. So, you better watch out."

Kenny grins. "Grandpa made this."

"**Really?**" Kaelah picks up the queen and her jaw drops and eyes almost pop out of their sockets. "It's beautiful." She strokes the board. "Wow! Mr. Snodgrass, you should have a shop and sell these."

"Pops, what did I say?"

"Fairs are enough."

Jim and Dottie give Barney Hartland Baseball figures Stan Musial, Duke Snider.

Jim and Dottie give Kenny a 1:18 scale diecast replica of a 1960 Ford Thunderbird Hard Top. Kenny wrinkles his nose and exclaims, "It's pink!"

Kaelah says, "It's pretty. I like it."

Kenny says, "Well—I guess I do, too. Thanks, Mommy. Thanks, Daddy."

"Boy, am I glad you're here, Kaelah," Jim says, and almost everyone chuckles.

Lastly, Dottie opens an envelope from Calista and pulls out a coupon. "Oh yes! Thank you, Calista."

"What is it?" Jim asks.

"It's for ten free dance lessons to learn Cha-cha and Rumba."

"Cha-cha lively, flirtatious, full of passion and energy," Calista says. "Rumba romantic and sensual, slow tempo, muito easy learn."

Jim smiles. "Now I know why the girls were smilin' when I said Dottie and I were thinkin' of takin' more classes."

"Yes. I no want them let cat out of bag," Calista says, shaking her finger at them.

"Momma, Pops, sounds like those are somethin' you'd like."

Joe looks at his mother and flicks his eyebrows twice. "Feelin' frisky, mon amour?"

Smiling, Bri shakes her head. "Don't know if we can do the Cha-cha, but the Rumba…" Her eyes widen friskily.

"Calista's a really good teacher," Jim says, and Dottie nods. "Dottie and I had lots of fun learnin' the Foxtrot and refining the Waltz. Think about it. In ten weeks, you'll be Fred and Ginger."

"Boys, why don't you show the girls your collections?" Dottie says.

"Okay." Kenny grabs Kaelah's hand and leads her into his bedroom. Galiena, Erika, and Barney follow. He points to the walnut shelf. "These are my die-cast cars. This one's a one-twenty-fourth scale 1956 Ford Thunderbird Convertible. It's my favorite. This one's a one-eighteenth-scale 1947 Cadillac Series 62 Cabriolet. It was the first car Daddy bought when he got out of the Army. This is a one-eighteenth-scale 1948 Ford F-1 Pickup. Grampa bought this when Daddy got out of the Army. This one's a one-sixty-fourth scale 1940 Willys MB Jeep. Daddy drove one like this after the war ended." Then he places his Christmas gift on the shelf, then shakes his head. "Don't know why Mommy got me a pink Thunderbird, even though I love Thunderbirds."

Kaelah places a consoling hand on his shoulder. "I like it. Pink's my favorite color."

Kenny smiles. "Wanna see my baseball cards?"

"Erika, Galiena, wanna see my Horse and Riders?" Barney asks.

"Sure." The two girls follow Barney downstairs into his bedroom. He turns on the light. "Wow! This is neat!" Erika takes a close look at the planes hanging from the ceiling over his bed, and posters showing the histories of aviation, automobile, and train. "You like history."

"Yeah." Barney describes his metal space banks on one shelf and the dozen horse and riders and baseball players standing, taking up most of two other shelves. "Grampa made the shelves. He made the coffee table upstairs, the shelves in Kenny's room, a jewelry box he gave Mom for her birthday a couple of years ago, and something else. But I can't remember it. **Oh**! I remember. Man, I can't believe I forgot this. He made a case for Daddy to display his medals from the war."

"I'd like to see them," Erika says.

Barney shakes his head. "He put the case in his closet and hasn't taken it out. It's still empty."

"Why?"

Barney shakes his head and shrugs, then names the Horse and Riders. "This is Roy Rogers and Trigger."

"And that's Dale Evans and Buttermilk," Erika says. "I always watched their show. I love cowboy shows."

"Me too! I'm sorry it ain't on anymore. This is—."

"Matt Dillon and Buck," Erika interrupts, then shrugs. "Sorry. I never miss *Gunsmoke*."

Barney smiles. "You know the rest of these?"

Erika looks at each one, then says, "That's Wyatt Earp. Everyone knows his Buntline Special. I **love** Hugh O'Brien. He's so handsome. And I never miss *Life and Legend of Wyatt Earp*." Then Erika puts her hands over her heart as she gasps. "**Oh**! I **adore** James Garner. We should watch *Maverick* together, I mean, if you want to."

"Sure! That would be neat. He's one of my favorite actors."

"That's Paladin from *Have Gun will Travel*, but I don't know the horse's name. I don't watch it that often—not like *Maverick* and *Wyatt Earp*."

"Rafter."

Erika nods before turning her attention to the baseball players and immediately exclaims, "**Don Drysdale!** You know the Dodgers are my favorite team."

"I know. Can you tell who my favorite team is?"

"I knew the Yankees were your favorite when the Pirates beat them in last year's World Series."

Barney shakes his head. "Let's promise to **never** mention that series again. Please."

Erika grins. "Okay." She looks at the four Yankees. "Mickey Mantle, Babe Ruth, Yogi Berra, and Roger Maris. You've got the big hitters."

"Mickey and Willie—are my heroes."

"I know who Willie Mays is. The Say Hey Kid. The Giants have beaten my Dodgers too many times."

"You have a lot of planes," Galiena says.

"Yeah. Mom thinks too many. I agree when I havta dust 'em." The girls chuckle before he names each one. Then centers on three. "This is the P-51D Mustang. My Uncle Frank flew this, protecting our bombers when they bombed Germany. He became an Ace shooting down these German planes, a Messerschmitt Bf-109K-4, and Focke Wulf Fw-190A-6."

"How do you become an Ace?" Galiena asks.

"When a pilot shoots down five enemy planes. My uncle was a double Ace. He was two planes short of becoming a triple Ace when he was shot down over Germany. They've never found his body, but we decorate his grave anyway."

"What's this?" Erika asks, looking at the door next to the bedroom door.

"My bathroom."

She opens the door and looks inside. "I have one, too."

"No, you don't," Galiena says. "We share a bathroom."

"Still mine when I use it."

"Nice bedroom," Galiena says, walking out of the room.

"Thanks. Ya wanna play Ping Pong?"

"Sure," Erika answers, and Galiena says, "I'll see if Kenny and Kaelah want to." She goes upstairs as Erika and Barney get the paddles and balls. A minute later, Galiena returns. "They'll be down in a minute. Kenny's about to 'mate her."

Barney grins. *He'd like to.* He stands the girls in a friendly game, just hitting the ball over the net so the opponent can easily return it. Then Kaelah walks into the rec room, Kenny following. "He kicked my you-know-what," she says, and Kenny chuckles. Then she points her forefinger at him and says, "But it's not nice to tell your opponent where she went wrong." Kenny's eyes get big. Then Kaelah chuckles. "I'm kidding. Any chance you'd teach me how to play better?"

"Sure!" Then he wipes his dry brow. "For a second, I thought you were mad at me."

"For a second I was—when you said 'checkmate' and I was just getting started."

Everyone laughs.

"Get used to it, Kaelah," Barney says. "Dad and I can't beat him, either. Who wants to play?"

"Kaelah and I will stand Erika and Galiena," Kenny blurts out. "If that's okay."

Barney watches as the four play a less friendly game of ping pong, especially between the girls. "Kenny, watch out," he says. "I think they play for blood."

"We're a bit competitive," Galiena says, hitting the ball over the net, and Kenny returns it, saying, "I think Kaelah and I can take 'em."

"Want to put some money on it?" Galiena asks as the game continues.

"How much?" he asks.

"Each loser pays each winner a dollar," Galiena says. "You win or lose at most two dollars. So, whadaya say, hot shot?"

Kenny looks at Kaelah, who nods. "I'm up for it. But it's up to you."

"Barn?" Kenny asks.

"Do we play round-robin?"

The girls answer, "Yes!" almost in unison.

"Okay," Barney says. "May the best and oldest man win."

A long and loud "BOO!" rushes out of four mouths. Barney makes up the table to keep track of who wins and who loses. Then, they draw playing cards to see who plays the first game. It is decided that the highest two cards play the lowest two cards.

After the ten games to eleven, a laughing Kenny rushes upstairs as the other four look at each other. "I can't believe he won **every— single**—game," Erika says. "**Every** game."

Barney shakes his head as he puts up the paddles and balls. "The li'l shit's good at everythin'." The girls laugh. "And don't play him in any memory games, like *Concentration*. He forgets **nothin'**."

"Well, Gal, at least **we** didn't lose any money." Kaelah smiles arrogantly at her little sister.

"Guess we better go upstairs and get the braggin' outta the way." Barney sighs.

Sure enough, as the quartet walks into the kitchen, they hear Kenny saying, "Shoulda seen me! I beat 'em all. My backhand was perfect." They stop at the entrance of the dining room and listen as Kenny continues, "Erika's pretty good even though she lost three games—like Barney." He laughs. "I think he let Erika win her game." Again, he laughs mockingly. "I'll **never** let anyone win—at anything." Then he thinks for a moment. "Maybe I should've let Kaelah win. She probably doesn't like me anymore."

Galiena nudges Kaelah in the ribs. "Go," she whispers, and the group walks into the living room.

"Kenny teach you how to play ping pong?" Calista asks, smirking.

"We let him win," Kaelah answers, and Kenny bursts out laughing. "I mean, he's so little. If we all beat him, he'd cry that we ganged up on him." Kenny's mouth drops as he stares, dumbfounded, at the girl of his dreams. Then Kaelah grins and steps over and gives Kenny a hug. "Yeah, you're pretty good—for a little guy."

Everyone laughs.

"Rock 'Em Sock 'Em Robots, anybody?" a wide-eyed Kenny asks.

Barney and the girls look at each other, then shrug.

"I get first dibs," Kaelah says, giving Kenny a daring stare. "But no betting!"

Everyone laughs. He then stares back at her as they make their first bout a staring match. The other three watch closely to see who blinks first. Then, everyone moans as they see the fleeting dimple crease on Kaelah's left cheek.

"How do you do that?" she asks, shaking her head. "It was like you were in a trance."

"He was," Barney says, and Kenny punches him on the arm, which gains Jim's rebuke, "Hey, let the robots do the punchin'."

As the men watch the kids' red and turquoise robots box until one head is knocked off its shoulders, Jim says, "Stanley, looks like we're gettin' deeper into Vietnam."

"I know. A couple weeks ago, we sent the first helicopters to Saigon with 400 personnel."

"Just the other day, the first American soldier was killed."

"Yeah. I'm glad I don't have any sons. Sorry. I wasn't thinking."

"No problem. I hope that war'll be over before Barn's eighteen." Jim shakes his head. "I just can't believe any war would last seven years."

And like the ping pong tournament, Kenny defeats Barney, Erika, and Galiena. Then Kaelah steps into the ring and grasps the controls. With the same daunting stare, she waits for Barney to say, "Go!" With a one-two punch, the red robot's head pops up, Kenny's jaw drops, and Barney yells, "**Kenny got beat by a girl!**" However, instead of boasting about her victory, Kaelah says, "Nice game," and holds out her arms for a hug, which the defeated cannot resist.

"Now that's sportsmanship," Jim says. "Good job, Kaelah."

"Thank you, Mr. Snodgrass." Then she looks at Kenny. "Rematch?"

The robots get more of a workout, and everyone gets a taste of victory.

At five o'clock, Dottie announces, "Dinner's ready," and everyone takes their place around the two tables. Then she asks, "Barney, would you please say Grace?"

"Yes, Mommy." He puts his hands together and waits until everyone has bowed their heads, then he says, "Grace. Amen."

Everyone laughs, especially the Hortons and the girls. Dottie does not. Staring at her oldest, she shakes her head. "I should've known. If it isn't one, it's the other." Again, laughter fills the house. Then she turns to Calista. "We usually eat leftovers for supper."

"We do! Some food better next day."

"Who wants to watch some movies after supper?" Jim asks, passing the plate of ham.

"Movies?" Galiena takes a serving of potato salad.

"They're eight-millimeter black and white silent cartoons."

"I'd like to see them," Erika says. "Mom, can we?"

"They're only about five minutes long or so," Jim says. "And there's four or five."

"Okay."

By six o'clock, bellies are full, the dishes washed and put away, and everyone is in the living room—the adults sitting on the sofa and chairs, the kids on the floor. Then, for the next hour, two Popeye cartoons, Laurel and Hardy, Our Gang, Kiko the Kangaroo, and a couple of Walt Disney cartoons thoroughly entertain the audience.

Calista stops laughing. "James, that was maravilhoso!" Her husband and daughters agree and thank him. "Where you get this film?"

"I bought 'em here and there. My plan was, after the war, to open an antique shop."

"Oh, you want sell those beautiful things you brought from Europe?"

"That was the plan. Hopefully, by next Christmas, I'll open a store—God willin' and the creek don't rise."

"What creek?" Calista asks.

Jim, Dottie, and Grandpa chuckle before Bri says, "Yes. It stumped me, too, until Jim told me. It's an expression that means a person is hoping God will help and nothing will prevent the success of the plan."

Calista nods. "God willing, and creek no rise."

"Exactly," Jim says, grinning.

"If you want to sell anything now, a couple thing caught my eye."

An hour later, as the grandparents exchange pleasantries with Stanley, Calista, and the girls, the boys retrieve their coats.

"If you no have plan for New Year Eve," Calista says to the grandparents, "please come to our house. We love have you. James and Dorothy and boys coming." She looks at them. "Yes?"

"We can't wait," Dottie quickly answers before Jim can open his mouth.

"Excelente! You no bring food. We have finger-food about six o'clock."

Grandpa says, "We can't come empty-handed. You tell Dottie what we can bring."

Calista nods as Barney helps Erika on with her coat. "What a cavalheiro!"

"Mother—gentleman," Kaelah says calmly but sternly as Kenny stands behind her, holding her coat. Then she turns and, seeing him, smiles. "Thank you, Kenny. You're a—cavalheiro, too." She looks at her mother, whose disapproving stare turns into a faint grin.

"You're welcome. I'm glad you came." He gets Galiena's coat as Barney assists Calista on with hers.

"Obrigado, Barney." As she buttons her beige chinchilla coat, she says, "You should be proud of you boys. They are perfeito gentleman."

"Thank you for saying that," Dottie replies. "They're not perfect—they are boys."

Everyone chuckles except the boys.

Then Erika leans over and whispers to Barney, "I think you're kinda perfect—except for the Yankees." She smiles. "Thank you for the Barbie. I hope to collect every one that comes out, like your cowboys and baseball players."

The guests thank the Snodgrasses for their gifts, and they, in turn, thank them.

Then, before they leave, Bri says, "Calista, I would love to have the recipe for that *Farofa.*"

"I happy you enjoy it. I give to Dorothy."

Jim, Dottie, and the boys escort the Hortons and the girls to their car, the boys helping carry gifts. Per custom, leftovers stay with the host.

"Next Friday, Kenny, we play Pool," Kaelah says in a challenging tone.

"I've never played Pool, so you'll have to teach me."

She grins. "Oh, I'll teach you alright."

They laugh before she joins her mother and sisters in the car. As they drive off, the Snodgrasses and Hortons wave at each other.

"Boy, it's cold out here," Dottie says, rubbing her arms as she rushes into the house.

"Dear, ya don't know what cold is." Jim closes the door after his boys come in. "Bastogne, Belgium, December 20th to the 27th." He sits in his recliner. "I've never felt colder."

"What happened, Daddy?" Kenny asks, squeezing beside him.

"The Battle of the Bulge," Barney answers. "The 101st Airborne, the Screamin' Eagles, kept the Nazis from takin' the town that a lot of roads came into."

"Thanks, Barn. I'll just say it was so cold—uh—well—," he clears his throat and looks at the flashing lights on the Christmas tree, "uh—frostbite took a lot of guys' fingers and feet—and uh—took a lot of guys."

"Kenny, I'll take the blue robot," Grandpa says, hoping to change the atmosphere.

"Okay!" Kenny quickly kneels on the opposite side of the coffee table and grabs the control handles.

"You like Kaelah," Grandpa says. As a wide-eyed Kenny nods, Grandpa punches and the red head flops back.

"Hey! That's cheatin'," Kenny protests. "You didn't say, 'Go'!"

Grandpa shrugs. "Go."

This time, Kenny is quicker at the jab, and the blue head springs up.

Then, just before they can start their third bout, Grandma says, "Joseph, we should go."

"Okay. Right after," BAM, BAM. The red robot's head jerks back.

"Grandpa!" Kenny exclaims. "I wasn't ready."

"The first rule of fighting—ALWAYS be ready." Grandpa looks at Barney. "That goes for both of ya when it comes to that bully."

"I know. Daddy's already told us."

"Is he still pickin' on you two?"

"Not as much since Daddy knocked the crap out of Charlie's dad."

"I didn't knock the crap outta him," Jim corrects. "I hit him, and he was smart enough to stay down." He taps Barney on the shoulder. "That's what you need to do next time he picks on you or your li'l brother."

"Can we practice before we go to bed?" Kenny asks.

Jim shakes his head. "After I read the paper tomorrow morning."

"Promise?"

Jim grins and says the magic word.

"That was a fun Christmas. We got to know Calista and her family, and they got to know us."

"The men seem to get along swimmingly."

Barnard nods. "And the women. Mom was proud to show Granma and Calista her latest sewing project. Calista was really happy that everyone was going to her home for New Year's Eve. Dad was delighted that Calista and Kaelah knew how to play Bridge and suggested a night they could get together for a game."

"She put you to work on the Saturday before New Year's Eve."

"Did she ever! I knew she had a mansion, but I had no idea it was so big—with so much wood to clean—baseboards, trim around doors and windows, not to mention the floor. But enough about cleanin'. Where to next?"

The angel takes his hand. "May 22nd."

When she starts to walk towards the blackness, he does not move. She looks into his eyes. "I know. But you must. Come on. I'll be with you every second—like I was thirty-seven years ago."

*"Well, you sure did a bang-up job then. Didn't ya, Angel? **C'mon, Kenny. Stop workin' on me. Let me die. Please!**" Then, he looks at the angel. "Let's go somewhere else. Please. Anywhere else."*

The angel holds his hand. "You know we can't. This moment changed you—changed you dramatically."

"You don't think I know that?"

"Barnard. I'll help you get through this. But—."

*"**Like ya did the first time? Hellava job, Angel! It was wing-worthy.**"*

The angel stares at him. "I understand how you feel."

*"**Of course you do! You know everything!**"*

She stares at him for a moment. "If you're finished with your temper tantrum…"

*"**I'M NOT HAVIN' A TEMP**—well, maybe…"*

"I was with you. You didn't do what you wanted to do." As Barnard contemplates his next words, the angel says, "And I'm with you now. In

Sixty-two, you didn't know the full story. Now you will—if you want."

"I knew it then!" Barnard barks. "They told us what happened." Then he shakes his head and sighs. "Ahhh shit. Let's get this over with."

Together, they walk into the blackness.

One-half pint of blood has been transferred.

"How you feel?"

"Fine. Wish the ambulance would get here."

"I see if OJ in fridge."

"Call 9-1-1 again. Tell 'em to get a move on."

12:50.

20

Lives Forever Changed

MONDAY, 21 May 1962

6:04 p.m. Central Daylight Time. The phone rings, and Kenny runs to answer. "Hello? **Daddy**! You on the way home? No? Why? Oh. Okay. I finished *The Great Crusade*. It was **really** good. Tomorrow I'll give a book report on it. So, did you meet General Eisenhower? **WOW!** That's cool. Of course. From 1953 to 1961. Okay. Here's Mommy. Love ya."

"So, did I understand you're not coming home tonight?" Dottie sits on the chair beneath the wall phone and listens. "Oh, that's nice. I hope you enjoy the game, too. You know, all work and no play makes Jim a cranky guy." She chuckles. "The boys'll be disappointed. But what's another day? Right? He is." She looks at her oldest as she puts her hand over the transmitter. "Barney, Daddy wants to talk to you."

"I'm busy," he says, bluntly.

"Barney, you haven't spoken to Daddy since he left."

"I don't care."

"He's gluing his plane together. Yes, he's still mad. Pouting like a little baby. I know. Pretty childish for a twelve-year-old boy who'll be in the seventh-grade next year," she says more for her son's ears than her husband's. "Okay. Enjoy your visit and the game. Bye." She hangs up.

"Daddy's not coming home tonight," Kenny says.

"No. He's at the Tigers-White Sox ballgame with a war buddy. Tomorrow night he'll come home. Be here around midnight or one o'clock." Then she stares at Barney. "I'm very disappointed in you." Receiving no response, she adds, "I have a notion to take away your TV privileges until school's out." Seeing that he still ignores her, she says, "Okay. No television for you until after Memorial Day—and no playing after school with your friends."

"**What?**" He glares at her.

"So, you did hear what I said. Good. You know what your punishments are."

"That's not fair!"

"I'll tell you what's not fair, young man—you not speaking to your father. It was wrong for you breaking your airplane."

"I bought it with my own money. I can do anything I want with it, including crashing it!"

"You didn't crash it! You broke it in a fit of rage. Your father is teaching you to respect your property, especially what you buy with your hard-earned money. Now, take your work in the kitchen so you can't watch television."

In a huff, Barney folds the newspaper in half, capturing the loose parts, and carries it to the kitchen, where he lays it on the table, then flops down on the chair and resumes repairing Revell's 1/32 scale German WWII Junkers JU 87-B Stuka Dive Bomber.

6:30. Kenny pushes the channel button, and the dial clicks to ABC. He watches *Cheyenne*.

7:30. He watches *The Rifleman*.

8:00. He goes to his bedroom to finish his homework while his mother watches *The Danny Thomas Show*.

8:30. She watches *The Andy Griffith Show* on CBS.

9:00. After completing his sixth-grade math homework, he joins his mother to watch *Ben Casey* on ABC. Forty minutes later, Kenny looks at the clock sitting on the television. "Daddy would be landing in K.C. about now—if he was coming home tonight."

"Yes," Dottie says. "Bedtime after this show."

10:00. As Kenny prepares for bed, Dottie watches the local news.

Without saying anything, Barney dumps the loose parts in the plane's box and starts to go downstairs to his bedroom.

"Barney. Come here."

Leaning on the kitchen/dining room archway, he stares, indignantly, at her.

"Tonight, I want you to think about how you're acting. You should not be mad at your father, not this long. You were wrong to break your plane, and he was right to discipline you. He could've punished you in so many different ways. But this way should teach you not to lose your temper—especially on minor stuff—and value what you have."

"I bought it with **my** money and I can do what **I** want with it."

"You're right. But those pieces could've hit your brother in the eye. He was sitting right there." She points to where her youngest was sitting. "I think that's the main reason Daddy punished you. So, think about what you're going to do tomorrow when he calls. Good night."

Barney turns and goes downstairs without replying.

Barnard bows his head, tears and snot flowing. "God, please forgive me for I did not honor my father. Dad," he bursts into tears, "please forgive me for gettin' mad at ya. Please."

The angel wraps her arms around his neck. She says nothing. Sometimes there is no need for words.

3:42 p.m. CT. As Joe and his friends are walking home from school, Continental Airlines Flight 4, tail number N70775, a Boeing 707-120, takes off from LAX in Los Angeles, California, to begin its 2,028-mile flight to O'Hare International Airport in Chicago, Illinois.

4:15 p.m. After the boys get home from school, Kenny rides his bike to the park to play ball with the gang while Barney stays home to serve out his sentence. In his room, he works on his schoolwork—until he hears the purring of a very enticing kitten.

Meanwhile, Flight 4, at a cruising speed of 500 mph, is just south of Las Vegas, Nevada.

6:00. While Flight 4 is just crossing the Kansas-Nebraska border between Topeka and Lincoln, Dottie and the boys are devouring a delicious dinner their mother has prepared.

6:30. As Flight 4 passes south of Des Moines, Iowa, Dottie tasks Barney with washing the dishes while Kenny sits in the living room to watch *Combat!* on ABC.

6:45. With the dishes washed and put away, Barney retires to his bedroom to finish his homework and continue gluing his model together as Flight 4 makes its final approach to O'Hare International Airport.

7:13. Kenny is three-fourths through watching *Combat!* when Continental Airlines Flight 4 lands at O'Hare.

There, the plane receives routine service and inspection for the return flight to L.A. as Flight 11, with a temporary stop at Kansas City, Missouri. No important anomalies are found, and the aircraft is deemed airworthy. Its scheduled departure time is 8:35. Its scheduled arrival time in K.C. is 9:36.

8:07. Jim arrives at the airport and checks in at the counter. After buying his ticket, he walks to a payphone, deposits the correct change according to the scale listed on the placard, and calls home.

The phone rings, and Kenny runs to answer. "Hello. **Daddy!** I got all A's on my tests today! I know. And Mrs. Morgan said that's what I'm getting on my grade card. **Five dollars!** Don't know about him, but I've been good. Just ask Mommy." Dottie steps up to her youngest. "Mommy wants to talk to ya. Okay. Love ya. Bye." He gives the phone to her and runs into the living room and flops down on the sofa to continue watching *Hawaiian Eye* on ABC.

"So, how was your visit last night?" Dottie asks. "That's good. Hopefully we'll see him and his family at the reunion in three years. And the game? Oh, my mouth is watering. I can smell 'em from here. Maybe we can all go to Kansas City when the Yankees are there. Well, I'd go for the hotdogs." She chuckles. "**You did?**" Okay, I won't. So, you'll be home around midnight? Okay. I won't stay up. Oh yes, the weather's wonderful." Barney walks into the kitchen, and she holds the phone out to him. "You're up. It's Daddy." As he reluctantly comes to the phone, Dottie says, "See you tonight. Have a safe trip home."

"Hi," Barney says, halfheartedly. "Yeah. She said I'm gettin' A's and B's, but didn't tell me how many. Guess she wants it to be a surprise. You did? Who won? Really? Three homers. Both shortstops? Wow. You know I have Rocky's and Luis' figures. Yeah, I glued the pilot so he won't come out." He takes a deep breath. "Sorry, I lost my temper. Yeah. I should value what I have. Yeah. Okay. See ya tomorra. Bye."

*With hands covering his face, Barnard cries uncontrollably, and the angel tries to comfort him. "I should've said I loved him. **That was the only time I didn't!** GODDAMNIT! Please. Please, let's go somewhere else. I can't relive this! Please."*

Barney walks into the living room where Dottie is reading a Better Homes and Garden magazine. "I'm done with the plane."

She looks up at him. "I'm glad you talked to Daddy. Sounds like you grew up during the night."

He shrugs, then Kenny asks, "What aren't you gonna tell us?"

She grins. "You'll find out tomorrow."

"Top secret?" Barney gives her a kiss on the cheek. "Good night."

"Good night, Honey. Sleep tight. Don't let the bedbugs bite."

"What are bedbugs, anyway?"

As if reading directly from the dictionary, Kenny says, "It's a wingless bloodsucking hemipterous bug sometimes infesting houses and especially beds and feeding on human blood."

"**Gross!**" Barney's eyes squint. "Now how am gonna sleep?"

"You don't have bedbugs," Dottie says, emphatically. "You didn't have them last night, and you don't have them tonight. So, sweet dreams."

"Why didn't ya say that?" As Barney heads for the kitchen, he says, "Good night, Mister Webster."

"They'll only nibble on ya the first night." Kenny chuckles as his mother gives him a disapproving stare, then shakes her head, grinning.

8:15. Jim checks his suitcase at the counter and carries on board his briefcase. Along with his business papers is the autographed Tigers-White Sox program. He stores the briefcase in the overhead bin and sits in the seat next to the exit door above the wing because it has a little extra legroom, a godsend for his ailing knee, arthritis from a war wound. After fastening his seatbelt, he stretches his legs, then opens Harper Lee's 1961 Pulitzer Prize-winning novel, "To Kill a Mockingbird," moves the bookmark to the back of the book, and begins reading where he left off the night before.

8:25. At the airport gate, a man buys a $75,000 life insurance policy for $2.50. He now has policies worth $300,000. Then the married man and father of a darling five-year-old daughter rushes through the terminal to the Continental gate where Flight 11 has closed its doors. Per the airline's policy, once the aircraft doors close, they are not reopened. However, on this night, one passenger arrives late at the gate. In violation of their policy, Continental personnel reopen the doors and allow the man to board. As the captain and first and second officers go through the preflight checklist for the Boeing 707-124, the four stewardesses, dressed in dark A-line skirts and jackets, and red berets, make sure the thirty-seven passengers are comfortable and ready for takeoff.

8:35. Kenny begins watching *The Untouchables* on ABC as Capt. Fred Gray, 50, guides Continental Airlines Flight 11 down one of O'Hare's runways, on schedule, and into the air just as the U.S. Weather Bureau issues a severe weather warning.

Its gross takeoff weight and center of gravity are well within set limits. It is the crew's last scheduled flight of the night back to Los Angeles, with a brief stop in Kansas City at 9:35.

The night sky sparkles with stars as Flight 11 cruises smoothly to its prescribed altitude.

8:40. Forecasting heavy thunderstorms, with a ceiling of 50,000 feet, between Chicago and Kansas City, the U.S. Weather Bureau renews the severe weather warning, predicting heavy thunderstorms with severe to extreme turbulence and the possibility of tornadoes.

Flight 11 is heading directly into an active cold front and prefrontal squall line.

8:52. The pilot requests and is granted a slight course correction to avoid the storm cell. Then, after reaching an altitude of 39,000 feet over Bradford, Illinois, Flight 11 heads due west.

9:01. Just east of the Mississippi River, the pilot asks Chicago Air Route Traffic Control Center if it has a radar picture of the storm. They do not. Chicago hands the flight over to the Flight Following Radar Site at Waverly, Iowa.

9:02. Flight 11 requests information concerning the storm area. The Waverly controller says the flight can divert north or south, and suggests the southerly route. The captain chooses to go north. The plane passes to the north of the storm and experiences some minor turbulence.

Moments later, the controller informs the pilot of a direct course to Kirksville, Missouri, that will miss all inclement weather. The crew replies they are starting the turn, and requests clearance direct to Kansas City. The Waverly controller informs the captain that they are processing the descent clearance.

9:11. The aircraft finally flies out of the turbulence and turns from a magnetic heading of 270 degrees (90 degrees to the left) to a heading of 247 degrees (113 degrees to the left). Holding this heading for approximately thirty seconds, it turns further left to 230 degrees. Finally, descent clearance is granted as the man who came in late gets up and walks to the rear lavatory. The crew announces to the passengers the upcoming normal descent to an altitude of 36,800 feet.

9:14 Waverly informs Flight 11 that they are unable to contact Kansas City. The captain replies, "Okay, we can probably reach them on your radio, do you want to send us over?" It is the last transmission from Flight 11.

9:15 A flight attendant knocks on the restroom door. "Sir, please return to your seat. We're about to begin our descent." The plane is twenty-two minutes from Kansas City. The man places six sticks of dynamite he bought for $1.74 two weeks prior in the used towel bin beneath the sink of the right rear lavatory, lights the short rope fuse, sits on the toilet, and watches the flame quickly travel to its catastrophic detonation.

9:17. The explosion blows off the aft thirty-eight feet of the tail section, sucking the bomber, the flight attendant, and six passengers into the cold air more than seven miles above the ground. Debris begins fluttering to earth, including human parts. The remaining structure, violently pitching nose down, spins uncontrollably towards earth. Its four Pratt and Whitney jet powerplants rip off the wings, which they are designed to do to reduce or eliminate fire in the event of emergency landings—or rapid descents.

9:20. Witnesses in the proximity of Cincinnati, Iowa, and Unionville report to authorities of hearing loud, unfamiliar noises. One thinks it is thunder. Two witnesses see a large flash and a short-lived fireball in the sky.

9:22. The commander of a B-47 Stratojet Bomber flying out of Forbes Air Force Base in Topeka, Kansas, is flying at an altitude of 26,500 ft. in the vicinity of Kirksville, Missouri, when he sees a bright flash in the sky forward and above his position.

Swift decompression causes fog in the cabin. The flight crew initiates the emergency descent procedures and dons their smoke masks. The plane continues disintegrating as the Waverly controller finally establishes contact with Kansas City Center and tries to transfer Flight 11's radar to them. They also attempt to contact Flight 11 for them to establish communications with Kansas City. They are unsuccessful. Finally, Waverly attempts to identify Flight 11's radar target location to the Kansas City Center. The Kansas City controller briefly observes a vague target about ten miles south of the intersection of Airways J45V and J64V, moving in a southerly direction. However, after two sweeps of the antenna, the signature disappears.

9:24. Three miles south of the Iowa border, and about six miles north-northwest of Unionville, Missouri, and one-and-a-half miles west of State Highway No. 5, Continental Flight 11, tail number N70775, crashes into an alfalfa field at a twenty-degree angle, the nose screwing into the ground. With part of the left and most of the right wing intact, the fuselage telescopes just aft of the cockpit. Passengers and flight attendants smash against seats, finally piling on top of each other toward the front of the aircraft. The remaining badly broken fuselage does not telescope. There are no drag marks down the hill. The landing gear is down and locked per emergency descent procedures. Wing flaps are up to maintain as much lift as possible during the rapid descent.

Still clutching the controls in a futile attempt to avoid the inevitable, the pilot and his first officer have done everything their training has taught them to do. They did their jobs.

9:30. *The Untouchables* conclude, and Kenny gives his mother a kiss on the cheek. "Good night, Mom. Love ya."

"Love you, too, Sweetie. Good night. Sleep tight. Don't—." He stares at her, and they both burst out laughing.

Dottie watches *Chet Huntley Reporting* on NBC.

10:02. As usual, Dottie is watching the local news. They know nothing of the crash. The Kansas City air traffic control calls the Federal Aviation Administration's Office of Accident Investigation and Prevention about Flight 11 being twenty-four minutes late and missing from radar.

With his bedroom door closed and locked, Barney sits at his desk, gazing at his favorite photo of his other dream woman, Lilly Christine. With his right hand, he slowly strokes his erection until he climaxes into the facial tissue he holds in front of his budding manhood. Then he washes and goes to bed. Lucky for him, the image of The Cat Girl chases away any thoughts of creepy crawly critters.

10:15. Witnesses and townspeople rush to the crash site in hopes of finding survivors. Two men bring large pieces of twisted aluminum to the Centerville, Iowa, sheriff's office.

A Centerville doctor is alerted and hurries to the crash site. He is a volunteer medical examiner with the FAA. From experience, he knows how crucial it is in assuring evidence is preserved and deterring souvenir hunters from carting off pieces of the wreckage.

In Cincinnati, Iowa, someone finds a blood-splattered lavatory door. On the door is the Continental eagle logo. Sandwiches, pillows, napkins, and other debris are scattered for miles along with a thirty-foot section of one wing. The lavatory door smells like a recently exploded firecracker. Authorities are called.

WEDNESDAY, 23 May 1962

Shortly after midnight, a crew of twelve FAA investigators rush to the scene of the crash. They verify the possibility of a crime and quickly call the Federal Bureau of Investigation. They immediately begin an intense investigation.

2:00 a.m. The son-in-law of a Unionville farmer discovers a portion of the fuselage lying on its belly in a muddy pasture of his family's farm. It is missing its nose and tail, and most of its wings. He runs to the house and dials for help.

When the investigators arrive, they cannot find the main crash site. However, all they have to do is follow a trail of mangled, twisted metal. Walking all night, they pass shards of metal, bloody blankets, and other debris, finally discovering the body of a man lying in the grass. He is staring from where he had come. He wears nothing but socks and an ID bracelet. The name on the bracelet: Thomas G. Doty. He was the last person to board Continental Flight 11. One investigator stays with the body as the search continues for the main crash site.

Continental Airlines Customer Service representatives in Kansas City begin calling next of kin.

3:12. The phone rings. Barney is sound asleep—until he hears his mother scream. He jumps out of bed and rushes upstairs to find her collapsed on the floor, Kenny holding her head in his lap, the phone dangling at the end of the spiral cord. He picks up the receiver, hears a female voice say, "Hello? Are you alright? Is anyone there?"

"Hello?" he says, kneeling on the other side of his mother. "This is Barney Snodgrass. No, she ain't. What did ya say to my mom?" His jaw drops and tears fill his eyes. He drops the phone and falls against the wall. With tears flowing, he stares at his mother and brother.

"Daddy's not comin' home?"

Slowly, Barney shakes his head, and hugs the rest of his family as all three cry, uncontrollably. Finally, their mother regains enough strength for her boys to help her onto the chair. The caller is still on the line.

"Hello?" Barney says through sobs. "Okay. I'll tell her." He hangs up the phone. "Mom. Mom. Someone from Continental Airlines'll be here sometime before noon to tell us what happened."

She stares at nothing in particular. "Call Gramma and Grampa." Then she shakes her head. "This'll kill 'em."

Barney takes a deep breath. "Okay."

"Call Dr. Genezer. He needs to know. And Dr. Hickey. He's in the book."

Barney dials his grandparents' number. It rings four times before the phone is answered. "Grampa—Grampa—this is Barn. No." He bursts out crying.

Kenny takes the phone. "Grampa, Daddy's dead. We need ya here." Uncontrollable sobs prevent any other words. Hanging up the phone, he composes himself long enough to dial the two doctors, telling them his father is dead.

"I'm not goin' to school tomorrow," Barney says.

"Me either," Kenny says.

Dottie just shakes her head,

4:00. A seventeen-year-old begins finding parts of the plane in the fields near his family's farm as the two doctors arrive. Dr. Genezer examines Dottie while Dr. Hickey talks with the boys in Kenny's bedroom.

"I knew your dad in the war," Hickey says. "Met him one time when he was recuperating from his wounds."

"Daddy was wounded four times," Kenny says. "He gave me a Purple Heart when I was little for almost choking to death."

"He gave me a Silver Star for savin' him," Barney says. "Well, I yelled for Dad and he came to…" Anguish overwhelms him, and he cries uncontrollably.

5:15. Before both doctors leave, Dr. Genezer tells the grandparents, "I gave Dottie a sedative to help her sleep." He leaves. Then hugs, kisses, and tears fill the Snodgrass home as rescuers arrive at the crash site. Assuming all lives are lost, to their astonishment, they do find one survivor—unconscious. Investigators attempt to find out what had happened, but the young man, suffering from massive internal injuries and shock, dies ninety minutes later, taking whatever he knows to his reckoning.

5:49. The sun rises as local police officers, county sheriff's deputies, FBI agents, and Civil Aviation Board investigators scourer the hills about five miles northwest of Unionville. At the crest, they see a crowd of police, medics, reporters, and bystanders surrounding the clutter of twisted metal and dead bodies. Most of the fuselage is found near Unionville. The engines and portions of the tail and left wing are scattered up to six miles from the main crash site.

Morning newspapers in Chicago, Los Angeles, and Kansas City speculate an electrical storm or a tornado brought down Flight 11. The Los Angeles Times reports a midair collision. The Kansas City Star surmises the jet was "wrenched apart in the air by a squall line of fearful intensity." The thunderstorm is the main suspect. But the investigation continues.

6:15. Andrew Mace of Chicago reads the front-page headline in the Tribune and at once calls Jim's phone number. Grandpa answers.

"Jim?"

"No. This is his father. Jim was killed in a plane crash last night."

"Oh God. I was afraid of that. I'm Andrew Mace. Jim and I went to the ballgame Monday night. I was one of Jim's platoon leaders. In 1955, I met Dottie and the boys at the first ten-year reunion of our Army unit. I won't keep you, but I want Dottie to know that Jim's VFW Post will take care of all the funeral arrangements. I'll give you my phone number when she wants to get in touch with me."

Grandpa takes down the information, then thanks Mace for the call.

The next call Mace makes is to his former noncoms, informing them that their leader has died. They, in turn, start making calls until everyone in the company has been notified. Almost every single man volunteers to be a pallbearer. They all order flowers.

7:00. The Valium Dr. Genezer gave Dottie is working its wonder, and she sleeps in her bed. Grandpa calls Mrs. Horton and the school to inform them of the situation.

7:30. Calista Horton arrives at Dottie's home with a beautiful bouquet of home-grown flowers.

9:00. A Continental Airlines representative arrives at the house. He tells the family, "The cause of the crash is not yet authorized for release."

"What does that mean?" Grandpa asks. "You know what brought the plane down or don't you?"

The representative repeats his answer verbatim, then apologizes for not being able to say more.

The visit lasts five minutes, ending with Grandpa saying, "Come back when you have something useful to say."

10:50. Dottie wakes, and Grandpa tells her of the phone call from Andrew Mace.

She sighs and wipes away a tear. "What a relief. God bless those guys. I love 'em all. And Jim loved 'em, too."

11:00. Delivery of flowers from friends and neighbors, the school, classmates, and Jim's co-workers and Army buddies begin to arrive. Mrs. Horton adds them to hers.

5:30 pm. After Calista gets her girls from school, they carry in enough food to last a week. The girls hug and kiss Dottie, her boys, and their grandparents, while giving their sobbing, heartfelt condolences.

7:00. Calista tells Dottie, "You need or want anything, call me. Yes?"

Dottie nods. "Thank you. You're a good friend, Calista." She sees them to the door.

Kenny watches, blankly, as Kaelah walks to their car, then looks at all the bouquets of flowers covering the dining room table, the top of the television, and on every end and corner table. "We could open a flower shop."

"Who's gonna water all of 'em?" Barney says.

"You are, mon amour," Grandma Bri says. "Your mother will need much help in the days ahead." She caresses his cheeks with her weathered hands. "You are man of the house, now. We are counting on you." She gives him a kiss on the forehead. Then, she buries her face in her husband's chest and silently weeps.

"Okay. That's over. Where to next, Angel?"

"Half is over. But before we get to the end, I think you'd like to visit the next day."

"Next day?"

"Yes. Thursday, the day before the last day of school. C'mon. You'll enjoy it."

Apprehensively, Barnard takes the Angel's hand, and they walk into the light.

Linh hands Ken a glass of orange juice. As he takes a couple of gulps, she calls 9-1-1.

12:52.

21

Commandos Retaliate

THURSDAY, 24 May 1962

6:45 a.m. CST. Barney, Kenny, and Dottie are sitting in front of the television as Cape Canaveral counts down to the launch of the Aurora 7 capsule carrying astronaut Scott Carpenter. The boys are watching the Atlas D rocket lift off from the launchpad. However, Dottie is reading the paper she holds in her hand. Then, with the capsule safely orbiting Earth, Barney says, "I'm goin' to school."

"You really don't have to. No one'll expect you back this soon."

"Tomorrow's the last day of school. And I need to do that." He points to the sheet of paper she holds in her hands.

"You really want to give this to him?"

"Yes!" With an emptiness in his heart, he stares at his father's easy chair.

"You don't want to ask him to reimburse you for your medical bills?"

His stare goes to his mother. "I'm not **askin'** him to pay me. He'll pay me one way or another."

"Barney." She places her right hand softly on his left arm. "You think Daddy would want you to fight him? He hasn't bothered you boys for a month."

"Yeah. He'd approve. For almost three years, he taught us to fight like he did. Now I'm ready!"

"You forgot your medical bills," Dottie says.

"I know what they are," Kenny says. "I just thought that was a bridge too far."

"It ain't," Barney says.

Kenny jumps up and hurries into the dining room, then quickly returns with a pencil. He takes the sheet of paper from his mother and begins writing. A moment later, he gives it back. "That's the dates and reasons. Mom, you'll have to put the amounts."

Dottie reads the new entries. "1. 9/21/59 Barney's bruised ribs, 2. 9/21/59 Kenny's chipped tooth (even though a baby tooth, I went to the dentist), 3. 5/26/61 X-ray of Kenny's shin, 4. 5/26/61 Stitches on Barney's forehead from Charlie's ring." Again, she puts her hand on Barney's arm, this time squeezing it, and stares into his eyes. "You make sure you kick his ass."

"And I'll help," Kenny says.

"You help only if his buddies show up," Barney says. "But Charlie's mine!"

"He beat me up, too. Besides, who has the brown belt in Taekwondo?"

"I'm sure when we meet after school, his buddies'll be there, so there'll be plenty of bums to go around."

"What do you want for breakfast?" Dottie asks, but both boys decline. "You have to eat something so you have the strength to fight." She steps to the refrigerator. "I'll fix lunches, too, while you eat breakfast."

"When are ya goin' to give him the bill?" Kenny asks, and Barney shrugs. "Better have a battle plan."

Only the sound and smell of sizzling bacon fills the room until Dottie places the plates of three slices of bacon, two eggs, and two slices of buttered toast in front of her boys. Then Kenny says, "Wow.

This would be my choice for a last meal." He looks up to see his brother and mother glaring at him. "I'm kiddin'."

After breakfast, the boys get ready for school, then hop on their bikes for the one-mile trek. As they ride in the comfortable seventy-three-degree morning air, in Washington, D.C., the FBI laboratory is testing the residue collected on fragments from the right rear lavatory and surrounding structure. The result: the explosive used is dynamite. With this knowledge, investigators hypothesize that the serial numbers from the dynamite might be found in the body of someone near the explosion.

7:59. Just before the beginning bell, Barney and Kenny enter their combination fifth and sixth grade classroom, their eyes and minds totally focused on one mission. Their target is turned to his right as he talks at a disinterested Erika. As Kenny takes his seat on the front row nearer the door, he watches his brother walk up to Charlie and hand him the piece of paper. Then Barney sits at his desk next to Charlie and in front of Erika. "Mornin', Erika." Barney never takes his eyes from Charlie.

"Good morning, Barney."

Charlie unfolds the paper and smirks at Barney as he slowly wads up the paper, snickers, and tosses it in Barney's face. Barney does not flinch. The wad bounces off his face, the desk, and onto the floor, finally coming to rest next to Erika's desk.

"Charlie!" the watchful teacher exclaims, "Pick up the paper and give it to me."

Charlie stares at the teacher as Barney stands and retrieves the ball of paper. As he turns around, Charlie reaches over, grabs Barney's sack lunch and flings it out the open window to the collective gasps of the other classmates.

"**Charles Tyran!**" the teacher scolds. "Shame on you. You get that—right now."

"No," Barney says, staring at Charlie. "It's mine. I'll get it." He flattens the wad of paper against his chest, folds it, and sticks it in his jeans' pocket; then casually walks out of the room, glancing at Kenny and winking.

A moment later, his classmates sitting nearest the window, including Charlie, see Barney outside. Charlie lets out a scornful belly laugh as Barney bends over and picks up his paper bag, then his tinfoil-wrapped sandwich, and the baggy filled with potato chips. He puts them back in the half-torn paper sack as Charlie's laughter seems to grow louder. Then, in one fluid motion that would make Brooks Robinson proud, he scoops up the dark red apple and, with all his might, throws a fastball through the window. **SPLAT!** The apple smashes into Charlie's left eye, exploding into dozens of not-so-delicious pieces.

A collective **"HAAA!"** fills the room as the teacher yells through the window, "Barnard Joseph Snodgrass! You go straight to the… Charles Tyran, you get back here, right now!" Charlie runs past her, his right fist ready for a beatdown while the left covers his throbbing eye. Focused on one thing, he runs towards the door. Quickly, Kenny stretches out as far as he can. His left foot nudges Charlie's back foot enough to move it behind his planted foot. Like a **B-47 Stratojet** crash landing, Charlie nosedives through the doorway, his left shoulder and hand crashing against the doorframe. Another **"HAAAAA!"** gasps from opened mouths.

An enraged Charlie jumps to his feet and glares at Kenny, who is already standing in the Taekwondo junbi stance (ready stance), preparing himself for the hopeful possibility of Charlie's third—and probably last mistake in the last three minutes.

"You'll get yours after I take care of your brother," Charlie bellows.

"Charlie, you settle down!" Mrs. Dabir commands.

Ignoring her, he storms out of the room and down the short hall. Before he makes it to the entrance doors to the school, all the students crowd along the windows to see the expected ruckus.

"Charlie's comin'," most of them warn Barney, who is watching for the attack and hearing his father say, *Step into your enemy, duck, block, punch.*

A moment later, the enemy bursts outside and runs straight for Barney, his right arm cocked to throw the haymaker. Instead of standing there to receive Charlie's planned knockout punch, Barney steps forward with left arm up to parry the punch, ducks, and with his right, launches his own coup de grâce. Pow! Charlie's fist lands first. But it is a glancing blow off the top of Barney's head as Barney's body twists as if throwing a fireball, his shoulders, hips, and right arm moving in perfect unison as his entire 116 pounds shifts behind his fist. Charlie sees Barney's fist coming, but is helpless to avoid it. With the precision of a Norden bombsight and the power of an atomic bomb, Barney's fist does not miss its target. **POW!**

Charlie may have felt the impact, but he does not hear the two bones in his nose shatter. He does not feel his left cheekbone crack. He does not feel his head jerk backward as it leads his limp, weightless body in an unimpeded descent to the grassy ground. He does not comprehend how clear the blue sky is as he stares blankly upward. He does not hear the uproarious **"YEAA!"** of his classmates celebrating the first-round knockout and them chanting the new champion's name, **"BARNEY! BARNEY! BARNEY!"** He does not hear the teacher yell, **"Barnard Joseph Snodgrass! STOP THAT RIGHT NOW!"** He does not feel the **POW! POW! POW!** of more punches knocking loose his front teeth. He does not hear the teacher order, **"You go straight to the office young man!"** Lastly, he does not see the victor bend over him and casually stuff the neatly folded paper in his shirt pocket, then leave the field of battle without celebration—or an aching hand.

Barney walks into the principal's office and his eyes widen as he looks at the other detainee. Then he says, "Mrs. Varsh, I hit Charlie. He's layin' outside."

For a moment, the shocked principal stares at him, then stands. "Is he hurt?"

"Sure hope so. He was bleedin' pretty good." As the principal hurries from the office, Barney sits on a chair next to the other student. "What are you doin' here?"

"I tripped Charlie, so Mrs. Dabir sent me here," a smiling, proud Kenny answers.

"So, you didn't see the fight?"

"What fight? I saw him throw one punch, then you beat the shit out of him. I don't call that a fight. I call it an **ass-whoopin'**."

The boys chuckle.

As he looks at his little brother, he says, "I did just like Dad taught us—close the distance when bein' attacked." A wry grin slowly curls his lips. "It worked." He looks to the ceiling. "Thanks Dad." Then, he sees tears well up in Kenny's eyes. "What?" Kenny shakes his head. **"What?"**

"I was just thinkin' 'bout Daddy teachin' us how to fight."

"Me too." Suddenly, tears well up in Barney's eyes and the brothers grab each other in bear hugs and cry—but only for a moment. They hear voices and see the teacher follow the nurse and principal as they assist a dazed Charlie to the nurse's station, the nurse holding a bloody hand towel over Charlie's face. Then they glance at his classroom to see Erika, Dick, Tommy, Willie, Mikey, David, and the rest of the class waving and applauding through the open door. Kenny holds up Barney's hand, acknowledging the new heavyweight champion of Schweiter Elementary School. Barney shyly waves back.

Then the principal returns to the office. "Barney, I think you broke Charlie's nose."

"Good."

"You don't sound like you're sorry."

He shakes his head. "Only thing I'm sorry about is he didn't get up so I could knock him down again."

Mrs. Varsh leans back in her chair. "Did Charlie do something to you that prompted this fight?"

He glares at her. "You kiddin'? For the last three years, he bullied me, my brother, other kids. Mom and Dad both told ya Charlie was a bully, stealing our lunches and money, beatin' us up. But ya did **NOTHIN'** to stop him." He shakes his head in disgust. "Then today, I gave him a bill for everything he cost us, and he threw my lunch out the window."

"He owes ya an apple," Kenny says, then the brothers burst out laughing.

"You think that's funny?"

"Yeah," they say together.

The door opens, and Mrs. Dabir walks in. "The nurse is taking Charlie to the emergency room." She closes the door and turns to Barney. "Well, what do you have to say for yourself, young man?"

He looks up at her. "I wish I had done this last week so I could tell my dad I finally got the **sonofabitch**." Then they watch the nurse escort the weeping Charlie out of her office.

The principal and teacher look at him in silence, both trying desperately to fight back tears of laughter. Then Mrs. Varsh says, "You know I have to call your mother."

"Don't bother," Kenny says. "When you were outside, I called her. She should be here any minute."

"I have to go settle my class down," Mrs. Dabir says, and the principal nods. "But first, you need to know Charlie hit Barney in the face with a wad of paper, and then threw his lunch out the window."

"Thank you for telling me."

Then, they wait.

Two minutes later, Dottie arrives, shakes hands with Mrs. Varsh, sits, and listens to what had transpired, and the charge of fighting on school grounds. "It doesn't matter if it's provoked or self-defense," the principal says. "We must expel everyone involved."

"Does that include Charlie?" Kenny asks.

The principal nods. "He won't be back."

"The boys warned me last night that would be the punishment." Dottie looks at her boys. "You think that's fair?"

The boys nod.

"However, the rules don't state when the punishment should be carried out." Mrs. Varsh looks at the two boys. "Since tomorrow is the last day of school, I don't see why I couldn't expel you—let's say— the day after tomorrow."

"School'll be out," Kenny says, and Barney gives him an elbow to the ribs.

"Hmmm. So, it will. Go back to class."

The boys jump out of their chairs. **THANK YOU, MRS. VARSH!**" They hug and kiss their mother.

"You're hurt!" Dottie exclaims, seeing Barney's hands.

He shows her his bloody fists. "**Ain't my blood!** First punch, right in the kisser, just like Daddy taught us. **And it didn't even hurt.**"

As the boys head for the door, Mrs. Varsh says, "Wash your hands before you go back to class."

They hurry back into the classroom to a rousing round of cheers and applause from their classmates—and a more subtle ovation from their teacher.

"One Punch Barney," a smiling Kenny says. "Archie Moore would be proud."

Barney grins as he walks to his seat and sits down as his classmates begin chanting, "One Punch Barney! ONE PUNCH BARNEY! **ONE PUNCH BARNEY!**"

"Daddy'd be proud," Kenny says.

Barney flops down in his desk. But instead of relishing the moment, tears shoot out of his eyes. Burying his face in his folded arms, he cries.

Erika leans forward and pats him on the back. "Cassius Clay would be proud, too."

As the teacher restores order in her classroom, in D.C., the autopsy of the flight attendant who was knocking on the lavatory door at the time of the explosion discovers a small piece of beige wax paper. The paper is from a dynamite cylinder. By the time school is out, that cylinder is connected to a stick of dynamite Doty had purchased a month earlier. That night, the evaluation of all the evidence logically leads to the conclusion that a dynamite device was placed in the used towel bin of the right rear lavatory with the express intent to destroy the aircraft.

11:41 a.m. CST. As the children eat lunch, they watch Aurora 7 splash down in the Atlantic, returning the fourth American astronaut safely to Earth.

FRIDAY, 25 May 1962

For the last day of school, Dottie serves her boys a special baked breakfast casserole of ground sausage, whipped eggs, shredded cheddar cheese, black olive halves, mushroom pieces, green bell pepper chunks, with a touch of salt and pepper in a bread-lined casserole dish.

At school, it is a festive day of games, songs, signing yearbooks, and eating lunch the mothers Snodgrass, Horton, and Wainwright cater, and being thankful that one classmate is absent.

*"Forgot about that. That was a **damn good day**."*

The angel looks at him, her head cocked to the right. But no fluorescent blue or electrical shocks. "Well, the next day was not so good. C'mon." The angel escorts him into the blackness.

"Ambulance on way."

"Good."

22

Bad News

SATURDAY, 26 May 1962

9:00 a.m. Barney and Kenny ride their bikes to Charlie's house. Barney knocks on the door, and Charlie's father answers. "Charlie here?"

"Just a moment. Charlie! Somebody's here to see ya!"

A moment later, Charlie walks to the door, but does not open it. "Whadaya want?" His question is nasally. Tape is over his nose and gauze in his nostrils.

"Payment," Barney says.

"Ain't payin' ya."

"I was hopin' you'd say that."

"Me too," a smiling Kenny adds. "Heal up quick." He slams his right fist into the palm of his left hand. "C'mon, Barn."

They get on their bikes and ride back home. As they coast up the yard, they find their grandparents' car parked in the driveway and another car parked in front of their house.

"Hope Mom's okay!" The boys rush into the house to find their grandparents sitting on the sofa with their mother and the Continental Airlines representative who had been there before sitting on their father's easy chair. They look at each other but say nothing. They stand and listen to what he is saying.

"The FBI's investigation is complete. The cause of the crash has been determined to be a suicide bombing committed as insurance fraud."

"Insurance fraud?" Grandpa asks. "Who brought the plane down?"

"The FBI hasn't given Continental authority to release his name."

"How do you know it was insurance fraud?"

"The bomber bought $300,000 of life insurance, which…"

"Daddy was murdered?" Barney asks, his chest heaving with fury.

"That's what it sounds like," Grandpa says, his upper lip quivering with his own anger.

The representative tries to regroup. "Life insurance. Brings me to your payment," he says as Barney leaves the room.

Suddenly, the kitchen door slams shut, followed by the slamming of the basement door.

"Kenny, go see what Barn's doing," Dottie says.

As Kenny opens the basement door, he hears his brother screaming and plastic breaking. At Barney's doorway, he yells, "**Barn, whadaya doin'!**" and watches his brother take a mighty swing of his baseball bat, then shields his face as pieces of the model airplanes hanging from the ceiling over his bed explode everywhere. Then, before he can take a swipe at his Hartland collection, Kenny charges him, tackling him around the waist and pushing him onto the bed. Struggling to wrench the bat away, Kenny uses his Taekwondo training to finally win the battle. Without taking his eyes from Barney, he tosses the bat into the utility room and immediately gets into the defensive stance. "I don't wanna hurt ya, Barn, so settle down."

"**What the hell?**" Grandpa exclaims. Patting Kenny on the shoulder, he steps into the room, scooting the pieces of plastic out of his path before brushing more pieces off the bed. He sits beside Barney. "I know exactly how you feel. I'm pissed off, too. Why does some sonofabitch think he has to murder innocent people to collect life insurance—or to lash out? If he wants to die, just kill yourself. You don't have to ruin other people's lives." He looks at Barney and puts his hand on his grandson's shoulder. "You feel better?"

Without saying a word, Barney shakes his head and begins crying.

Wrapping his arms around him, Grandpa says, "Let it all out, Barn. There's a lot more cryin' in our future." Then he looks at Kenny. "Come here." Kenny sits on the other side of his grandfather, and the three cry. After a few minutes, Grandpa says, "Kenny, get a broom and dustpan."

"No." Barney wipes his face. "I did this. I'll clean it up."

"That's okay. I don't have anything else to do."

Barney and Grandpa stand and hug. "Thanks, Grampa. I love ya." *I love ya. That's what I shoulda said to Daddy.* A second wave of tears flows.

"I love you, Barn." He looks into his bloodshot eyes. "You gonna be okay?"

Barney nods, then looks at his desk and bursts out laughing. His brother and grandfather look. On the desk stands the only model airplane still intact—Revell's 1/32 scale German WWII Junkers JU 87-B Stuka Dive Bomber.

Linh monitors the men's vitals. Then…

"It took me all summer to gather all the pieces of the seven airplanes and sort 'em out. Then it took me 'til Christmas to glue 'em back together. Kenny was a big help. He was a lot better in separatin' the parts than I was. But then, he was always good at puttin' puzzles together, especially those darn 3-D ones."

"You two grew closer after your father died."

"Murdered," Barnard corrects the angel.

The angel nods. "Murdered. Tell me what happened to Charlie."

"Nothin'.

"Charlie didn't pay, and when your mother confronted his parents, they were not receptive to the idea either, so—"

"Made Mom sue 'em in Small Claims Court, which really pissed 'em off."

"Not as much as losing just under a thousand dollars, including court costs."

Barnard smiles. "Got that right. And to rub salt in an open wound, the judge tossed out their countersuit wantin' restitution for Charlie's medical bills from my one punch knockout."

"To be accurate, one punch knockout and seven punch beatdown."

Barnard smiles. "Judge said it was an additional penalty suffered for allowing their child to bully."

"They didn't pay the judgment."

"Nope. Made Mom put a lien on their house. As you know, the feud didn't stop there."

"We'll get to that in a sec'. But first, we need to bring the jury full circle before it's too late."

"What do you mean?"

"We need to show the jury what happened before." She leads Barnard into the darkness.

23

Before

FRIDAY, 31 December 1999

The eye not buried in the depth of the pillow opens, blinks clear the blurriness, then stares at the lime green LCD numbers on the face of the alarm clock. *6:39. Well, shit.* The man sighs, closes his eyes, pulls the sheet, cover, and comforter over his head, and buries his face into the nest of his pillow.

Peeking from under the warmth of the bedding, his top eye stares at the clock. ***6:40!*** **"Ah, shit! You kiddin' me? One fuckin' minute?"** In a huff, he throws the covers off. Instantly, cool air rushes over his naked body, awakening his full bladder. He jumps out of bed and rushes into the master bathroom, barely making it before the floodgate opens, emptying the bladder's orangish contents into the black porcelain throne. "Whew! That was close. Feels like my legs are lighter." He washes his face, sprays deodorant under each arm, and dresses in sweats and sneakers.

The stove's clock reads 6:48 as two pieces of whole wheat bread toasts, and a scrambled egg, sausage, and cheese TV breakfast microwaves. The man chases a handful of vitamins down his throat with a couple gulps of cold orange juice—from the jug, then does the same with his AM medications including a pill to prevent heart attacks and strokes, one to prevent blood clots, two diuretics, two for high blood pressure, and 600mg of Gabapentin, an anticonvulsant used to combat nerve pain in diseases such as DPN (diabetic peripheral neuropathy). He smears butter and jelly on the toast, sets them on a saucer, retrieves the TV breakfast from the microwave, places everything on a tray, and carries it into the living room. After sitting in his recliner, he turns on the television with the remote and switches to NBC to watch the tail end of the first hour of *Today with Katie Couric and Matt Lauer.*

The lime green LCD readout on the VCR reads 7:00 AM. After placing his glass, fork, and spoon in the sink and the microwave tray in the trash, he returns to his recliner, picks up the first handwritten letter and shakes his head. *My penmanship has gone to hell. Mom's probably spinnin' in her grave. Maybe I should've typed it. But then— who's gonna give a shit?* After reading the words, he folds the 8.5-by-11 sheet in thirds, inserts it in the envelope with Ken on the front, licks it closed, and lays it on the arm of the sofa. "Hope ya had a nice Christmas—Brother."

He reads the second letter, wipes a tear from his cheek, places the letter in the envelope with Tori on the front, kisses her name, licks it closed, and places the envelope next to the first.

Then, he reads the last letter. After wiping more tears now flooding from his eyes, he puts the sheet in the third envelope sporting the name, Allie, licks it closed, and leans it on the end table against the 8-by-10 framed color photo of a six-year-old girl standing at the edge of a lake waiting for her very first fish to bite.

He turns off Matt and Katie.

The digital alarm clock reads 7:10 as he turns on the CD player and cranks the volume up. Before he can begin stripping the bed, the fast-paced instrumental of Meat Loaf's "Bat Out of Hell" booms throughout the house from the surround sound speakers hidden in the walls. The song follows him as he carries the bedding downstairs to the utility room along with this week's dirty laundry. He loads the bedding into the washing machine and sends the washer's agitator into action.

7:20. The man starts reciting the words "You Took the Words Right Out of My Mouth (Hot Summer Night)" as he opens the vertical blinds in front of the sliding glass patio doors and stares outside. As he sings along with Meat Loaf, he thinks, *Your kisses always could take the words right outta my mouth.* He stares at the six or eight inches of snow on the deck. *Still comin' down. Should I or shouldn't I? Now or when it stops? If it stops.* He shrugs. *Like the old saying goes: Put off 'til tomorra what ya don't wanna do today. If ya have a tomorra.* He continues singing as he begins cleaning the dining room.

7:25. As he sings "Heaven Can Wait," he grins, remembering when he tasted paradise. Then the grin quickly vanishes as he wishes he could taste it again.

7:41. With the dining room and most of the living room dusted, "Paradise by the Dashboard Light" booms throughout the house, and the man starts singing and jumping and twirling and shaking his body that could have taught Joel a move or two in *Risky Business*.

7:50. Huffing and puffing, the man leans against the wall between the living room and dining room. "Whew! **I love that song!**" He returns to the utility room, shakes loose the sheets and blankets before throwing them into the dryer with a cling-free sheet. Then, he dumps the rest of the laundry into the washing machine, turns it on, and walks upstairs.

7:58. With the bedding in the dryer and the clothes sloshing in the washing machine, the man finishes dusting the living room as he joins Harry Chapin in singing the opening song on the singer's album, *The Gold Medal Collection*. And when "Taxi" ends, the man sadly mutters, "Yep, another man would've never let ya go."

While listening to his favorite songs—and singing the ones he knows, like "I Wanna Learn a Love Song," he dusts his office and the spare bedroom where the most important person in his life would have slept—if things had been different.

9:04. The man returns to the basement as Disk 2 begins playing "A Better Place to Be." Even though he knows the words, he does not sing. He puts the warm bedding in the basket and the washed clothing in the dryer. As the song concludes, he carries the bedding upstairs. "I know I'm goin' somewhere," he mutters, "and that's gotta be a better place to be."

9:22. With the bed made, Joe begins cleaning the master bath. While listening to "Mr. Tanner," he remembers the one time he dared sing from his heart and sing from his soul. He knew how badly he sang. But it did not matter. It just made him whole.

10:00. Sitting in his recliner, the man watches his favorite morning game show, Bob Barker hosting *The Price is Right*. "Calista or her girls would've made great Barker's Beauties."

11:05. He retrieves the clothing from the dryer and carries it to his bedroom, where he dumps it on the bed. Folding his shirts, he stares at the queen-size bed. *How I miss cuddling with ya, feelin' every inch of your gorgeous body, kissin' those deliciously soft lips, starin' into your mesmerizin' eyes, hearin' your sexy voice talkin' dirty to me—your contagious laugh.* "Damnit! Why didn't ya want me to come with ya?" A deep sigh. "Ya know I would've." He pats his left breast. *I'll always wear your heart over mine.*

Noon. After taking his noon meds, including 600mg of Gabapentin, the man sits down to watch the local news while eating a microwave enchilada dinner and drinking four ounces of Merlot. Since Merlot, which is one of the most alcoholic wines, containing 13 to 15 percent alcohol, and Gabapentin can cause drowsiness or slow breathing, they can also slow body and brain functions.

12:35 p.m. As the man starts to stand to take his things to the kitchen, dizziness attacks and sends him back into the recliner. "Holy crap! What the hell!" He shakes his head. "Ah—parent—ly—I can't hold my—my boo-boobs." Sighing, he relaxes, giving the spell time to leave him.

12:45. Finally, the dizziness is gone, but drowsiness arrives. Like a hippopotamus, the man's mouth opens and his chest swells as he sucks in a huge yawn. He can barely lift his eyelids to see what the television offers. It would not have mattered. His brain does not register what his eyes see. He falls asleep.

5:30. The man opens his eyes and stares at the television. After a few blinks, he finally realizes that he is seeing *ABC World News Tonight with Peter Jennings*. He shakes the cobwebs out of his brain in time to hear Jennings say, "We begin our newscast with breaking news. Reports are that Boris Yeltsin has resigned as the president of Russia and Prime Minister Vladimir Putin will act as president." ***Holy shit!*** *Dad's probably spinnin' in his grave. I think Vlad's a former KGB officer. Pure Commie, that's for sure.* His belly growls. He walks into the kitchen and puts a lasagna meal in the microwave.

6:00. With his evening medications—including another 600mg of Gabapentin—the man feeds the belly beast, washing everything down with more Merlot, then makes the kitchen spic-and-span.

6:15. He carries the bottle and glass of wine into the bedroom, turns on the CD player, and runs water in his whirlpool tub. As the melodious voice of Irish singer Enya fills the house, the waterfall of steaming hot water fills the black, two-person tub, the man empties his bowels, then slowly and carefully shaves his short gray beard before gingerly lowering his naked body into the hot water. He pushes the button, and the twenty jets activate the water, massaging almost every inch of his body. He closes his eyes and thinks about the two women he most enjoyed bathing—one in this tub. *Oh, how I miss ya. If I could only turn back the clock…* After downing the final drops of wine, he empties the bottle into the glass, only filling it half full. *Man! Hope I got another bottle.* He shakes his head. *Bought a six-pack for Ken. He knows I don't like that shit except when it's scorching hot.* His face contorts. *That shit tastes like piss.* Then the corner of his lips curl. *Well, depends whose it is.* In his mind's eye, he sees… Slowly, his shoulders, then neck, chin, and left ear sink below the surface of the water. Suddenly, his arms and legs thrash as water seeps into his left nostril. He sits up coughing and blowing the water out of his nose. "**GODDAMN!** Drown why don't ya! Ya dumbass!"

7:30. Dressed in a thick hooded bathrobe and moccasin slippers, the man brings his father's .45-cal. revolver and a gun-cleaning kit to the living room. He sets them on the end table with another bottle of wine. As he cleans the revolver, he watches Regis Philbin host ABC's *Who Wants to Be a Millionaire*. "I think it's the first answer," he says. "But ya better call a friend." He chuckles. "Yeah. Call a **fucking** friend."

8:00. The network begins covering the New Year's Eve festivities from around the world as the man tosses the gun-cleaning items back in its box.

8:15. The man did not learn his lesson at lunch, and again the wine/Gabapentin combo gangs up on him. He fumbles the .45-caliber shells, scattering more on the tabletop and carpet than he inserts in the cylinder of the revolver. He laughs at his awkwardness, then tries shaking some sense into his foggy brain. He grabs for the stemmed flute, half-full of wine. His fingers lose their grip, and the glass tumbles onto the carpet, pouring its purplish liquid over the carpet and shells. "Oops." Again, he laughs.

His eyelids grow heavy. Big yawn. He tries fighting the sleep. The sandman is too strong. Sleep engulfs him. And the man, sprawled on the recliner, with the hood covering his head, looks like the exhausted Jedi Knight, Obi-Wan Kenobi, relaxing in a galaxy far, far away.

8:37. The phone rings, and the male caller leaves a message on the answering machine.

9:25. The phone rings and the same caller leaves a message on the answering machine.

11:57. The phone rings and the female caller leaves a message on the answering machine.

George Bailey's smile fills the large television screen as the bell on the Christmas tree jingles. "Attaboy, Clarence!" he exalts as *It's a Wonderful Life* concludes, "Auld Lang Syne" resonating from the surround sound speakers hidden in the walls of the house. Instantly, the lime green LCD readout on the video recorder changes to FRI 12/31/1999 11:58:00 PM.

11:58:12. "Jingle Bells" resonates from the doorbell chime hanging on the hallway wall.

Suddenly, his eyes shoot open. His heart pounds against his chest cavity. Horrified, the man looks around the room, not recognizing anything, his foggy mind playing tricks on him. Confusion. Panic. His right hand grabs the hard item on his lap, fumbles with its odd shape, its three pounds abnormally heavy and strangely awkward to handle. Finally, a firm grasp controls it. But the thumb against the double-action hair trigger is the wrong place for such pressure. The metal firing pin at the end of the hammer pierces the primer at the center back of the cartridge. The primer's small explosive ignites, which in turn ignites the propellant in the cartridge. The propellant's chemicals burn, rapidly generating gas which produces high pressure in the cartridge. This pressure separates the cartridge from the shiny copper .45-caliber bullet, forcing it through the well-oiled barrel of the Colt D A 45 at about 830 feet per second (fps).

11:58:15. **BANG!**

"YOU GOTTA BE SHITTIN' ME! I shot myself—by accident?"

Shaking her head, the angel sighs. "Barnard, Barnard, Barnard. And you were doing so well."

Instantly, blackness. His body glows a fluorescent blue; his fingers and toes tingle as if asleep. ZAP. His digits curl into painful knots. He shrieks, flesh quivering, hands and feet jerking in spasms, arms and legs twitching uncontrollably. At last, a final groan gurgles in his throat, and his naked body lies silent. The blue slowly fades to black. Then the small, bright white light reappears.

A grimacing Barnard huffs and puffs. "Wow. That was intense."

"You obviously haven't learned what's acceptable and what isn't."

"I apologize for what I said."

"I know. And again, you're forgiven. So, let's move on. A new year is almost upon us! And now we must see what happened—after." The angel takes Barnard's hand, and they walk into the flickering light.

24

After

FRIDAY, 31 December 1999

11:58:15. The man's body jolts and legs spasm, flipping one tattered leather slipper onto the wine-stained gray carpet, the other dangling on the man's toes about to join its partner. Flesh and bone are no match for the seven-sixteenth-inch projectile as it rips through skin, fat, and muscle before severing the superficial femoral artery. The man quickly pulls apart the front of his robe. His eyes bulge as he stares at the blood spurting from the gaping hole at a rate of 10.5 pints a minute. There is no pain—the shock of the horrific scene prevents it, except for a little burning sensation from the hot bullet. At once, he presses down on the wound, reducing the bleeding, on top of his leg.

The rumble of the electric opener lifting the two-car garage door, a key rattling inside a doorknob, the kitchen door slamming against the cabinet, and quick footsteps tapping on the tile floor indicate help is approaching. But is it approaching fast enough?

11:58:57. Forty-two seconds have passed, draining 1.1 pints of blood—more than what a person donates at the Red Cross and nine minutes faster. The victim becomes lightheaded. The pressure he is exerting on the wound lessens. His heart beats faster. Blood spurts higher. His right arm jerks, and the barrel of the revolver lying in his lap rests against the remote control's channel selector. And in one-second bursts, Xena yells and freezes in midair, balloons rain down from another party, a giant alien stands before the U.N. pledging to serve man, Ron demonstrates the Veg-O-Matic, and a pink cloud moves across the central states. Even a glimpse of the mouthwatering ad for his favorite pizza cannot whet his appetite. No fleeting peek at the bikini-clad bombshell Marine JAG colonel can command his manhood to stand at attention as she has so many episodes before. Nor can the howling wind whipping sheets of sleet against the nearby window send a chill down his spine. And the phone ringing and the female voice on the answering machine cannot attract his attention.

The frosty air chases the man inside the house. He turns into the living room and stops. Seeing the blood, the man exclaims, "**Shit!**"

11:59:05. Eight more seconds pass in Barnard Joseph Snodgrass' life, and another one-tenth of a pint drains through his fingers. His heart and respiratory rates increase, but not from the leggy brunette swaggering out of the interrogation room as Fox Mulder leans to the right to prolong his view of the stunning woman in the chain and silver micro miniskirt. "I don't know about you, Scully," he says to his slightly amused partner, "but I'm feeling the great need to blast the crap out of something." The *X-Files* episode, "First Person Shooter," continues, the remote now resting on the floor, the revolver lying upside down between the man's bloodied thighs. Blood pressure falls.

The victim stares at the big-screen television. It is a blank stare— a stare of indifference, even though the clear picture and sound equal those of any theater with THX.

The man taps the victim's cheek. "**Joe! Stay with me!**" He presses on the wound as a woman rushes into the living room carrying two red satchels labeled with a white cross above the words, FIRST AID. "**Linh, call an ambulance!**" He pulls Joe off the recliner, lays him on his back, and elevates the wounded leg as Linh calls 9-1-1 from her cell phone. "**Damn!** It's through and through. Linh, give me the QuikClot!"

As she talks to the dispatcher, she removes the QuikClot dressing from the package and packs the gauze in the wound, on top of the leg and bottom. Then the man applies pressure on the wound as Linh quickly puts an oxygen mask over Joe's nose and mouth, a pulse oximeter on his finger, and a blood pressure cuff on his upper left arm. She pushes the ON button and the machine automatically monitors his vitals as the man whips off his overcoat and lays it over Joe's upper torso.

11:59:20. Another fifteen seconds pass along with another four-tenths of a pint—totaling 1.6 pints.

"Ken, BP 120/80, pulse 65, resp 20." She feels Joe's cheeks. "Skin cool, pale, sweaty. Stage 1 Hemorrhagic shock."

Joe's head bobs to the left, then right.

"JOE! Stay with me!"

Joe's head stops bobbing.

11:59:50. Thirty seconds and eight-tenths of a pint join their predecessors. Compensating for the blood loss, the body constricts the blood vessels in the arms and legs. The skin is cooler and paler. A festive Times Square pours into the living room, a room the living is quickly leaving on this joyous night.

11:59:55. Five more seconds pass, and a total loss of precious blood—3.2 pints or thirty percent of the total amount in the body. "BP 110-75. Pulse 100. Resp 25. Breathing shallow." The body cannot maintain circulation and adequate blood pressure. Joe loses consciousness. "Ken, Stage 2 Hemorrhagic shock."

The television jubilation shifts to a Dallas ballroom as a younger host takes over for the ageless Mr. New Year's Eve. "Okay, Central Time Zone, this is for you. Three. TWO. **ONE!**" The VCR acknowledges the new era: SAT 01/01/00 12:00:00 AM. "**HAPPY NEW YEAR!**"

Brilliant bursts of fireworks spray the television screen. Dazzling flares of light dance in the glass fireplace guard, in the golf artworks hanging on a wall, and in two pictures of a young girl proudly displayed on the end table. Even the man's eyes reflect the sparks of color, but do not flinch as the old millennium gives way to the first moments of a new thousand years and the hope for a brighter future.

"Wow, Barnard! Things are getting exciting."

"You tellin' me! I think Ken and Linh got there in the nick of time."

"Well, I wouldn't be counting my runs until the last out is made. And before it is, why don't we get this over with?" The angel grabs Barnard's hand, and they hurry into the darkness.

The VCR's LCD reads 12:01 AM. Blood loss is four pints.

"Still bleeding." Ken grabs another QuikClot pack and sticks more gauze in the wound as Linh checks Joe's vitals. The automatic blood pressure monitor beeps.

"BP 90/60. Pulse 122. Resp 35. Stage Three. Ken—transfusion?"

Suddenly, the monitor whines.

"He crashing!" At once, Linh begins administering thirty chest compressions and two breaths as Ken puts a tourniquet around Joe's leg near his groin. "**C'mon Joe! Fight!**"

12:04. The automatic blood pressure monitor beeps. "He back."

"Good. Linh, better get the AED ready."

Linh sets up the automated external defibrillator, placing the two sticky pads on Joe's bare chest, one below his right shoulder and the other below his left nipple. The defibrillator monitors Joe's heart rhythm. She monitors his respiration. "Resp 38."

12:05. Again, the monitor whines, and the AED indicates a shock is required.

"Stand back! Three, two, one, SHOCK!" Linh presses the shock button, and Joe's upper body lunges off the floor, then collapses. She checks his heart, then resumes CPR for another two minutes.

12:07. "I'll take over. You get the DBT." Ken assumes CPR while Linh gets the Direct Blood Transfusion equipment. "When did they say the ambulance would get here?"

"She say snow make very difficult to travel."

"C'mon Mother Nature. Help us out!"

12:07:25. The AED whines. Linh says, "Stand back! Three, two, one, SHOCK!" She presses the shock button and Joe's upper body again lunges off the floor—then collapses. "Weak pulse."

"We've gotta MTP now!"

12:08:05. Linh retrieves the telescoping IV pole from the Massive Transfusion Protocol items as Ken monitors his brother's vitals. She extends the pole before getting one bag of Ken's low-titer, Group O blood type from the storage bag and hangs it on the pole. After cleaning Joe's arm with povidone iodine, she inserts the needle into the vein in his right arm and starts the transfusion at a rate of one pint every fifteen minutes.

"I'm gonna see what's keeping EMTs." Ken takes Linh's cellphone and dials 9-1-1.

12:08:22. "Okay. Please hurry!" Ken turns the phone off. "They can't risk getting stuck. Almost twelve inches on the ground." He shakes his head. "Don't understand. We got here." He gently combs his fingers through his brother's damp hair. "Why didn't ya wait 'til Spring to clean the revolver—AND DRINK?" He shakes his head. "You know better."

"You think accident or suicide?"

Shrugging, Ken again shakes his head. "He's always had the uncanny ability to miss a gimme."

"You were quite the fighter. Guess you didn't want to join my flock?"

"Don't know 'bout fightin'. All I did was lay there." His eyes caress

the angel's sultry body. "If I had known you were my guardian angel..."

"You should have. You fantasized about me for years."

They watch the action. "Be a damn shame—DARN shame—to lose the game after all that Ken and Linh have done."

"Well, you know they're not finished. But, so far, they've given it the old college try."

"Well, the game ain't over 'til the fat lady sings. You hear any hummin'?"

"Not yet. But I do hear a throat clearing and a 'me, me, me'."

"Ye of little faith. And I couldn't have a better team: a Green Beret medic and an APRN specializing in trauma."

"Yes. You had your own dream team."

1:08. Ken and Linh look at the blood bag hanging on the IV pole. Then they look at each other. "That's it. He's still bleeding." After Linh pulls out the blood-soaked QuikClot gauze, Ken quickly stuffs more gauze into the wound. "If that doesn't do it, then we'll need to hook me up."

Linh sets out the apheresis pack of PLTS as the last of four units of blood transfuse from the bag into Joe's body. Suddenly, the AED whines. "Stand back! Three, two, one, SHOCK!" Linh presses the shock button and Joe's upper body lunges off the floor—then collapses. "Weak pulse."

"Hook me up."

1:12. Linh cleans Ken's arm before inserting a needle into the artery in his left arm. Then, she draws his blood into the apheresis machine, which separates the platelets from the blood, then returns the remaining blood back to Ken. The platelets form clots in Joe, but diminish the clotting ability in Ken. The rate of transfusion is one pint in fifteen minutes without the donor suffering side effects.

However, in a person who is rapidly losing blood—like Joe—the rate of transfusion must be faster.

1:20. One-half pint of blood has been transferred.

"How you feel?"

"Fine. Wish the ambulance would get here."

"I see if OJ in fridge."

"Call 9-1-1 again. Tell 'em to get a move on."

1:21. Linh hands Ken a glass of orange juice. As he takes a couple of gulps, she calls 9-1-1.

1:21:20. "**Ambulance on way!**"

"Good."

Linh monitors the men's vitals.

Then…

"Do You Hear What I Hear?" The voice of the angel brings Noël Regney's and Gloria Shayne's Christmas song into the light.

"Wow! You have a really beautiful voice."

"Angelic?"

"Most definitely."

"Thank you. But I sang it because I hear something. Don't you?"

"Finally! Hope they're not too late."

The whine of the siren grows louder, then slowly dies. However, the flashing red lights continue.

"**EMS!**"

"**In here!**" Ken and Linh answer.

Ken tells the technicians what they have done. One tech checks Joe's vitals. "Got a pulse. Weak, but got one."

The other tech says, "Okay. We'll take over from here."

"Well, I guess we can resume your reckoning."

"Where to?"

"June 16, 1962."

Barnard stares at the angel, then shakes his head.

"You have to, Barnard." The angel holds his hand as she escorts him into the blackness.

The End of Book One